CONQUER
YOUR
LOVE

...

J.C. REED

Cover art by Larissa Klein

Editing by Shannon Wolfman and JM Editing

ISBN: 149033274X
ISBN-13: 978-1490332741

To all who've loved and lost:

Love is a battle. It needs to be seized and conquered.

"Love is fragile. Love can easily be broken. Love is not always perfect. And sometimes love makes mistakes. When everything's broken, everything seems lost. The only way to get your love back and repair it...is to conquer it."

—CONQUER YOUR LOVE

BROOKE

Love happens in the blink of an eye. One moment your heart is yours, and the next it belongs to someone you never intended to give it to. There is no transition. No earning on his part. Just foolish trust and hope for a future of happiness and emotional fulfillment. As much as we all hope for a happily ever after, life doesn't work that way.

Love's a bitch. I had to learn that lesson the hard way in the form of a green eyed, sexy as sin, six foot two sex god.

Jett Mayfield.

My first and only foray into love and the second biggest mistake of my life.

PROLOGUE

MAYFIELD REALTIES WAS situated on the sixtieth floor of _Trump Tower_ in the bourgeoning business district of New York City. A little after eight a.m. Jett Mayfield sat in his office overlooking the busy street below. The people and yellow taxis looked like ants in constant motion: always hurried, always tense. Like the city, Jett had once been abuzz with life—or his former interpretation of it: live hard, work even harder. Until he met _her._ There was something about Brooke Stewart that had changed something inside him. It wasn't her beautiful chestnut eyes, nor the way she moved—confident and yet reserved. She had talked to him on a deeper level, touching something he had thought untouchable. His initial intention had been different though. His agenda had been to make her fall for him, not through words, but through actions and sex, lots of the latter, because he had wanted something she had. Not for himself, but for the man and for the company to which he owed everything. But events took a couple of turns he didn't expect.

When the plan backfired, she disappeared.

A shadow belonging to the past: gone but not forgotten.

For the past hour he had been staring at the cell phone, leaving him a tangled mess of fury and frustration. And more pain, which caused even more anger.

How stupid of her to go and not listen to him.

How stupid of her to turn off her phone so he couldn't reach her. And no matter how many times he called and how many messages he texted, Jett knew instinctively none reached her because if they had, she would feel his agony. She would feel just how important it was that she *listen* to what he had to say. It wasn't about his feelings. Fuck them. There was something else he needed to tell her; something that had rendered him sleepless at night, always worried for her, for them, for everything he believed in. And if his suspicions were true, then they needed each other just as much as they needed air to breathe.

"Mr. Mayfield—Jett?" Emma's head appeared in the doorway, jerking him out of his thoughts. He rewarded her with a frown. It wasn't like him to be rude, but the girl was a receptionist temporarily promoted as his personal assistant until he could find someone more suitable. As such, she wasn't yet accustomed to his preferences, which included not bothering him when he didn't want to be bothered.

Wide-eyed like a deer caught in the headlights, she made no sign to get to the point and then fuck off again, leaving him to the darkness clouding his thoughts and the unusual soreness in his chest. He sighed impatiently. "What is it?"

Emma seemed to remember how to speak again, but her wide eyes continued to mirror her insecurity. Jett liked his employees like that. Even if they thought he was a real son-of-a-bitch, they worked harder in order to please him.

"Someone's here to see you. I told him that you're busy and to arrange an appointment, but he won't go away. He's been here for half an hour." Emma's words rained down on him like a waterfall. All he caught was something about a guy being here to see him when he was indisposed.

"Tell him I'm not available."

"He said it's important."

They all did. "Then tell him you came to see me and I *specifically* told you I'm not available."

Emma's eyes widened just a little bit more, if that was even possible. Her frantic glance swept over him in fear. Obviously she wanted to keep her job, but the visitor

3

seemed to frighten her even more than the possibility of displeasing Jett. He had two options: send the girl back out and risk her coming back, interrupting his obsessing about Brooke, or deal with the visitor. In the end, he decided option two was a tad more appealing.

"Show him in."

Emma's expression relaxed instantly and she almost bounced out of his office. Glowering, Jett sat back in his chair and began to massage his temples to get rid of the increasing throbbing behind them. If he knew where Brooke was he wouldn't have to deal with this crap, and everything and everyone else could just go screw themselves. But as things stood, he had to maintain a façade of normalcy before things blew completely out of proportion.

"Jett, my man." The familiar voice coming from the door jerked Jett back to reality. His attention snapped to his life-long friend, and some of the pressure weighing him down lifted. As usual, Kenny had managed to dodge any dress code and looked like he was about to step into a bar—or jail—rather than into the office of the realty business's hotshot of the year. Ripped jeans, short sleeved black tee, tattooed upper arms, and pierced eyebrow. Then again, that had been Jett's style, minus the piercing, for many years before he traded Kenny's wild lifestyle for his father's business. He still had the tattoos and the almost faded scars to prove it.

Jett closed the door, briefly registering the curious glances from his employees staring at both him and Kenny. They probably wondered what a man like Kenny was doing in one of the most successful companies in real estate, meeting with no other than the CEO. His employees didn't know the true Jett. No one did. If they did, they'd run. But not Brooke. She had sensed his dark side and fallen in love with him nonetheless.

"You said you wanted to talk and it was urgent," Kenny began as soon as Jett had closed the shutters, leaving them sheltered from prying eyes.

"I never said here."

Kenny shrugged and slumped into Jett's chair, propping his legs up on the polished oak desk, expertly ignoring the brown leather couches set up near the door, chosen for such an occasion. Jett's eyes narrowed but he didn't comment. "I assumed you needed me and that you knew what you were doing," Kenny said. "You should've specified a place. Not my fault you're being incautious, bro."

Fuck it. He was right, of course, but the knowledge didn't stop Jett from glowering. To hide his irritation, he poured two glasses of double malt whiskey from the carafe on the coffee table and pushed one toward Kenny.

"It's barely morning," Kenny remarked, his fingers

clutching at the glass with remarkable eagerness.

"Who the fuck cares?"

"Point taken."

The whiskey tasted like expensive honey. A bit too sweet, with smoky and earthy undertones. He hated it, but it was the beverage that went down best with his clients and as such he always had a bottle available in his office. In his five years working for Mayfield Realties he had never touched it—until today.

"I need you to find someone because my private investigator's doing a shit job, and you're the only person I trust," Jett said, barely noticing his friend's half full glass.

Kenny didn't blink. "How urgent is it?"

"Major deal."

"A good hookup and can't find her number?" Kenny grinned. He had no idea how close he was to the truth.

"Something like that," Jett remarked dryly as he retrieved a brown Manila envelope from his cabinet and tossed it to Kenny. "Here's everything you need to know about her. And there's something else you need to get me."

Kenny's brow shot up as he flicked through the envelope and Brooke's details. His stare remained glued to Brooke's sleeping face with her wavy hair spread across the pillow like a halo. The picture had been taken with Jett's cellphone in his luxurious Manhattan apartment, on the last day they spent together. Jett had been sitting in the chair opposite from the four-poster bed, torn whether to spill his secret because she had opened up to him a few days previously, telling him about her painful past and why she didn't want a relationship. He felt he owed her the truth, but in the end he decided not to spoil the moment. It had been a big mistake because the next thing he knew they had a fight, and she was gone.

Missing without a trail. And he never had the opportunity to explain things.

"Hey, you still with me?" Kenny said, observing Jett, assessing him. "Why did she leave?"

"I dunno. Ask me something else!" Jett grimaced and refilled their glasses. He swigged down the golden liquid in one gulp while Kenny stared at his, leaving it untouched this time. The whiskey burned down Jett's throat and probably messed with his brain. The beauty of oblivion. If he couldn't find her, then that was the state he was aiming for.

Kenny just shook his head and pointed at the now closed envelope, his look devoid of emotion. "She's pretty." He had always been good at not saying what he thought. It was the reason why he stayed out of trouble—unlike Jett.

"Yeah."

"When did you last see her?"

"Twenty-four hours ago."

Kenny's pretend frown barely hid the beginning of a

sarcastic grin. "That's a really long time."

Jett knew what he sounded like. Desperate. But it didn't matter.

"I'm serious." His voice was cold. Menacing even. He didn't like it when people made fun of him. "I need to find her. You have a problem with that?"

"Jesus. What happened to you, man?"

"I fucking messed up. I fucked up. I wouldn't have called you if it wasn't important."

Kenny leaned back. He didn't seem in the least bothered by Jett's outburst—they had remained friends through tougher shit than that.

"Do you have any idea where she could be? Friends? Family? An ex or a secret boyfriend?" Kenny asked.

If I did I wouldn't be here wasting my time with you, would I?

"I *was* the secret boyfriend." Jett's hand shot through his dark hair as he tried to calm down the angry voice inside him. No good in lashing out at the people around him. They weren't to blame.

"I tried calling her mother who didn't seem particularly worried, but claimed she had no idea," Jett said. "The roommate's gone with her, so I can only assume they both took a road trip. The detective and his team called every hotel in the state of New York." Jett frowned at the memory. He was no professional, but even he knew no woman and her best friend would move out of their cozy apartment and into a hotel for no reason. Talk about wasting precious hours. "I can only assume she's staying with her friend's family."

"Your guy checked credit card companies?"

Jett nodded. "Last time she used it was at some grocery store across from her building."

"What can you tell me about her friend?"

Jett shook his head grimly, signalling that was a dead end. "I know nothing about her. Only that her phone's switched off, too."

Kenny nodded and for a moment silence ensued. Jett's heart began to beat a million miles an hour, though whether it was from the amount of alcohol coursing through his blood or from the seriousness of the situation, he couldn't tell.

"Maybe she's left the country." Kenny eventually resumed the conversation.

Jett had thought about it and discarded the option quickly. "How could she have paid for it without her credit card? I need you to dig deeper than that." He looked down at Kenny who remained silent, his displeasure clearly visible in the frown line on his forehead.

"I'm out of the business, Jett. You know that."

"I wouldn't ask if it wasn't important," Jett whispered.

"You're my best friend and I'd do anything for you, bro. But last time I barely got away with it. I vowed to stay out of trouble."

Kenny's hesitation reflected in his dark eyes, and for a moment Jett was sure his friend would leave him hanging. And then his gaze met Jett's and Jett knew he had won.

"You like her, don't you?" Kenny asked.

"More than I care to admit." It was the truth.

"Then I'll do it. Just promise to have my back if the wrong people come knocking on my door."

Jett smiled, and for the first time since the fight with Brooke he almost felt enthusiastic. Hopeful. Because Kenny always knew what to do. He wasn't one of the most feared hackers for no reason.

"Thanks, man. I appreciate it," Jett said.

"I'll call once I have a lead." Kenny stood and Jett walked him to the door.

***

At 11.45 a.m the cell's screen buzzed to life with an unknown caller. Jett had been stuck in a meeting for the last two hours, barely paying attention to his father's endless rambling about a few new acquisitions and the consequent profits the company could make.

Jett excused himself and shot out of the room, pressing the cell to his ear but not speaking until he reached the men's restroom. The faint scent of roses wafted past as Jett peered into each cubicle, making sure it was empty.

"She boarded a plane to Europe," Kenny said as a means of introduction.

Had the private detective missed the credit card charge?

"Wait until you hear the next part," Kenny coaxed. "You sure you were the *only* secret boyfriend? Because it looks like someone else paid for the tickets."

Brooke wasn't like that. And yet did he really know her?

"Who?" Jett's voice was a layer of ice.

"Ken Clarkson. He's a lawyer from London. Owns a successful firm. Not married."

Why the heck did he need to know the last part? Was he supposed to feel better about the fact that Brooke might be seeing a *not married* guy? When did they meet and why did she trust him enough to let a stranger whisk her away on vacation? Could he be an ex?

"Jett?" Kenny's tone was strained with something. Certainly not worry. More like humor.

"Give me a sec."

The pressure behind Jett's eyes intensified at the thought of Brooke in the arms of another man, claiming what should be *Jett's*. He moistened a hand under the cold water tap and ran it over his feverish nape. The cool moisture provided enough diversion to help him gather his thoughts through all the brain fog. And that's when he began to put two and two together. A lawyer. Paid-for tickets. Europe.

"Where exactly in Europe?"

"Let me check." The sound of flicking papers carried down the line an instant before Kenny said, "Some place called Bellagio. Never heard of it."

He had found her in—

Bellagio—Italy.

Fuck!

That wasn't good. On a scale from one to ten, this was a hundred. A disaster.

"When?"

"Last night," Kenny said. "She landed earlier this morning."

Jett's heart began to thump just a little bit harder. If he jumped on a plane now, he'd be there in eight hours. The actual work would begin now but he wasn't worried about that. He'd never been scared of giving his best—be it working at his job or getting a woman. What worried him was that he could be too late. He had to get to her, and quickly.

"Do you need me to find out more about the lawyer?" Kenny asked.

"I need something else." Jett paused as he looked around to make sure no one could hear him. The restroom was still empty, but he lowered his voice nonetheless to be on the safe side. "Find me a gun dealer in Bellagio."

A pause then, "You're not going to kill her? Or the

lawyer?" He could sense Kenny's doubt.

What the fuck?

Jett had done many stupid things in his life, but he had never been even remotely inclined to harm a woman. He took a deep breath to steady the waves of anger rushing through him. "Just find me the right guy, Kenny."

"I was just—"

"Don't," Jett said, interrupting him. He had no time for questions. It was getting late and he had to get the company jet ready. "Just do what I said."

His father's meeting was still going strong as Jett returned to the conference room. He wasn't keen on wasting any more time, but as a CEO he couldn't just leave without notice—or without anybody noticing. It wouldn't bode well with his reputation. As Jett slipped back into his seat, Robert Mayfield's stare fell on Jett and his brows shot up. The old man didn't like to entertain the idea that something else might be more important. Jett scribbled 'business meeting in Europe- -critical' on one of the notepads carrying the company logo and pushed it across the table toward his father. Signalling Emma to approach, Jett instructed her to gather his stuff, get the company pilot on the phone, and cancel all appointments for the week. He drove home to change and get his passport, then straight to the airport where the company's private jet would take him all the way to the place he visited not that long ago. With her.

1

BROOKE

LOVE HAPPENS IN the blink of an eye. One moment your heart is yours, and the next it belongs to someone you never intended to give it to. There is no transition. No earning on his part. Just foolish trust and hope for a future of happiness and emotional fulfillment. As much as we all hope for a happily ever after, life doesn't work that way.

Love's a bitch. I had to learn that lesson the hard way in the form of a green-eyed, sexy as sin, six foot two sex god.

Jett.

My first and only foray into love, and the second biggest mistake of my life.

I smirked as I adjusted my sunglasses so my best friend, Sylvie, wouldn't catch the telltale signs of betrayal in my eyes. God knows I had shed enough tears over Jett. You would have thought they were depleted by now. Fat chance. It seemed I still had a few left, whether I wanted it or not. Not only did I realize that love can grow in the absence of the person you love, but so does the pain resulting from a broken heart.

It was funny, really, because I couldn't figure out why I started loving him in the first place. Was it his good looks? Or the way he made me feel? The sex? He sure as hell didn't deserve it.

It was barely ten a.m. but the sun stood high on the horizon, bathing the Malpensa Airport building in a glow. Already I could tell it was going to be a hot day, which wasn't surprising given that we were in one of the most beautiful and expensive vacation spots in Italy.

"Let me help you," Sylvie said decisively, snatching my suitcase out of my hand before I could argue. I watched her in silence as she heaved it into the taxi trunk, ignoring the driver's awkward attempts at helping her. She had been protective and caring for the last two days, ever since the thing with Jett blew up. She had been tripping over her own feet to help me 'survive' the raging storm within my heart. In the last forty-eight hours I had been served and massaged, had my hair brushed, my bags packed, and my makeup done by her. I drew the line at having her feed and carry me. Sylvie had always been a good friend, but being caring didn't come naturally to her. So the sudden attention scared the crap out of me. I didn't know whether to run away or hug her.

"Hey, Brooke?" Sylvie tapped my shoulder to get my attention. I turned to face her, realizing I had been spaced out. Again. My brain just switched off momentarily like a computer on standby and needed to be tapped back into work mode. It wasn't natural for a twenty-three-year old. I knew it. She knew it. The whole world probably did. I wished I could make it stop. Get my old life back where I was just 'Brooke'—an overworked, underpaid college graduate naïve enough to hold on to her dreams.

Just forget.

If only I could.

"Get in," Sylvie said, holding the taxi door open for me. I nodded thanks and slumped onto the backseat. Sylvie joined me and grabbed my hand, giving it a firm squeeze, while her smile said everything there was to say. My best friend was here to support me. She'd take care of me until my heart mended and the pieces of my world glued back together.

"You're awesome. You know that?" I whispered to Sylvie.

"That's what friends are for." She moistened her lips and her expression clouded over, as though she wanted to say more but decided against it. I scanned her flawless face and long blond hair. Her outward, gentle beauty revealed none of the hard shell coating her heart. Just like me, she had been bent and broken by men but, unlike me, Sylvie never gave up on love. She kept jumping into the next relationship, only to have her heart broken once more. We were different in this respect. I certainly wouldn't make the same mistake twice.

"Did Clarkson say when you're going to meet the old man?" Sylvie asked, changing subject.

I shook my head as I thought back to the English lawyer I had met with in New York. "He said he'd call once we landed." Absentmindedly, I began to play with the metal clasp of my handbag—a birthday gift from Sylvie—and traced my fingers over the soft faux leather. At that time I had been reluctant to accept it because it had been so damn expensive and I wasn't used to luxury. To think that I had just inherited a multi-million dollar estate from a relative I didn't even know I had completely blew my mind. To think that Jett had tried to trick me into selling the estate so he could build luxury lake-side accommodations for the rich and famous blew my mind even more—and not in a good way. I smirked and leaned back against the smooth leather seat.

"What's the plan?" Sylvie asked.

"He's showing me the property first, then we'll move on to the next step."

She nodded slowly. "Which is looking at the estate's accounting to make sure the old man's not passing any debt to you."

"I know that."

"It was just a reminder, Brooke, in case you forget."

I shot her a dirty look and she smirked back. I never forgot anything and Sylvie knew it. This was her way to tell me that I was playing in a completely different league here. Basically, well over my head, while she was the one who knew everything about high society, and she was determined to take the role of mentor.

Not that I had ever asked her for her guidance. Or that I needed a mentor. But I let her do and say as she pleased because every now and then Sylvie's advice hit the spot. I had no idea what to do with a mansion and thousands of acres of land, with an entire legal firm on speed dial, and a bank director wanting to meet me personally to commence our 'business relationship.' The coming days would be tough, and I was thankful to have someone like Sylvie by my side.

"You'll do okay, chica," Sylvie said, misinterpreting my silence. "I don't doubt you for a second."

I smiled. It was easier to let her think I was nervous because of my first meeting with Alessandro Lucazzone. I couldn't tell her that my heart was fluttering like a delicate butterfly throwing itself against its prison because the hour-long drive to Lake Como brought on more pain than I cared to acknowledge. And now my demons were officially out of the cage and I had to face them.

"He'll be here eventually. You know that, right?" I whispered.

"I know," Sylvie said. "But it doesn't matter. You won't have to talk to him if you don't want to. You don't have to see him ever again. He's part of your past and he'll stay that way."

Taking a deep breath, I propped my head against the window and stared out at the stunning display of sparkling blue water and mountaintops, wondering whether I could really stay away from the one man who broke my heart.

2

TINY GRAVEL STONES crunched beneath the tires as the taxi came to a halt around the corner and parked neatly in the vast driveway of the Lucazzone estate. I paid the driver and exited the car, barely paying attention as he helped with the luggage. He took off down the unpaved private terrain that seemed to be the only way to reach the Lucazzone mansion, unless you didn't mind a rocky boat ride across the lake on the other side of the estate. Both were secluded areas.

I knew I shouldn't gawk and yet I couldn't help myself. From up front, the magnificent building stretching three stories into the sky looked like a miniature of a Venetian palace, stuck in the middle of the countryside. The grand three-opening loggia with pillars and dovecotes on the roof was reminiscent of the fortress-like villas of the early 1500s, but it had a personal flair to it: a beauty that transcended place and time. A warmth that instantly made me feel at home, and at the same time a soft shiver ran down my spine because I realized that one day everything would be mine.

"It's so beautiful." Arms stretched out, I resisted the urge to spin in a slow circle. Instead, I inhaled the fragrant air. It wasn't just beautiful—it was haunting, mesmerizing. So silent I could hear the chirping birds and the soft wind rustling the leaves. Sylvie didn't answer. I shot her a sideway glance and caught the drawn brows. I didn't dwell on it because old houses and nature weren't exactly Sylvie's thing. A margarita and a nightclub were more her locale.

"Let's ring the bell," I said, grabbing her arm and pulling her up the stairs to the front door.

"Shouldn't the lawyer be expecting us?" Sylvie asked.

"He's probably inside and didn't hear the taxi. It's a huge house."

Sylvie mumbled something that resembled a 'maybe.' I paid her no attention as I pressed the bell. A moment later the door opened and Clarkson's tall figure blocked the view inside.

"Miss Stewart." He reached out his hand, and the lined skin beneath his eyes crinkled as though he was genuinely pleased to see me. I shook his hand briefly, then moved aside to introduce Sylvie.

"You're the lady who wouldn't open the envelope,"

Clarkson said good-humoredly.

"You're the gentleman who wouldn't stop pestering me about it," Sylvie returned. I laughed because they both nailed it. I had been in Italy when Clarkson first called to inform me that I was about to inherit the Lucazzone estate. Naturally, he didn't disclose that information to Sylvie, but his secretary had sent a form letter, which Sylvie was too scared to open.

"It's lovely to finally make your acquaintance," Clarkson said. I could tell he was smitten with her by the way his eyes seemed to linger on her, taking in every detail of her designer-clad body. He seemed like a nice guy—genuine, well-mannered and, judging from the lack of a wedding ring or tan line on his finger, definitely not married. He was too old for her though, at least twenty years her senior, and that gave me peace because I wouldn't want my best friend to date my lawyer.

"Thanks for inviting us," I said, drawing his attention back to me. A flicker of disappointment appeared in his eyes and disappeared just as quickly.

"It was Mr. Lucazzone's wish to meet his heir before—" He dies, I mentally filled in the blank. Clarkson cleared his throat. "Anyway, he's still in hospital and cannot be with us for another day or two, until his tests are performed. But he's instructed me to show you to your rooms and make your stay a pleasant one."

Clarkson helped with the luggage as we followed him down the hall and up the stairs, past several closed doors into what looked like a large drawing room. He tried to maintain a light conversation, asking about our flight and drive over. I let Sylvie handle it as I took in the house.

Outside I had described it as beautiful, but the word did it no justice. It was magnificent and huge with cream marble floors, expensive paintings adorning the walls, and a huge staircase leading to the second and third floor balustrades. Suiting the Mediterranean style, several vases with flowers were set up in the corners, brightening up the minimalist look. It was my style: no clutter, everything neat and orderly, just the way I liked my life.

"This is the west wing. It's all yours. You'll find all rooms have a spectacular view of both the lake and the mountains behind," Clarkson said, keeping up the small talk. "I'll let you settle in. We can go over the financial reports in the next few days."

"Sounds perfect."

He nodded and his eyes twinkled again. I figured many people would have felt at least a pang of jealousy for my unexpected windfall, but not Clarkson. He seemed genuinely pleased for me.

"Absolutely," he said. "All members of the staff will gather later this afternoon to introduce themselves. They come and go as they're needed so you'll have the house all to yourself until Mr. Lucazzone's back. If you need anything, please don't hesitate to call. I'm staying in Bellagio, which is a stone's throw away."

"Thank you for everything," I said, meaning every word.

"My pleasure," he said, opening the first door. "I hope the ladies will have a pleasant stay." His look swept from me to Sylvie and lingered there a bit too long as he handed me what looked like a leather pouch with a silver ring dangling from it, which I assumed were the keys to the house. I nodded a 'thanks' and Clarkson reached out his hand to shake mine. And then he was gone and the house was silent. For a few seconds I felt disoriented—surreal. We were in Italy. Alone. In a huge house that would soon belong to me.

"You still have time to run," Sylvie whispered. I smiled at her weak attempt at humor to ease my nerves.

"I think I'll stay." I smiled and pointed at the open door. "Now, have your pick before I change my mind."

***

"What do you think?" I asked Sylvie as soon as we had unpacked our suitcases and opened the balcony doors to let in the fragrant air of the nearby woods. We were sitting on the expensive lounge chairs, soaking up the warm rays of sun as we stared onto the lake. The sun caught in the sparkling water and reflected in a million facets. I sighed with pleasure as I relaxed into the soft pillows, figuring the only thing missing was a big hat, orange lemonade, and an umbrella straw.

She hesitated. "I like it. You'll be fine. Big old house, plenty of silence and a lake to swim. Let's hope you have internet, so we can stay in touch when I'm back in New York."

Her eyes were closed and her face a perfect mask of indifference, but I didn't fail to catch the slight bitter tone in her voice. She didn't want to lose her best friend, which was understandable given that we had known each other for so long. I felt uneasy at the thought of not seeing her every day, but I wanted to give this new development in my life a chance. It wasn't going to be forever; just for a while—until the Jett episode blew over and I managed to get a job I liked—far away from him and his world. How could I make this clear to her?

"It's not the city life we're used to but I agree it'll be a nice change for a while." Emphasis on *while*. "You could stay with me. Explore the country. Do all the things people do. You've got to admit it's an amazing opportunity."

Her head inclined to the side. "We could learn Italian. Maybe attend a cooking course. Get married. Have four kids. And talk about diapers and skin rashes the entire day."

I groaned, ignoring the sudden urge to roll my eyes. As

usual, she was being sarcastic at the outlook of not visiting a club every night. She wasn't a country girl. She loved the fumes, the stress, the constant mental activity, and lack of sleep. Me? Not so much. If I wanted her to stay with me, I needed a different tactic.

"I've heard Italian guys are hot."

Now I had her attention. Sylvie's eyes snapped open and her lips curled into a smile. "You're back in the game? I wouldn't mind one of those charming, sultry, suave Latinos who can set the room on fire with a single sway of his hips. Imagine the passion, the drama, the intensity." She threw her head back and took a deep breath, fanning herself with her manicured fingers.

I knew I might be letting the she-wolf out of the cage with my casual remark, and yet I honestly didn't expect so much enthusiasm coming from her. In Sylvie's world there was only success, sex, parties, and variety—and any combination of those. No doubt Lake Como could provide any of those but was I really keen on it?

Sensing my hesitation, Sylvie pulled a face, misinterpreting my silence. "No club? What about a bar? I don't even mind a bit of walking or a long drive, as long as there's any sort of music and alcohol." She pouted.

Lie, Stewart.

If I lied and said there were no bars or clubs, Sylvie would leave me hanging within the week. I just *knew* it. If I told her about Bellagio's nightlife, I doubted we'd get to see any sights, other than the bottom of a tequila shot.

"To get to a club we'd need to cross the lake, walk up the hill, and then take a taxi to the city," I said slowly. It wasn't the shortest way but certainly not a lie.

Sylvie jumped up and regarded me with a smug smile that told me I had just lost the battle.

"Or we could go the way we came. I don't mind the extra miles." She pulled a card from her back pocket and waved it in the air, inches from my face.

"What the hell is that?" I tried to grab it out of her hand but she pulled it away and stepped back, pressing it against her chest like a piece of treasure.

"Our very own personal taxi service. I figured it wouldn't hurt asking the driver whether he offered private trips. Turns out he does. How cool is that?" Her eyes sparkled again and I knew I had, indeed, lost the battle.

"Isn't that expensive?"

She shrugged. "So?"

The girl came from a rich background; she grew up as part of the upper class society. Of course she had no objections to throwing money out the window—unlike me.

"Come on, chica. My treat." She rolled her eyes. "Not that you need it."

I sighed. Just because I'd inherit an estate didn't mean it came with a bank account set up for nights out.

"Brooke." Her blue eyes bore into mine and she pouted again. "Let's go out. Only tonight. You know me. I can't be *this*." She smirked and pointed around her at the stunning house and the setting, like it was a bad thing. "I honestly don't mind a long drive or a huge taxi bill. Any small club is better than no club. Please."

Puppy eyes again. My hesitation faltered because, first, I knew a lost cause when I saw one. And second, come to think of it, a bit of fun wasn't such a bad idea. I was single—I cringed inwardly at the thought—and in one of Europe's most famous vacation spots. I had sworn off alcohol for good but I could at least dance the night away.

"We'll be back by midnight?" I asked.

"Sure." Sylvie shrugged and averted her gaze, which was a dead giveaway that she was lying. In that moment, I knew I wouldn't be able to pry her away from the clubs with a crowbar—unless the bouncers threw us out.

With a strange sense of dread gathering in the pit of my stomach, I watched Sylvie pull out her cell and dial the number on the card. A moment later she had agreed on a time and hung up.

We hadn't even fully unpacked our bags yet, and she had already secured a trip to a local nightclub. Talk about priorities!

I followed her inside as she began to rummage through her suitcase, and I sat down on the bed, watching the mess she was about to unleash upon her room. Soon her clothes were scattered all over the floor and bed. Judging from the half full suitcase, there was more to come.

Back home Sylvie insisted we pack everything we might need, which in Sylvie's dictionary was the equivalent to cramming everything from her overflowing closet to the contents of her bathroom cabinets into the oversized suitcase she wanted to take with her. Needless to say, we had paid the price for extra baggage at customs. But at least she knew how to dress. I stared open-mouthed at one designer dress after another, some barely resembling a dress at all. More like pieces of sheer fabric that left nothing to the imagination.

"You need to get laid," Sylvie said as she pulled out two short dresses and compared them. "And pronto. Jett might have been hot, but newer is always better."

Where the hell did that come from?

"I never said I wanted to get laid," I said through gritted teeth.

"Of course you didn't." She smirked and tossed one dress aside, then picked up another. "But I know you want to. Or at least that's the way to go if you want to rid your heart of him once and for all."

I slumped against the pillows as I regarded the dress in her hands. She was right about that. In her own way. Ever since I came back from my trip with Jett, she seemed to have recovered from her own heartache. If I wanted to move on, all I had to do was be like her. Forget the world. And just have fun, even if that meant dating lots of men within a very short time. She wasn't cheap. She didn't sleep with most of them—she just liked soaking up the attention and then moving on to the next.

She winked. "Whatever you do in Italy, stays in Italy. I promise my lips are sealed."

Oh, Lord.

She tossed the first dress to me. I caught it in mid-air. "Try this."

I held up the strapless dress and eyed it suspiciously. The black material felt soft in my hands, almost weightless. It was so tight and thin, I had no doubt people would see my underwear—particularly under the neon lights of a club. Definitely not the kind of dress I had in my wardrobe.

Under normal circumstances I'd have objected to wearing something that daring, but today was different. I wanted to be someone else, preferably someone that wouldn't remind me of my old boring self.

What do you want to prove, Stewart?

Ignoring my rational mind, I shrugged out of my jeans and casual shirt. Sylvie dangled a pair of black pumps in front of my face.

"I don't think I'll be able to walk in them," I said, slipping into the shoes nevertheless. The heels were so high

I almost toppled over and had to hold on to the dresser for support.

"You can't say no to *Jimmy Choo*. It'd be a sin. Plus, you look hot. If I were a guy I'd totally do you." Her dead serious expression told me she wasn't kidding.

I inspected myself in the large mirror. This was a dress I'd never wear back home, but we weren't back home. No one knew me here. Besides, Sylvie was right, I looked hot. The dress hugged my body in all the right places, emphasizing my curves, of which I had always been ashamed until college when I realized men liked them. The heels made my legs appear thinner and sky-high. Maybe not as long as a model's, but I could certainly see the benefit in wearing them.

"Told you," Sylvie said, grinning. "Now, let's rock this town."

Biting my lip, I nodded and averted my gaze. How could I tell her that Bellagio wasn't exactly a town? More like a village. I was yet to find out just how tiny it actually was.

3

SITTING IN THE backseat of the taxi with my arms wrapped around me, I realized Sylvie's dress choice had seemed a good idea in the privacy of our four walls. Not so much in public. I kept pulling the hem in the hope of giving it more fabric, or length—anything that would help me feel less naked.

"You look so hot," Sylvie whispered, probably misinterpreting my fidgeting. "I bet every guy in that club will be all over you the moment you enter the door."

Did I want that?

Not really.

I wasn't the attention seeking type or the one who wanted to be in the spotlight, but I couldn't share that with Sylvie. She wouldn't understand.

"No, I bet they'll be all over *you*." I pointed at her little black dress, which seemed to ride even shorter than mine. Or maybe it was the effect of her long and toned legs stretching up forever.

"You think?" Sylvie's face lit up like a Christmas candle. Not only was she stunning, she also had a constant need to be reminded of it.

"I know," I said, happy to no longer be the topic of the conversation.

I stepped out of the taxi into the balmy night air. My curls framed my cheeks and brushed my naked shoulders like soft butterfly wings, making my skin tingle. Club 66— the only club in the nearby area—was a tall, tower-like building with a glass front. The front doors were open and the faint beats of some Top Forty song carried over. A broad shouldered big guy stood to the side, eyeing us. I wasn't sure whether he was supposed to be some kind of bouncer or just a guest waiting for his date, lighting up a cigarette or looking for phone reception.

"That's all you could find?" Sylvie glared at me from under heavily mascaraed eyelashes.

I shrugged. "Want me to quote you? Like you said, 'better than sitting at home, growing roots.' If you don't like it, we can still grab a pizza on the way back home and watch reality TV."

Actually, I wouldn't have minded that.

Just thinking about it—sitting around in pajamas, eating

ice cream and watching a really sad movie, preferably where the male main character died, because Jett was as good as dead to me—sounded like the perfect night to me.

Sylvie scoffed and walked through the doors into what resembled a dimly lit reception area, leaving me behind smiling. With her it was all a matter of priority. *Any* sort of club was better than no club. At times I wondered how the heck we managed to stay friends for so long when we had so little in common.

The reception desk also served as a coat counter, which was obvious from the few jackets dangling from hangers and a lady standing there, cashing in. Sylvie and I weren't wearing jackets, but we paid the cover charge and our hands were stamped, and then we entered the actual club area.

Being one of the few entertainment opportunities for those aged eighteen and up within a fifty-mile radius of Bellagio, the room was filled to capacity, overflowing with dancing girls and young men vying for their attention. The walls were covered in mirrors. Manufactured smoke wafted in the air, creating a dreamlike haze. Surreal but also a bit tacky. In the middle of the room was a huge staircase leading to a second story that, gazing up from my position, looked like it was bathed in darkness. I could already tell the music—the same fast beat I had heard outside—would make any sort of conversation hard. I mentally prepared myself for a long silent chat with the bottom of my glass as

Sylvie and I maneuvered around the gathered crowds of people, heading for Sylvie's most preferred spot: the bar.

"You order while I'm looking for a table," I yelled at Sylvie so she'd hear me over the background noise.

"What?" she yelled back, her gaze fixed on her right where three people worked behind the bar, mixing and serving at a fast speed. I couldn't tell whether she was so transfixed by the outlook of getting hammered, or the music was indeed way too loud. Tugging at her arm to get her attention, I leaned in to repeat in her ear and watched her flinch. Nope, it wasn't the music. Just the anticipation of an alcohol-infused night.

I didn't wait for her reply. Making my way past the staircase with a rope running across it and marked as 'VIP area', I scanned the tables and chairs lining the walls. They were all occupied, apart from one table. I dashed for it like a maniac, eager to 'claim' it before someone else spied me and beat me to it. I didn't even care that my dress exposed way more of my thighs than was acceptable as I slumped onto the plush leather settee and bumped my knee against the table in front of it.

Long pangs of pain shot up my leg. I cringed to hold back a startled yelp, already missing my jeans, which would have provided a layer of protection.

"You okay?" Sylvie said, sliding next to me.

I nodded and grabbed a drink from her outstretched

hand, realizing she had made the effort to remember I had sworn off alcohol for good because every time I so much as took a sip, something bad happened.

Like me waking up half-naked in bed next to a man who turned out to be my boss.

Or revealing all the things I wanted to do with said boss, which reminded me that I was jobless now, and probably had bad references. Talk about stupid!

I took a sip of my water with a slice of lemon, and placed the glass on the table as I watched Sylvie gulp down half of her margarita while searching the area for prospective male targets. Half a minute later they had spied her, and the first suitor found his way to our table. I looked away and tuned out because I knew he most certainly wasn't going to offer *me* a drink, ask for a dance, or whatever he was about to say.

"You okay if I go for a dance?" Sylvie whispered in my ear. "He's quite cute."

"Have fun." I smiled at her encouragingly. In all the years we had known each other, I had grown used to guys probably thinking I was the less hot friend, the baggage, at times even the gatekeeper of the hot tall blonde.

For a few minutes I just sat there listening to the club music; my mind wandered off to the estate and my own life plans. I had no job but would inherit a property that was worth quite a bit of money. Not that losing a job had happened to me before, but it wasn't my style to live off someone else's cash. As soon as I figured out how long I'd be staying I knew I'd find employment, even if just for a few weeks. The language barrier might be a problem, but I hoped in a tourist area someone might have something for me that wouldn't require fluent Italian language skills.

"Thanks for saving our spot," Sylvie said, sliding back into her seat. I looked from her to the full margarita glass in her hand. It was at least the second drink and that barely twenty minutes within our arrival.

"You should slow down a bit. We're not in New York where we know the place." I wasn't usually the voice of reason—or a buzz kill—but we were in a different country.

She waved her hand and shot me a dazzling smile. "Relax, Brooke. You weren't this boring when you were still guzzling down tequila shots with me."

I smirked. Granted, she had a point, but still. Nothing wrong with being careful. Better safe than sorry, right?

"Look at that hot Italian guy." Sylvie pointed past a group of dancing girls to a guy with a tattoo on his neck and a black leather jacket draped across the stool beside him. He looked like he belonged to a gang. I couldn't really judge whether he was hot, or not. Obviously I didn't have Sylvie's hawk eyes when it came to spying an attractive specimen of the other gender in a dimly lit club. From the distance I could barely make out more than his height and cropped hair, ripped jeans, and what looked like lots of ink covering his bare arms. For all I knew, he could be between twenty and fifty years of age, with a hideous face.

"He looks like a drug dealer," I remarked dryly.

Sylvie laughed that tinkling laughter of hers that told me she had probably heard the opposite of what I just said, and she grabbed her glass. "Time to get acquainted."

Oh God. Not him.

I grabbed her arm and yanked, forcing her to face me. "Please don't hook up with the local mafia. I don't want them knocking on our door, or burning down the house the moment they realize you go through men like others change their underwear. He looks like trouble and trust me, I have a keen eye when it comes to spotting trouble." I raised my brow, not stating the obvious.

Something flickered in her blue gaze. First I thought it was a spark of realization that I was right—and then her mouth pressed into a tight line and I knew it was determination. She was about to try to prove me wrong.

"Oh, come on, Sylvie. That's so stupid." I rolled my eyes. Sylvie yanked her arm away.

"Just because he looks like a bad boy doesn't mean he is one. Besides, I'm not interested in dating him. Just in having a drink and then chatting for a few minutes. You know, meet new people, and maybe improve my Italian."

Sylvie didn't speak one word of Italian. During our flight

she had been using her meager Spanish and French vocabulary, think 'muchas gracias' and 'merci' when talking to the flight attendant.

"Chatting? Really? Do I need to remind you that's what you always say?" I crossed my arms over my chest and regarded her coolly.

"Chill, Brooke. I know what I'm doing. Besides, we're here to have fun. You might as well start having it." She shot me her most reassuring smile, which wasn't reassuring at all. If there was one thing I could say about Sylvie, it was that her taste in men sucked almost as much as mine. Given that mine had just hit rock bottom, I could only hope she wasn't going to try to top me.

She leaned in to place a soft peck on my cheek, and then she was gone before I could mentally devise a strategy to keep her away from a natural human disaster. My eyes following her through the crowd, I leaned forward in my seat and craned my neck so I could watch Sylvie's every move—just in case she was aiming for more than a drink. As if sensing the blonde behind him the tattooed guy turned, and then they were engrossed in conversation. Just in the blink of an eye. My heart fell in my chest as I observed their body language. Both leaning into each other, Sylvie smiled at something he said, and then he smiled. The next thing I knew they were on the dance floor, his arms wrapped around her. Her body grinded against him as the

DJ switched the tune to something fast but sexy. The kind of music that invited you to let the guy you've barely known for five minutes play acrobatics with your tongue.

My gaze glued to Sylvie and her conquest, I took another sip of my water when something tickled my neck and someone's hot breath caressed my ear.

"Brooke, what the fuck do you think you're wearing?"

I jumped in my seat at hearing the familiar voice in my ear, and my heart skipped a beat. Turning, I looked up to see *him* leaning over me, barely an inch away. The way he made my heart hammer, I knew I was far from over him.

4

HOLY MOTHER of sins!

What the hell was *he* doing here?

The question played over and over in my head as I swallowed hard to get rid of the sudden lump in my throat. It wasn't just my throat that felt constricted, but everything else—from my stomach to down below, as though every inch of my body remembered the good times he and I once had.

That was before I found out he was planning to steal my future estate.

"J—" My mouth opened and closed again, unable to utter his name, while my eyes remained glued to him like a moth to light. I wanted to run; I wanted to scream, and yet I did none of those things. My whole being was too hurt to react, too stunned by his presence.

It couldn't be. He couldn't be here because he couldn't possibly know where I was. No one did. I took a deep breath to calm the alarm bells ringing somewhere at the back of my mind. I was in deep crap. No, make that the deepest and crappiest of crap, because Jett was at least twice as sinfully gorgeous as I remembered him and thrice as dangerous—to my heart. The soft spot I thought I had for him in my heart and in my lower abdomen, magnified in the blink of an eye.

Dark hair that brushed his collar, eyes as deep and green as sin, a white shirt that only managed to emphasize his broad shoulders and sculpted chest—the guy was a walking hazard to the female population. He certainly was to me. Even though he had crushed my heart and I *knew* about the kind of jerky trick he had tried to pull on me, I *still* couldn't help the tiny butterflies fluttering in the pit of my stomach. Maybe it wasn't my stomach, but something else. Something remembering his exploring fingers and the way he had filled me, making me come over and over again.

I rolled my eyes at my sudden onset of stupidity. Okay, we had amazing sexual chemistry and he definitely knew what he was doing, but whatever he had to say I wasn't going to listen to him. Or bed him. Even though I sort of wanted the latter. A lot.

"You know what I'm going to do to every guy who so much as looks at you?" Jett's lips brushed the lobe of my ear as his mouth moved to the corner of my mouth, his deep tone with just a hint of a Southern accent caressing my every nerve ending, making me want to—

Hell, no!

I jumped to my feet to put some much-needed distance between us and almost toppled over the bistro table. My eyes bore into him and the music died around us. The whole room began to spin and the people turned into a blur of distorted faces and colors. Closing my eyes, I gripped the edge of the table for support and forced myself to take deep breaths until my heartbeat slowed down to a bearable level. When I opened my eyes again he was still there. Still towering over me. Still gorgeous. The room began to spin again and my resentment started to slip away, which angered me. I needed to be angry because he was the bad guy.

"Sit down." He closed the distance between us, the deep frown between his eyebrows barely taking away the breathtaking perfection of his face.

My mind screamed at him to stay the hell away from me, but my throat remained constricted, incapable of following my brain's command. I raised my arm to stop him. Jett flat out ignored it as he clutched my upper arm and pushed me back into my seat. He dropped down next to me, so close I might as well have sat on his lap. I watched him sniff the contents of my glass and push it into my hand, seemingly satisfied that it wasn't alcohol.

"Drink up. You're dehydrated." His tone left no room for discussion. I hated to give him the satisfaction of following his command, and yet I found myself taking one sip after another until the glass was empty. He took it from me and placed it on the table, then turned to regard me, his head cocked to the side, his jaw set. His stunning green gaze wandered over me, drinking me in, making me feel completely naked. Even though the lights were dimmed, I could see a nerve twitching beneath his right eye. With every moment that passed he seemed even more pissed. I crossed my arms over my chest, wishing I was wearing more than the thin layer of nothing Sylvie called a dress.

"You still haven't answered my question, Brooke," he said slowly, emphasizing my name.

I returned his icy stare and my tongue finally regained its ability to speak. "Sorry, did you say something? I was too busy figuring out whether you were stalking me."

Jett's expression darkened. "What the hell are you wearing?"

"This?" I looked at my half exposed chest and laughed. It sounded a bit strained and nervous, but he certainly couldn't tell with the music in the background. The tune changed to something about a girl not letting a guy trick her twice. I snorted.

How fitting!

The DJ was sending me a message.

"Okay, I'll bite," I said. "What's wrong with it?"

"You're giving every guy in here a hard-on. Including me." His fingers brushed the inside of my thigh, riding as high as the hem of my dress, which was mere inches away from my thong. At his warm touch, heat immediately travelled through my belly and pooled between my legs. I pressed my thighs together and tried to push his hand away. He didn't move.

"Maybe every *other* guy was the plan," I said. "Because I wasn't planning on seeing you. How did you find me?"

"Once I figured you were in Italy, it wasn't hard. Knowing you and Sylvie, and given that this is the only club in the area—" He shrugged. I cringed at his audacity. Who the fuck did he think he was?

"Seriously, you're such an arrogant jerk," I hissed.

His icy stare dropped a few degrees, if that was even possible. I narrowed my eyes in the hope he'd feel my distaste for him.

"Didn't I make myself clear enough in New York? It's over between us. Get the fuck away from me, Jett. I don't want to see you."

If my words reached him, he didn't react. Didn't even blink. For a second I thought he didn't hear me. I opened my mouth to repeat myself when he raised his hand to cut me off. "Look, I know what I did was a shitty move but I can explain. I was trying to protect you."

The protection crap again. "What are you protecting me from? An inheritance you'd rather have for yourself?" I rolled my eyes. "Please, spare yourself further embarrassment and just leave me alone because I'm not buying your lies."

His hand grasped my upper arm so fast and hard, I flinched. He inched closer until I could feel his breath on my lips. "Listen to me. I don't want the Lucazzone estate. There was a time when I did, but that changed after I met you in that bar and we got to know each other."

There was something in his eyes, a glint that begged me to believe him, a flame that forced me to search through our history for signs that he hadn't been trying to deceive me all along.

"Fuck you, Jett."

He was so close, barely an inch away from me; I could barely breathe. I needed to get away from here, from him, from the whole situation. And yet I remained seated, not even yanking my arm away even though his grip was beginning to hurt.

As though sensing my discomfort, Jett loosened his grip but didn't let go of me. "I know you don't trust me and I can't blame you. I probably wouldn't trust myself, but this is serious, Brooke. You don't know what you're getting yourself into." His calm tone and sharp gaze sent a shiver down my spine. Somewhere in the back of my mind I realized he had said exactly the same words before, and the realization made me uncomfortable. Not to mention it managed to ignite my curiosity.

"Protect from whom?" I almost choked on my words. The entire situation sounded like something out of a Hollywood movie. And yet I didn't laugh. Maybe it was the dead serious expression on his beautiful face. Or the way his thumb brushed my thigh, both soothing me and setting my skin on fire. Or his voice that conveyed a magnitude and significance I somehow seemed to fail to grasp.

"It's complicated," Jett said, hesitating. "Go out with me and I'll tell you everything I know."

He almost got me.

I snorted at my idiocy. He was playing mind games again, and this was just another ruse to get me alone so he could seduce me or get whatever he was after.

"No way."

"Fine. No date. Just breakfast, coffee, or whatever you want." He cocked a brow and a glint of amusement lit up his eyes. Green as sin—the kind of sin I couldn't wait to dive into and stain my body with. No way was I going to be alone with him anywhere.

"What are you afraid of, Miss Stewart? That you won't be able to resist me?"

Oh God.

How could I have forgotten his inflated ego? I bit my lip hard so I wouldn't smile, not because it was funny but because he was so spot-on—I might not be able to resist him. Not only was he scorching hot, he knew the effect he had on women, and that's never a good combination. Jett raised a brow in challenge.

"You're not God's gift to the female population." I hated to admit it but he sort of was. At least his good looks were, thanks to his inherited hotness gene. Not sure about his shitty character. "I'll give you five minutes over coffee, just to explain, and that's it. Then you'll leave me alone. Deal?"

He seemed to consider my suggestion for a moment. I felt my heartbeat speed up again as I regarded him. Even though I was fuming mad and the scars of betrayal he had left behind would take years to heal, if ever, I couldn't help the bubble of happiness growing in my foolish chest. Now that the shock was slowly wearing off, I was happy to see him.

"Make it dinner."

I laughed at his self-assured expression and the amused glint in his eyes. He obviously thought I was going to give in. The guy definitely needed to be taught a lesson.

"Lunch, and that's my final offer. Take it or leave it."

"You drive a hard bargain, Miss Stewart."

"I'm known for my bargaining skills," I said proudly.

"Throw in a drink and a dance today, and you have a deal." He moistened his lips, his tongue leaving a moist trail. I stared at it for a moment longer than I should have, unable to peel my gaze off him.

"I'm not drinking tonight," I said.

His leg brushed my thigh. It was just an inch, but enough to remind me just how close we sat. My breath hitched and the walls began to close down on me. The air felt too hot to breathe.

"A dance, then. And I get to pick the song." He grinned.

No way was I letting him pick the damn song. He'd probably go for something slow and sexy. Something that would invite a lap dance. That was way too personal, not to mention the last thing my crumbling self-control needed.

"I pick the song," I said decisively.

"What about we retreat to the VIP area and no one picks the song?"

I shook my head. "We stay here, on the dance floor, where everyone can see us."

"Fine by me, Brooke. I've always been into public performance. I'm glad to know I could give you a taste for it." His voice was low and hoarse, his stare intense, the glint of amusement gone, leaving no room for misinterpretation.

Oh God.

My cheeks flamed as I thought back to the one time we had sex on the shore of Lake Como, where people could have seen us. I realized I had just said the most stupid thing ever and probably managed to inflate his ego even more. Soon it'd grow to monstrous proportions, and he'd need a bulldozer to push it through the door.

"Let's just dance before I change my mind," I said. At least he didn't get to choose the music.

Jett stood and reached down to help me up. I placed my hand into his outstretched palm, trying hard to ignore the electric shock running through my arm, playing havoc with my nerves.

As he pushed through the crowd making room for me to follow, I scanned the dance floor and bar, realizing Sylvie was nowhere in sight. She had taken off with Tattooed Guy.

Unbelievable!

My mood plummeted.

The dance floor was crowded but not to the point of strangers touching you. The neon lights over our heads flickered with the beat, bathing us in a seizure-inducing white glow. Above us I could see the staircase leading to the darkened VIP area; to our right was what looked like a DJ booth. Jett turned to face me but didn't move. I frowned, wondering what the heck he was waiting for.

The music was louder here. I leaned in to shout so he'd hear me over the noise. "One song, Mayfield, and that's it. No touching, grinding, or any other funny moves. Or I'm gone."

"What? You think I can't keep my hands off of you? You're damn right about that, baby."

As though to prove his point, his hands moved to my ass and pulled me against him. Balancing on seven-inch stilettoes, I barely reached his chin. His hand forced my chin up until our gazes interlocked. His lips neared mine, scorching my skin with his hot breath. For a moment I thought he'd kiss me but he just hovered there, leaving me both wanting and fearing his kiss.

"What are you doing?" I managed to say through ragged breaths.

"Waiting for the right song. I'm going to make the best of my one and only dance."

The music slowed down a bit as the DJ made an announcement in Italian. I looked around, confused, wondering what was going on. An instant later, half the dance floor cleared and other people joined us. Most were couples. I realized the DJ was about to change the music and none of us had asked for it. Damn! I had been pretty comfortable with the last fast-paced song.

"What did he say?" I asked Jett, frowning.

His lips curled at one corner but he made no effort to explain as the beat morphed into a different song. A love song. I groaned inwardly.

Great, just great!

Jett must've had a lucky day.

"That's more like it," he whispered as he pulled me closer to him—so close I could feel his heartbeat.

I knew this song and instantly wished I hadn't agreed to a dance. The female vocalist began to sing something about love never dying, lurking in the deepest crevices, bypassing time, and resurfacing once more, stronger than before. It was just one song, albeit a stupid one. I chose to ignore her voice and let the beat lead the way.

It was all so slow and sexy, the way my chest trembled against his, the way Jett's body began to move against me, his hips molding into mine, his breath tickling my cheek, sending my heart into overdrive. I wanted to run and yet I couldn't move, as though he had put a spell on me and frozen me in his arms forever.

As the music pulled us in, our bodies moved in accord. I inhaled his scent—a mixture of manly aftershave and *him*—and let his arms envelope me, pressing me so close against him I could barely breathe. Maybe it was the way he smelled or the way his hands possessed me, but something about him drove me wild and daring. I felt his body brushing against mine and my mind dissolved into nothingness as our bodies merged to the hot beat. I don't know how long we just danced, clutching at each other, wanting, owning. By the time we stopped, I had lost track of both time and myself. I had long forgotten why I was so pissed at him. All that mattered was that I had never felt so *right* in anyone's arms.

"You smell so good. Like wild roses in a warm summer night's breeze," Jett said in my ear as he led me through the crowd and back to my table.

Smiling, I averted my eyes so he wouldn't see how much his words affected my sappy heart. What woman wouldn't want to hear she smelled like roses?

We reached the table and Jett pulled me against him, forcing me to meet his cryptic gaze. "Brooke—" He trailed off, hesitating, as though he wanted to say something but couldn't decide whether to continue, or not. We stared at each other in silence, relishing the other's presence. Eventually he said what he had started, though I could tell by the guarded look on his face that it wasn't all.

"I'm sorry."

His eyes looked so earnest that my breath caught in my throat. No words could convey so much and yet so little. What was I supposed to say? That I believed him and that everything was all right—when it wasn't? It'd be a lie because I didn't believe him. I didn't trust him.

Jett squeezed my hand gently but combined with his words, it was too much. A sting of disappointment and pain washed over me. I pulled my hand away and stepped back to put some much-needed physical space between us. This stupid song! Love wasn't supposed to hurt.

His eyes bore deeper into my soul, cutting through layers of hurt and mistrust. I could feel him in my heart and in every fiber of my being.

"I know you don't trust me, Brooke, and I'm ready to give you as much time as you need, just don't back away from me. Give me a chance to prove that I was telling the truth."

His gaze was so intense, I found myself nodding. I *wanted* him to regain my trust, not to get back together, but because I knew deep down he wasn't a bad person.

"There's a bus station in front of the club. Meet me there tomorrow and I'll explain," he said.

"Okay," I said reluctantly, already regretting my decision. "And no more lies, Jett."

He took a deep breath and smiled that dazzling, lopsided smile of his that always managed to send my pulse racing. "I promise you the truth and nothing but the truth."

"Now go," I said. "I don't want Sylvie seeing us together, or she might decide to bite off your head." And then I'd certainly miss his beautiful face, but that I didn't add. Jett didn't need to know just how much he still affected me.

His face clouded over. "I'm not letting you—"

"I'll be fine, Jett. I've never been better. Now go, or the deal's off." I infused my tone with all the resolve I could muster. I knew I sounded brisk and unfriendly, but I didn't want him to get the wrong idea. Jett could be stubborn, but so could I. I wasn't going to spend the evening with him and risk falling deeper into this mess before he had told me his part of the story.

Countless emotions, ranging from annoyance to mulishness crossed his features, and then it all settled into compliance. Obviously, he was a clever guy and knew when to back off.

"Bus station. Twelve o'clock." His fingers trailed up my upper arm and settled beneath my chin, and for a moment I thought he was going to kiss me. I held my breath, anticipating the intimate touch of his lips, but it never came. "Please be careful. And Brooke—"

I raised my brows, barely able to breathe. "Yeah?"

"Switch that goddamn phone on now. I don't want to have to remind you again." His tone was menacing, carrying just a hint of a sexy threat.

I opened my mouth to tell him where he could shove his command, but he had already turned away, having the last word, as usual. Speechless, I watched his broad shoulders move away until he was swallowed up by the crowd. Only after sitting back down did I realize I had been holding my breath and my heart was acting crazy. And was that a hint of disappointment I detected?

I exhaled and pulled my phone out of my handbag, fighting the urge to do as he had bid. What would he do to me if I defied his authority? My heart skipped a beat at the countless possibilities flooding my mind, and my stomach clenched with anticipation at each and every one of them.

Did I want to find out what he had in mind?

Hell, no. We were done, so naturally I'd switch on the phone—after letting him steam just a little bit longer.

Twenty minutes later—enough time to calm down my nerves—Sylvie joined me at the table, blue eyes sparkling, cheeks glowing. She placed another glass of water in front of me and slumped into her seat.

"Thanks." I pointed at the glass as I eyed her carefully, trying hard to keep my expression as nonchalant as possible.

"Good catch! I'm glad you've met someone new," Sylvie said.

"What do you mean?" I looked up from my glass, startled. Did she see Jett? Oh God. I wasn't ready to explain yet when I didn't know what to say.

She pointed at a guy lingering near our booth. He had been standing there waiting for someone for the past ten minutes, and he just happened to look our way that very instant.

"No, it's not what you're thinking." I grimaced, unable to hide my annoyance.

"No?" She raised her brows knowingly.

I chose to ignore the irritating grin on her face and

changed the subject. "Had fun?"

"Got his number." She waved her phone and laughed. And then she went on to tell me everything about the guy. As much as I tried my best to listen to her gushing, I found myself drifting off, following my own thoughts to green eyes and a warning that had managed to instill discomfort in me.

"Hey," I said, cutting Sylvie off. "I'm really tired. Let's call it a night."

Maybe it was the disquieting undertone in my voice that reached her through the veil of alcohol and raging hormones, but Sylvie's gushing stopped instantly and her expression became serious. "Are you okay?"

"Yeah." I gave her a half-hearted smile. "Just tired."

"Okay. I'm calling our driver to pick us up early."

I nodded and mouthed 'thanks' as I followed her out into the starry night. Standing outside the club, the countless unfamiliar faces only managed to magnify my unease, and I couldn't wait to get home.

5

I SPENT THE night tossing and turning, always aware of Jett's presence in my thoughts. When the clock hit seven a.m. I tiptoed past Sylvie's guestroom, heading downstairs into the large living room.

Soft sunrays were streaming through the high bay windows, bathing the room in a bright golden glow. I opened the door to the veranda and let in the fresh country air and the sound of chirping birds. The clear blue water of the lake shimmered. In the distance, I could make out two sailing boats—probably early risers like me, unable to sleep for whatever reason. I took a deep breath and let it out slowly, enjoying every minute of nature I'd never experienced in New York. Everything felt dreamlike in this beautiful house on this beautiful island. I wasn't sure I wanted to leave. At least not for a while.

So much had happened those past four weeks. Being transferred to Jett's company. My sexual arrangement with him that turned into something else. Then Alessandro's will and finding out there was more to Jett's intentions. Was a month all it took to change my world?

Jett had hurt me by trying to use me to get his hands on the estate, yet I still couldn't deny the fact that we had amazing chemistry. The time we spent together was one of the best in my life—I was truly happy. At some point I honestly thought we belonged together. He was the first man to create so much contradiction inside me: love and hate. Lust and contempt.

I had thought by sneaking away from him I'd put enough time and distance between us so I could recover. He managed to shatter all my hopes in the blink of an eye. Even though things were definitely finished between us and I had no intention to rekindle our romance, it bothered me that I had been genuinely happy to see him. It was wrong in every sense of the word, but I could do nothing about it. After seeing him again last night, I had no idea where I was standing in terms of feelings. And I certainly didn't want to find out. He could break down my walls too easily. Shatter my resolution and make me want to give in to my foolish heart. He wasn't worth the pain nor the feelings of guilt. In the end, I knew I'd end up hurt again. With his green eyes and his strong body, he once possessed my body but I wouldn't want him to possess my heart and soul.

By the time I closed the doors and headed for the kitchen, the sailing boats were long gone and my stomach grumbled, reminding me that I hadn't eaten since the evening before. Opening and closing cupboards, I peered inside to familiarize myself with the contents. Whoever did the shopping had stocked up on everything from fresh fruit and vegetables, to bread, bacon, and cheese, probably expecting or believing Sylvie and I could cook. Sylvie barely knew how to make an omelet and I wasn't much better. As I filled the coffee filter the bell rang, startling me. My heart began to hammer in my chest and certainly not because I was scared. I hadn't told Jett I was staying at the Lucazzone estate, but for some reason I expected to see him here. Sort of looked forward to it. When I opened the door and realized it was Clarkson, I couldn't help the disappointment washing over me.

Forcing my mouth into a smile, I motioned him to come in. Dressed in a suit, he looked as though he was coming straight from the office and, judging from his no-nonsense expression, he obviously thought seven a.m. was the appropriate time for a business meeting.

"Good morning, Brooke." He returned the smile and his glance scanned the front of my bathrobe. "I hope I didn't wake you."

I ignored the urge to ask him to stop by later—

preferably when I was showered and dressed, and Sylvie wasn't still sleeping off her hangover. Instead, I wrapped my bathrobe tighter around my body and decided to lie.

"No. I've been up for a while." My voice sounded a little hoarse from the lack of sleep, but you could attribute it to anything from a sore throat to a heated verbal discussion the previous night. I headed for the kitchen, expecting him to follow. "Do you want coffee?"

"That'd be lovely."

"Cream? Sugar?"

"No, thank you. I have to watch my cholesterol level."

He laughed briefly and I smiled because it was the polite thing to do. It had always bugged me to laugh when people said that line. There's nothing funny about a health concern so why would you try to laugh it off? Opening a cupboard, I rose on my toes to reach a mug and filled it with the still hot coffee, then handed it to him.

"Please, take a seat." I pointed at the polished mahogany table. He sat down and I followed suit, choosing the chair opposite from his. My hand wrapped around my half-full coffee mug but I didn't take a sip until he did.

"It's such a beautiful day," Clarkson started. I hope you and Sylvie are enjoying your stay. Is she still asleep?" It seemed a harmless question, but for some reason I cringed inwardly. I didn't like him asking questions about her. He was twice her age and it felt creepy. Too personal.

Maybe he was trying to be polite, like most Brits I had met.

"How's Mr. Lucazzone today?" I had never been particularly good at small talk or changing the subject gracefully. Luckily, Clarkson didn't seem to mind.

He inclined his head and his expression changed into a frown. "I saw him last night and he was better than most days. But his health is declining rapidly. I'm afraid he won't last much longer, Brooke." His tone was layered with worry, and I wondered whether he and the old man had been close.

I was about to say that I was sorry when Sylvie entered the kitchen dressed in a bathrobe similar to mine, only she looked so much hotter. Her blond hair was tied up in a high ponytail and her blue eyes, even though rimmed by dark shadows, looked sparkling and energized. I had no idea how she did that when I felt as though a train had just hit me, and I hadn't even touched any alcohol.

At the sight of Clarkson, Sylvie's eyes popped wide open. I could almost hear her thoughts. What was he doing here so early? I waved her closer and pressed my coffee mug into her hands—not that she needed it.

Clarkson's eyes fixed on her and remained there for a long time. I bit my lip hard and begged my brain to come up with something—anything—to break the uncomfortable silence but, as usual, it remained surprisingly blank when it came to making small talk.

"I'll let you ladies get dressed," Clarkson eventually said. "Mr. Lucazzone wishes to see you today. If you could be ready in half an hour, I'd be more than happy to drive you to the hospital." His tone was friendly but I thought I heard a clear decisiveness of tone, a force that allowed for no objection. He smiled, and I realized I was probably over-analyzing things the way I always did.

I nodded and followed Sylvie upstairs.

***

Clarkson pulled the car into a visitor spot in the hospital's parking area, and we headed for the pretty yet inconspicuous building. With its yellow façade, it would have blended right in with the other buildings on the street were it not for the double security glass doors and the large windows. Like many clinics in Italy, this particular one was a private institution—a two-story, six bedroom home in a secluded Bellagio area, not far from the lake shore. The place was a surgically sanitary haven for the rich who were on the verge of leaving this world. As we entered and walked through the hall we were met by the sight of plush leather chairs, bouquets of flowers on every table, and soft music playing from invisible speakers. Smiling nurses in green linen uniforms pushed patients in wheelchairs along the spotless hallways into the stunning green yard that faced a small pond. Sylvie and I waited near the open terrace door as Clarkson announced our presence to the receptionist.

We followed Clarkson to the second floor and down the broad hall, past several closed doors. My stomach was in knots and my breathing came in whistling heaps. While I was nervous to finally meet Alessandro Lucazzone, I also harbored a strong dislike of hospitals to the point of having a panic attack. The smell of sanitizer and disease reminded me too much of my sister. Before she died she had been hospitalized for months, during which we came to visit often, each time working hard on putting on a brave face and maintaining a fake façade of normalcy. As a thirteen-year-old, I understood the importance of keeping up the protective walls that would shield our family from the devastating realization of having a drug addict as a sister and daughter. I had tried hard to see the positive side of our visits, and in my juvenile fantasy the hospital with its sickening scents and scary, white walls had been a safe haven that would help my sister get well. The impression was shattered when Jenna died and, in his grief, my father shot himself. In his last few hours, while he lay attached to various tubes and machines, the white sheets were soaked with my mother's tears, and the room echoed with useless prayers that didn't keep him alive. That's when I realized hospitals were places of death. You went there to visit your loved ones before they were taken from you forever, reminding you that life could be lost in the blink of an eye.

I had managed to avoid entering hospitals ever since my father passed away, but even years couldn't wipe away the memories of powerless dread, of endless prayers that would go unheard.

"This is it." Clarkson pointed at a closed door. I took a deep breath to calm my racing heart and wiped my hands on the soft material of my knee-length skirt. What would I say to this stranger who had never met me and yet had decided to leave his estate to me? Saying 'thank you' felt wrong because, even though I *was* thankful, I didn't want him to think that inheriting what belonged to him was all that mattered to me.

"Mr. Lucazzone wishes to speak with Brooke alone," Clarkson said to Sylvie.

"You still have time to run," she whispered to me, ignoring the lawyer. I smiled at her weak attempt at infusing some humor to ease my nerves.

"Ready?" Clarkson nodded encouragingly and knocked twice, then opened the door, stepping aside. Moistening my parched lips, I walked into the room, leaving Sylvie outside.

6

THE OLD MAN was sitting in a wheelchair near the high bay window overlooking the gardens, his head resting on a pillow, his veined hands, the color of parchment, were sitting atop a blanket. In the bright afternoon sun, the whiteness of his bones shimmered beneath the thin skin, building a strong contrast to the purplish hue of his lips. To his right stood a middle-aged woman in a pale green uniform, her black hair with silver-gray streaks was tied at the nape of her neck. A nurse, I thought, and yet her glance seemed far too protective—hostile, even. I knew instantly we wouldn't be friends.

As the door clicked shut behind us, the old man moved his head, his light blue eyes as sharp as ice. I inched closer on shaky feet, stopping a few inches away from him, unsure whether to speak or let Clarkson take the lead. My tongue flicked nervously over my parched lips, and it wasn't just because of my paranoia of hospitals. It was Alessandro Lucazzone who decided to address me.

"Seniorina Stewart. Brooke." Despite his high age, his voice was still clear and strong—like that of a man half his age—and out of sorts with his aged body. He eyed me carefully and a genuine smile lit up his face, erasing my unease at meeting him.

"How are you, sir?" Bending down to him, I grabbed his outstretched fingers and let him kiss my hand. His grip felt cold and dry, but not unpleasant.

"My niece—so beautiful. Already I feel better," he said in heavily accented English, releasing my hand. I smiled shyly. Even though his words were sparse, his tone was warm and welcoming. Not strange—just friendly, making me feel as though I was family. A feeling I hadn't felt since Jenna and my father died. The sparkle of pride in his eyes conveyed just how much he meant his words. Alessandro had been gay, marrying my ancestor for money. Or maybe he had loved her, in his own way. I didn't know and even if I did, it wasn't my place to judge. All that mattered was that my presence made him feel better, because no one deserved to suffer.

"Thank you for inviting me." I glanced from the nurse to Clarkson in the hope someone would translate. In the end, Alessandro made it clear he understood me perfectly.

"Alessia, bring us tea." He waved decisively at the nurse and watched her usher out the door, then motioned Clarkson to step closer. The lawyer pressed his ear to the old man's mouth but in the silence of the room I could hear his whisper. "Give me a few minutes with her."

Clarkson nodded and peeked over his shoulder at me. I looked away hastily, even though I knew he had caught me listening.

"I'll wait outside," the lawyer said, before shutting the door behind him, leaving Alessandro and me alone.

"Please." The old man's accent was heavy as he patted the chair next to him, offering me a seat. "We don't have much time. Alessia will return shortly and she won't leave us alone again."

I walked around him and sat down, unsure what to say.

"You remind me of my dear wife, Maria," Alessandro began. "You look just like her. I wish you had met her. She would have adored you because she always wanted a daughter." His eyes misted over, reminiscing as he traveled back in time. "She was so strong and kind. So beautiful on the inside and out."

"I'm sorry for your loss," I whispered past the sudden lump in my throat, but Alessandro didn't seem to hear me. His eyes filled with moisture.

"She died ten years ago, but I remember her like it was yesterday. She loved this estate. Sometimes that's the only thing I remember, yet I don't tell anyone because if I do, all will be lost." His gaze focused on me and for a moment his eyes sharpened. "You're my only heir, Brooke. You mustn't sell this estate and never to the wrong people."

This was the time to assure him that I never would. The estate certainly didn't hold the same emotional value for me that it did him, but I had enough respect to grant a dying man's wishes as long as I lived. And yet, as much as my heart wanted to speak out to him, to ensure him of my good intentions, my mouth remained shut, unable to utter a word in the face of so much passion emanating from him.

Alessandro gripped my hand softly, holding it as his eyes locked with mine. "I promised my wife to keep the property within the family. My health is deteriorating by the day and I know one day, very soon, I won't wake up again. It's my greatest wish to see to my wife's happiness even beyond the grave and respect her wish. Please promise me that you'll take care of this property when I am gone and it will be yours."

I stared at him, not seeing *him* but the fact that he was dying and he knew it. It pained me because I didn't want it to happen. I wished for him to live for many more years to come, to enjoy the estate and everything he ever missed out on. The face I saw in front of me would someday cease to exist, belonging to a past that would be forgotten. While it wasn't in my power to change time or fate, I could at least carry on his legacy.

"Family blood is the strongest of all," Alessandro whispered, sensing my thoughts. "We don't have much time to get to know each other, but you're part of this family and you'll always be—" his fingers gently touched my chest where my heart was located "—in here."

"I promise," I whispered, meaning every word and more. "I won't let you down."

He smiled and leaned back in his wheelchair. A few moments later Alessia returned with our tea and sat down near the window, not leaving us out of her sight, just like Alessandro predicted.

Alessandro and I talked for about an hour, during which he wanted to hear everything about my life. I told him how I grew up, leaving out the part with my sister and my father, because I didn't think it mattered. Besides, I didn't want to depress him. I tried to ask questions, but I could sense his reluctance at talking about more than his upbringing. He mentioned his son who died at birth and Maria's miscarriage a few years later. He told me of his wife's battle with cancer and how she lost it ten years ago, making me aware how lonely he must have been in the years after her passing. At some point, Alessia refilled our teacups, like a shadow slipping into my view and out of it, but never leaving the old man out of her sight. Alessandro and I talked some more until another nurse entered to remind him that it was time for his medication and therapy. Before he left, his shaky fingers pointed at an envelope on the table, bearing the conditions of his final will and photos he wanted to share with me.

"Thank you, Alessandro," I said.

He smiled and his shaky fingers touched my cheek gently. "Thank you, Brooke. Now that you're here I can finally rest."

His words hung heavy in the air as Alessia wheeled him out of the room. With a heavy heart and moisture in my eyes I watched him leave, vowing to keep my word to him no matter what. We had barely skimmed the surface of our lives, and yet I felt as though we were interconnected, our paths intertwined by fate, even if for a brief time. I felt as though I knew him on a deeper level, and that knowledge made it even harder to accept just how little time we had.

Call me naïve because I liked to believe in the good in people, but I knew that Jett's claims about Alessandro Lucazzone couldn't be true. I could feel it. I could see it in the old man's eyes. He wasn't flawless; like everyone else, he had made mistakes. He married my ancestor for money rather than live the life he was born to live—with a man. Or maybe he had loved her, in his own way. I didn't know and even if I did, it wasn't my place to judge. But he was no murderer. Whatever Jett's private detective thought Maria Lucazzone had written in her diary, I knew it couldn't be true and I would prove it.

Opening the window, I stared out onto the beautifully landscaped park-like garden as I took a long, deep breath to regain my composure, and then returned to Clarkson and Sylvie.

***

I found Sylvie on a bench on the veranda, sitting near the rosebushes and sipping lemonade. The sun was hiding behind light gray clouds, and a soft breeze coming from the lake ruffled the leaves and green grass, promising a light rain shower. The fragrant air was still warm though, as if not even the lack of sunrays could cool down the earth beneath our feet.

She frowned when I arrived, but if she caught my shaky emotional state she didn't dwell on it. "You've been in there forever. How was the meeting?"

"Great." I managed a half-hearted smile that wouldn't have fooled anyone. "It went really well." I sat down next to her and she pushed her lemonade glass toward me, silently welcoming me to take a sip. My fingers tightened around the glass but I couldn't bring myself to lift it to my lips. I didn't want to risk shattering it.

"Brooke," Sylvie said slowly. Sensing something in her tone, I looked up to meet her stare. A shadow clouded her blue eyes and a soft line formed between her delicate brows.

"What?" I said warily.

She took a deep breath before replying and let it out slowly. I could tell she was preparing her words carefully, or maybe she was hesitant to share with me whatever was bothering her. "I'm sure I'm just blowing it out of proportions and it's probably nothing."

"What?" I repeated. "Just spit it out."

"Okay. While you were in there, the old man asked to speak with Clarkson. Alone." She raised her brows meaningfully. "I found it a little strange and followed them to a room down the hall." Nothing strange about a client wanting to talk with his lawyer in private, but I didn't argue with Sylvie. She wasn't usually one to notice *any* sort of activity that didn't concern her so, naturally, my suspicion was roused.

"What did they talk about?" I asked.

Sylvie inched closer and peered over her shoulder as though to make sure no one was listening. "The old man asked Clarkson to make sure no one knows you're here. He also said he wanted to spend as much time as possible with you before—and I quote—the vultures descend upon their prey. I don't even know what that means. At least he didn't speak in Italian."

"He said that to Clarkson?"

Sylvie nodded. "I swear I was around the corner. They didn't know I was listening." She faked a shudder. "Seriously, old people give me the creeps. They're so weird. My grandfather was like that. He was so paranoid of children, kept saying he could see them and hear their laughter when no one was around. I guess it comes with age."

I grimaced. The poor guy. I could only hope Sylvie's relatives were accepting of his quirks. But she was right. Paranoia *was* a scary disorder of the mind and not easy to deal with.

"So where's Clarkson?" I asked, changing the subject.

"Don't know. I guess still with him. What did you talk about?"

I pulled out the envelope and held it out to her so she could peek inside. "Nothing big really. We talked about his life and the conditions of my inheritance. He made me promise not to sell the estate. Actually, he was pretty specific about that. He doesn't want me to alter it either. He also wanted to—" I saw Clarkson standing in the doorway to the backyard and dipped my head toward him, deciding now wasn't the right time to talk "—I'll show you later." I sat up and waved at Clarkson to get his attention.

"It's lovely here, isn't it?" Clarkson said.

I nodded. "I'm glad Alessandro is taken care of in such a nice place."

***

Clarkson explained he had some business to tend to. After a short talk we agreed that he'd be calling me with updates. Alessandro Lucazzone hoped to see me again in the next days and I was happy to oblige, not just as his heir but also as the last family member he had.

Anxious, I kept glancing at my watch. With every second that passed, I was moving closer and closer to 11.45 a.m. Jett and I had agreed to meet at noon and I couldn't wait. My only problem now was getting rid of Sylvie. She wasn't his biggest fan, so there was no way I could tell her about my lunch arrangement. If she found out, she'd only end up thinking I was still into him—which was true—and she'd try to talk me out of it. Not only did I promise Jett that I wouldn't back off, but his over-protectiveness had managed to spark my interest. My sole intention was to listen to his reasons and clarify what exactly he thought put me in danger. Maybe even discover a way to heal my heart, like parting on good terms rather than in anger and pain. Only the truth can set the heart free. With knowledge I could move on, learn from my mistakes. If I was lucky, his sincere apology would be enough to make amends and help me move on. Although it wouldn't stop the pain, I was sure it could heal some of my bruised ego.

By keeping our meeting short and to the point, there was no need for my best friend to know about it. I'd tell her eventually when I could deal with her angry outburst, but right now I sure wasn't going to listen to her ranting for the next hour.

So how best to distract her? Three things always managed to help Sylvie forget the world around her: fashion, men, and parties.

Considering it was late morning, the clubs were closed and Sylvie had no date, taking her shopping was my best bet, even if she probably had more clothes than Carrie Bradshaw from Sex And The City. But could I convince her to go on a shopping spree without me?

Probably not.

Throughout the first years of our friendship, Sylvie had always joked about how clingy she was. Turned out, it wasn't really that much of a joke. This left me with one other option: treat her to a spa visit.

Sixty minutes of sighing under the expert hands of a massage therapist should provide enough distraction so I could meet with Jett. I had another problem: Alessandro was stationed at a private hospital in a secluded area far away from the city center. According to Clarkson, the bus station was a half hour walk away.

"So what now?" Sylvie asked as we stepped out of the hospital. She sounded so bored already, and I hadn't even shared my plan with her. I scanned the area. The residential street was almost empty. Apart from a busy café at the corner and some parked cars, there was nothing that could possibly be of interest to Sylvie or help my quest. Until my glance fell on a parked taxi on the other side of the road.

"Let's drive back to the city," I suggested, interloping my arm with hers so I could use bodily force to push her in the right direction, if need be.

She eyed me carefully. "Why? What's there to see?"

"I want to treat you to a spa visit. I've heard nothing but amazing things about Italian spas, and I think you should try one. Come on."

Dashing for the taxi before she could object, or the driver could decide to take off, I pulled her after me. Sylvie opened the door and we both slumped onto the backseat. I instructed the driver to take us to the hotel Jett booked me in during my first trip to Italy. As he drove off I sat back in my seat.

"New city, new scene, and you're already forgetting Jett. My work's almost done," Sylvie said.

"Yeah." I cringed inwardly at hearing his name. She couldn't be farther from the truth. If only she knew. It was impossible to forget him, not least because he was here.

By taxi we reached the city in less than ten minutes. As it turned out the driver would have made a great sightseeing guide. Speaking half English and half Italian, he recalled everything he knew about Bellagio's history and ancient buildings. It wasn't exactly Rome, but I listened nonetheless and even Sylvie seemed fascinated. As we cruised down the busy main street, the driver pointed out the designer shops and even recommended the best places to get a bargain. Not that Sylvie needed to save cash. She had always been loaded—courtesy of her rich family whom she actually despised. But what woman is immune to the prospect of a mid-summer sale?

Eventually the taxi stopped on a bus lane. I paid quickly and we got out in front of the large sign advertising the spa hotel I had stayed at on my first trip to Bellagio.

"Not bad," Sylvie said, looking up at the impressive building.

"Good choice, huh?" I beamed at her and dragged her through the glass doors into the marble floor reception area. The spa center took in the entire basement. I paid for a full body and facial treatment package, and the receptionist handed Sylvie a white bathrobe and towel with instructions where to get changed.

"Aren't you coming?" Sylvie asked.

"Sorry, can't." Sylvie could always look right through my lies so I averted my gaze, hoping she wouldn't catch whatever gave me away. "I'm supposed to do something for Alessandro. Can't explain now because I'm running late, but I'll pick you up when you're done, okay?"

I pecked her cheek and headed for the door before she could start her interrogation.

"Don't be late," Sylvie called after me.

"Have fun," I called back. My guilt at lying to her flared up again. It was nasty, self-focused, and certainly not what real friendship stands for. I hated doing it but she wouldn't understand. I *had* to find out what Jett had to say.

Outside the hotel I glanced at my watch. It was 12.30 p.m. I was running half an hour late. I fished my phone out of my bag and switched it on with trepidation at the outlook of calling him to pick me up. The screen came to life with the usual swirls of colors. Three bars loaded together with a welcome message from an Italian service provider. I scrolled through my contact list when the text messages and call notifications began to come in one after another.

Holy.

Cow.

Ninety-eight messages. And all from Jett.

And then the phone started to vibrate and the display showed his caller ID.

I pressed the response button and held the earpiece to my ear.

"What did I tell you about switching on your goddamn phone, Brooke?" His deep voice thundered down the line. I gasped at just how amazingly sexy he sounded. He seemed slightly annoyed, but I could sense a hint of amusement in his tone. "Have you forgotten about our meeting?"

The idea that he still thought he was entitled to treat me like he was my boss annoyed me. If he could play this game, so could I.

"Sorry, is it noon already?" I faked a surprised pause, making sure I sounded sarcastic. "I didn't realize. It's been such a busy day."

"Really?" His voice changed, became softer. Did I detect a hint of jealousy?

"Where are you? You were supposed to be at the bus station in front of the club."

I communicated my location.

"Okay, wait there. I'll have you picked up. The driver will be there in five."

And with that he disconnected, leaving me more nervous than before. Was it really such a good idea to meet with him? Probably not but, damn, I wasn't going to back off now.

7

THE WAITER LED me through an almost empty restaurant, then up a broad staircase. Soft voices and the noise of cutlery carried over from what I assumed was the kitchen area somewhere below us, but apart from that nothing really stirred. I peered around me, wondering why a restaurant in a famous tourist area would be so unusually quiet at this time of day.

"Where are we going?" I asked the waiter. He continued to walk, ignoring my question, which led me to believe he either didn't understand me, or he was following specific instructions not to answer any questions. I clamped my mouth shut, both confused and fascinated. Surprises weren't my thing, however I had to admit this one was more than interesting.

We passed through a closed off dining room on the

second floor which—by the look of it—was probably reserved for special events and wedding parties. To our left, chairs were stacked on top of the tables. To my right, the whole wall was made of glass, allowing a clear view of the blue sky and the mountain backdrop. Soft Italian music played in the background—not loud enough to be intrusive, but loud enough to give a romantic flair. The waiter slid the terrace doors open and guided me out onto a panoramic patio decorated with flowers. In the middle, near the white stone balustrade, were a table and two chairs, the white brocade tablecloth shimmering unnaturally bright in the sunlight and building a beautiful contrast to the crystal vase holding pink roses. A bottle of champagne was perched between ice cubes in a silver bucket next to two champagne flutes. I swallowed hard to get rid of the sudden dryness in my throat.

Holy shit.

Did Jett pay to have the restaurant closed off to everyone but us? And I thought by agreeing to just having lunch with him I could avoid exactly this kind of shocker. From the way the roses were arranged, to the fine tablecloth and sparkling glass and cutlery, I could tell someone had mulled over every detail. It would have been the perfect spot for a marriage proposal.

A proposal, Stewart? Really?

I snorted at the mad and absolutely irrational direction

my thoughts were taking. Obviously I was still the hopeless romantic, and yet I didn't quite want to *be* in love. Not to mention the fact that I barely knew anything about Jett and his life, while I had already told him everything about me and my life. The good, the bad, and the horrible.

"Like it?" Jett whispered behind me.

As usual, my abdomen twisted and knotted at the sound of his voice, and my heart began to beat faster like a helpless butterfly in a glass cage. I spun around and smiled at Jett, barely able to keep my eyes off him. He was dressed in a V-neck shirt and tight jeans that barely managed to hide the perfect sculpting of his hard muscles. The sunlight caught in his eyes, reminding me of dark-green gemstones.

Oh.

God.

Oh God. He was stunning.

No. He was sinfully perfect, from his dark hair to the way his mouth twitched at the corners whenever he was about to smile.

Tiny butterflies came to life in the pit of my stomach. I wanted to hate him so much, to be done with him once and for all, because in some way he was like a drug—the more I tasted him, the more I became addicted. But the way he smiled at me, and the way he cocked his head to the side, expecting my reaction upon seeing him, reminded me that I was human. Weak. Prone to making mistakes. And I could only hope I wasn't about to make yet another one. Because in the end—no matter how much I liked him or he liked me—he was still Jett Mayfield. The man who played dirty. The man who played me.

My knees weakened and my mouth turned dry as he moved toward me—so confident in his stride—until he was close enough to touch me. I inhaled the earthy scent of his aftershave and let it slowly engulf my mind.

A sexy smile played on his lips. His green eyes looked alluring in the sunlight. The beginning of a stubble shadowed his tan skin, making me want to run my fingers over it. I turned away from him and toward the clear blue lake because it was easier than looking at him. There was still so much pain inside stemming from his actions and the realization that if he hadn't lied, if he hadn't tried to trick me, we might still be together. There might still be an *us*.

"Brooke." His voice was deep and strained. Guarded. Ignoring my disturbing attraction to him, I leaned over the balustrade as far as I could and took a deep breath as I tried to control the turmoil inside me. I might not be able to shake it all off, but I wasn't going to show him just how big a soft spot I still had for him either.

"I'm glad you could come. I thought this would be the ideal place to meet and talk." He touched the small of my back, oblivious to the storm raging inside me, reminding me how gentle he was. How amazing we once were together.

"I didn't expect this." I turned to face him and our gazes interlocked, making my knees go weak.

"You said you wanted a public place. I believe the exact words were 'outside, where anyone can see us." He leaned against the railing and shot me an amused look that brought with it the most gorgeous dimples. Dimples that made you wish you would drown in them.

I crossed my arms over my chest, as if the action could put some distance between us.

"Yeah, but I meant having other people around, Jett. Lots of people. Think fast-food chain." Being seen wasn't much of a put-off to him. He had made that pretty clear on the lakeshore.

"What's wrong with the people present?" He nodded at the waiter, amused.

I heaved a sigh in mock exasperation. Whatever I said, my arguments were lost. I had given in to his request to talk and was ready to listen. But I could already tell coming here was a mistake. The place was too beautiful; too perfect. Away from the distractions of a club or the people employed in his office, any ounce of determination to fight the stupid attraction between us dissipated into thin air.

"You wanted to see me, so let's get to the point," I said. "What did you want to talk about?"

"Let's have lunch first." His tone left no room for discussion. "We'll talk later."

"Fine." Hungry as I was I didn't argue with that, even though I doubted I'd be able to swallow more than a few bites in his presence. Jett guided me to my chair and held it for me. I slid into the seat, whispering a thank you. He sat down opposite from me and then we were gazing at each other again, soaking in each other's presence over the small table—the way we had ever since our fateful meeting in a club, which wasn't quite as accidental as I initially thought.

"What can I get you to drink?" the waiter asked, startling me.

"Champagne," Jett said.

"For me water, please."

Jett raised a puzzled brow, but didn't comment.

"Why champagne?" I asked him as soon as the waiter had left to get our order. "Are you trying to get me drunk?"

"We both know I don't take advantage of a drunken woman, even though I've got to admit it's nice to hear all the little things that come out of your sexy mouth. You know, the things I don't get to hear when you're sober."

The telltale heat of a blush rushed to my face. Jett had seen me drunk at least twice. Every time he made sure I got home safely, and every time I told him, in my drunken state, how much I wanted him. It seemed like my subconscious was programmed to reveal the truth regarding how I felt about him—whether I wanted it, or not.

"I have sworn off alcohol." I watched him take a thin

bread stick and break it into two, then hand me one while he kept the other half. "Thanks," I mumbled, nibbling on one end. "It makes me say stupid things I don't mean."

He snorted as he took a bite. "I doubt that."

For some reason, his statement annoyed me. Probably, because he was right. Yet, it brought up an issue that had me occupied for longer than I cared to admit.

"Why did you lie to me, Jett?"

He hesitated, avoiding my gaze. A moment later the waiter appeared with a trolley carrying our drinks and various dishes. He set the drinks in front of us and wished us "Buon appetite," and then he was gone again.

"I didn't know what you wanted, so I ordered everything on the menu," Jett said, not answering my question. I tried to ignore the various delicacies on the trolley, which was hard because everything—including Jett—looked so delicious. My stomach rumbled, reminding me I hadn't eaten since breakfast.

I watched him pile a little of everything onto a plate before handing it to me. I took it from him but didn't touch the food.

He noticed me watching him and sighed. I began to tap my foot impatiently, asking the obvious question with a mere raise of my eyebrows.

"I know you want answers but can we eat first?" He pointed at my plate. I eyed the food as I contemplated whether to give in to his plea, or remain stubborn in my decision to get this over and done with.

"Please, I'll explain later," Jett said slowly, his electrifying eyes piercing a hole into my soul.

There was something in his voice: hope that we wouldn't end up fighting. Hope to avoid the inevitable—the countless questions demanding honest answers. Whatever those answers were, I had a nagging feeling I'd need a strong stomach to deal with them, so I grabbed my fork and popped a cube of white cheese into my mouth, chewing slowly. It tasted delicious, of fresh milk and herbs. I took another one, followed by what looked like a meatball tasting of peppers and olives.

I looked up when he lifted his fork and helped himself—from the same plate. The gesture was so intimate it made my heart skip a beat.

Too intimate.

It wasn't what two strangers did.

"You're damn sexy when you eat," Jett whispered. "I'm glad you're not one of those anorexic girls on a diet."

I almost choked on my bite but continued to eat as if we were having a business conversation. "I don't believe in diets."

He smiled. "It's not just your attitude I like. I love the way you get lost in every new sensation. You show the same passion when you're under me."

Good gracious.

Red flags began to flash somewhere in the back of my mind. He was beginning to flirt with me, piling on the sexy compliments, which—given Jett and our history—wasn't a good sign.

Before I could stop him, he leaned forward and brushed his thumb over my lips and then sucked the tip of it into his mouth. I took a sharp breath and forced myself to let it out slowly.

In his absence, I had prepared all those kickass comebacks that would kick his ego to the curb. In my head I knew what I wanted to say and how to infuse just the right amount of sarcasm into it. Sitting in front of him, an arrogant, self-assured smile reflected in his eyes, my wit sort of dried up, and I found myself staring like an idiot, fighting for words while my brain remained surprisingly blank and my insides turned all mushy.

Dammit, I couldn't think of anything to say. Worse yet, I could barely breathe because of the delicious pull between my legs. My panties were beginning to melt just from watching him do *normal* stuff, reminding me of all the pleasure he and his fingers had once bestowed upon me. The awareness came to me that I could sleep with him anytime. Pull him to me, yank his shirt open, run my fingers down his chest to the happy trail I had once been more than eager to explore.

His sexy smile widened. As if he knew what I was thinking.

Damn him and his gorgeous body!

Damn him and his flirting!

Thankfully, our waiter arrived to ask whether we needed anything else. For a moment I seriously considered asking the waiter to stay during the rest of our lunch. Figuring that might be a little too awkward, I resisted the urge and watched the waiter leave again.

I was a grown woman, for crying out loud. I didn't need to hide behind anyone's back because I couldn't deal with a hot guy. Or maybe I could.

Play it cool and play it cold, Stewart!

"Jett, I want you to forget what happened between us," I started, my tone infused with as much frostiness as I could muster. "It's over. We can't go back to how things used to be."

Jett's eyebrows shot up. "It's never over. Not until every fight has been lost. And for you, I'd fight."

"There's nothing to fight for. You're not getting the estate."

"I already told you it's not about the estate, Brooke. This is about us. About your safety." His voice came low and dark. Like a menacing warning that he wasn't going to give up.

"I don't need your protection. He's just an old man.

What can he do to me?"

Hesitating, Jett put down his fork and crossed his arms over his broad chest. "It's not that simple."

"Then explain. I want to understand."

He took a sip of *my* drink before putting the glass down slowly, leaving his untouched. Hiding my annoyance at the intimate gesture, I wondered whether he was trying to make a point by helping himself, like wanting to say that what belonged to me belonged to him. Seriously, could he turn more *caveman-like* on me? My blood began to boil in my veins. It started to boil harder when he touched my hand. His fingers began to trace circles on the back of my hand, slowly but with just the right amount of pressure—the way he used to do when we were still together.

How the heck can you explain to a guy that it's over when you're having a hard time convincing yourself? Why is telling others what they have to do always simpler than applying your own advice in practice?

"Tell me what's going on. I want to understand," I said, pulling my hand away from him. "That's the only reason I'm here. Why do you think I'm in danger?"

I leaned back in my chair, regarding him coolly. The more I thought about this, the more his assumptions seemed ludicrous. Scary, yes, because Jett was persuasive. But still absurd.

"Like I said, Alessandro's just an old man. What do you

think he could possibly do to me from a hospital bed where he's *dying*, Jett?"

He frowned and a shadow crossed his features. I honestly thought he was going to start talking...until he lifted his fork again and began to eat, taking all the time in the world.

I groaned.

Damn!

He did it again—ignoring me. Letting me wait on purpose just because he felt like being in control.

Assessing. Testing.

Testing what?

I felt like leaning over that table and shaking some sense into him. Maybe even strangle him while I was at it, because his reasoning, or lack thereof, made no sense to me, and I was slowly losing my patience at his reticence.

"It's not just Lucazzone I'm talking about. It's the elite club he belonged to," he said slowly. "My father, Robert, was involved many years ago."

"What club?" I eyed him carefully, sensing the sudden change in the air.

Jett sighed and ran a hand through his tousled dark hair. His gloomy expression reflected the countless emotions fighting to gain control inside. In the end his shoulders slumped like he'd made a decision he didn't want to make, but his dark expression didn't change.

"I'll tell you everything I know, okay?" Jett said. "But I want you to just listen and listen carefully. Whatever I say today doesn't leave this table. You cannot tell anyone."

The sharp edge in his tone instantly raised my alertness. He grabbed my hand and gave it a hard squeeze until I nodded, silently giving him my word.

"A few years back, Alessandro Lucazzone was involved in my father's business. It was for a brief time and he was never officially listed as a shareholder, so I couldn't figure out why my father would let him make the decisions he made—decisions that cost us millions. I stumbled upon it when I checked our financial reports dating back to my time at college. A few weeks ago, Robert finally came clean and admitted something that could harm the company."

Jett paused and his eyes narrowed, the angry line between his eyebrows saying more than a thousand words. His grip on my hand tightened, hurting me just a little, but I didn't pull back. "They were both involved in this sort of elite club. You know, drugs and kinky sex practices, and lots of people to be paid off to keep quiet. My father and quite a few people—many of them rich and famous—were addicted to that stuff and paid whoever hosted the events millions. In my father's case, he paid it out of the company's accounts. When I joined the business the company was on the verge of liquidation, in which case we would have lost everything. I've pulled in enough business to keep us afloat for a while. But one wrong decision and it's all over the media, and we'll end up losing major deals and our good reputation. If anyone finds out, the company's done. You were right about everything."

"I don't understand. Right about what?" I had a hard time following him and the sudden change in tone didn't exactly help. His gaze settled on me, imploring me to understand. His hand squeezed mine again, silently asking me to relate, to feel his emotions, or maybe to believe him.

"Robert thought by buying the Lucazzone estate he could save the company. I first agreed it was a good idea because the land is valued at much more than we initially offered and tourists flood in every year. I thought, why not try to sell it as the next St. Tropez or Kitzbuhel?" He began to massage his temples.

"But you increased your offer. It was a huge gamble. You could have lost a lot of money," I whispered, my head still spinning around the words 'sex practices' and 'elite club.' It sounded like a bad Hollywood movie.

"I was against paying more because, like you, I know when the risk's too high but he wanted it and in the end it's still his company. After meeting you, that wasn't what worried me. I was afraid that once the people involved learned of your inheritance, they'd come after you to make sure you wouldn't find out their secret and talk."

His hands cupped my face, forcing me to look at him.

"Do you understand what I'm saying?"

I nodded, but not because I understood. He was nervous. I could feel tension wafting from him in strong waves. The glint in his eyes scared the hell out of me.

"You said 'club,'" I began slowly. "Are we talking about a few kinky preferences like a bit of BDMS or—"

He shook his head gravely and let go of my face but didn't break eye contact.

"All I know is that they've been fanatic about keeping their identities protected, which leads me to assume there was more to it than that."

"Wow." I bit my lip hard, barely feeling the pain. "Where did the meetings take place?"

A grimace crossed his face and a silent look passed between us. He didn't have to tell me that it was the Lucazzone estate.

"According to my father, many powerful people were involved," Jett said. "He made it clear that many of them would stop at nothing to keep their preferences hidden from the public."

"But why would they think I'd know anything about them?"

"Because you're the heiress. You're expected to inherit Lucazzone's secrets and no one knows the specifics. They're probably scared. I know I'd be." His expression remained earnest, but the sudden caginess in his voice didn't escape me.

"You were never involved?" I tried to instill nonchalance into my voice, like his past didn't matter. After all, we didn't know each other back then, so it wasn't really my concern. But it mattered. I didn't want him to be some pervert.

Shooting me a dirty look, he took a deep breath and let it out slowly. The way his fingers began to tap on the table told me he was having a hard time keeping his annoyance under control.

I raised my chin a notch and regarded him stubbornly. "Were you—"

Jett cut me off. "I heard you the first time and I'm fucking pissed you'd ever think that of me."

"I didn't. I—" My throat constricted at the angry glint in his eyes.

"What the fuck, Brooke? I thought you knew me." His voice came so low I had a hard time understanding him, which was worse than yelling. It made me feel bad—disappointed in myself—even though I had no reason to be.

"I don't know you because we've barely scratched the surface of your life," I said warily. My heart was beating a million miles an hour. "I'm sorry. It was just an innocent question. Anyone would ask the same thing, given the circumstances."

"Given the circumstances." His jaw set. He pulled his hand away and leaned back in his chair, putting as much distance between us as our sitting arrangement allowed.

He was angry and I couldn't blame him.

"I didn't mean to be accusatory," I said. "It was just a question, Jett."

He laughed slowly, still avoiding my gaze. I scanned his beautiful face. His scowl didn't distract from his beauty; it just made him look *different*, and I realized I really didn't know much about him.

"I wish I knew you better," I said softly. "The real you—not the mask you're putting on to hide what's inside."

His cloud of anger lifted just a little bit. "I'd love another date."

I laughed at his impudence. "This isn't a date."

"Whatever you call it, I'd love another one of those." He cocked his head, giving me the kind of smile I had been waiting for all day.

No, Stewart. Don't you dare!

"I'm not asking you." The corners of lips curled upward. "If you say 'no' then you leave me no choice than to do the next stupid thing, like kidnapping you because I want to earn your trust. I want to make things right again. What do you say?"

My heart skipped a beat and I had no idea whether it was because Jett's strong grip on me sent naughty thoughts through my head. Or because his threat both scared and fascinated me.

"You don't mean it."

"Try me." No smile. No blinking. Just pure, raw determination to get his way.

I swallowed down the big lump in my throat. This was supposed to be a formal meeting. Nothing too intense. Yet here I was, tempted to give him another chance, knowing I might be heading down a self-destructive path.

"Your whole story sounds kind of far-fetched, Jett. You don't have any real proof. Everything's based on assumptions. Give me one good reason why I should believe you."

"Because it's the truth." He didn't hesitate; didn't even blink. "I was never involved, Brooke. That's not the kind of person I am, and I hope one day you'll know that deep in your heart."

Maybe, but that time hadn't come yet. Jett was a convincing person who might or might not tell the truth. I needed proof before I was ready to trust him again.

I checked the time on my cellphone and brushed my hands over my skirt the way I always did when I was about to leave.

"I have to go. It's getting late and Sylvie's expecting me in ten minutes." It wasn't a lie. Without waiting for his reply, I grabbed my bag and stood, wondering why I wasn't as pleased with our meeting as I initially thought I would be.

Maybe because he hasn't given you any real answers.

True. In fact I ended up with more questions than before, and I didn't like it one bit.

"You're amazing, you know that?" Jett walked around the table and stopped in front of me, his height intimidating me, as usual. My eyes lingered on his lips. So close. So delicious. I held my breath as he brushed a stray strand of hair out of my face. His touch sent a shiver through me, making me all too aware of just how close we were standing. My heartbeat started to drum in my ears. I had experienced this feeling before—at the office back in New York the day I broke up with him, thinking I had lost him forever. Right before he told me that he loved me.

His lips moved just a little bit closer to mine, hovering inches away. Not too close but enough to make me aware of his manly scent and the sudden tension in the air. Aware that even though he had explained his reasons, it was *still* over.

"You really are amazing, Brooke," he repeated.

"Why are you telling me this?" I almost choked on my words.

"Because I should have told you before, when you would've still believed me. And I should have told you as often as I could so you'd never forget."

Damn him and his ability to say the right things at the right time. I didn't want to fall for him any deeper than I had already. He was gaining the upper hand again, turning the table on me.

"Jett please, just stop." I blinked back the telltale moisture gathering in the corners of my eyes.

"Why?"

Because you broke my heart once, and there's no guarantee you won't do it again.

"I don't believe you, Jett. Everything you said—I just can't believe you anymore. Not until you give me proof." It was the truth. Even if I wanted to, I couldn't trust him. "I should never have come here. Sylvie was right when she warned me about you."

"Not everyone's hell bent on screwing you over, Brooke. Some people genuinely care about you." I turned away but he grabbed my shoulders, forcing me to face him. "If you want to know the truth, don't ask a friend who'll tell you only what you want to hear. Check the facts and you'll see that, yes, I made a mistake, but I'm telling you the truth when I say I only tried to protect you."

I yanked my hand away from him. Awkward silence ensued. I knew I had hit a soft spot. I could see it in his face, in his eyes, the way he moistened his lips, pondering his next move. Eventually, he let out a frustrated groan.

"I lied to you one time when I didn't know you. Before

we decided to have a relationship. I know I did many things wrong, but I never stopped caring about you."

A liar is known to tell many lies but the one who speaks the truth will always stick to the same story. It was a universal knowledge I had embraced many years ago. In this case, however, the truth scared me. What if he cared about me but not enough to avoid hurting me again?

"I need to go, Jett." I checked the time on my cellphone again, silently praying he'd let me go. I was no match for him if he didn't. He stepped back but his gaze never left me.

I made my way across the terrace and down the stairs, minding my steps as Jett followed behind. I reached the waiting taxi in a few long strides. His strong grip on my upper arm told me our conversation wasn't over and, as usual, he was about to fight for the last word.

"Brooke. We never had a real date." His eyes were two glowing pits of smoldering heat. I had never seen so much determination in anyone. Then again, I had probably never seen the real Jett. "In spite of everything that happened and what I explained to you today, would you go on a date with me? I'm not asking you to trust me. I know that takes time. I'm asking you to give me a chance to earn that trust and make things right again."

My heart hammered in my chest. The attraction was still there, coursing back and forth between us like an intangible current. "I would. Just prove your claims are true."

"They are. Even if you don't understand things now, sooner or later you'll find out I never meant to hurt you."

"I still need evidence," I said coolly, holding on to my determination for dear life.

"And then you'll give me a chance to redeem myself?"

"Yes." It sounded fair enough. With proof I could understand his motives. "I really have to go now. Sylvie's waiting for me."

His smile returned with full force and brought with it the most gorgeous dimples. I held my breath as his mouth came closer. But instead of kissing me, he whispered in my ear, "I'm still thinking of you. Even though everything's messed up, I still want you by my side. I still want to be with you, within you, inside you, hearing you panting my name."

8

I HAD NEVER been one to deal with emotions easily. My heart was racing, my mind was spinning, and my body was floating in a vacuum as Jett drove me back to the spa. After our conversation and the few unexpected turns it took, I didn't know what to believe or think and, most importantly, I didn't know what to say to him when letting my guard down wasn't an option.

"Thanks for lunch." My hand hovered on the door handle but something kept me from pulling it open.

"My pleasure," Jett said softly. His gaze was focused on me, like always, but there was something in his eyes that made me instantly aware of the confined space we were in. He dominated everything: my thoughts, my space, even the air I breathed. My breath hitched. He was too close for comfort and I couldn't get away fast enough.

"I'm sorry, I have to leave." Without so much as a glance back I sprinted out of the car, heading for the safety of the spa's salon.

As I pushed the heavy glass doors open, I could feel his stare burning a hole in my back. Only once I was inside the reception area did I dare stop and take a deep breath, searching for him across the street, but the car had already sped off. I didn't know whether to feel relieved or disappointed. Either way, I had to conceal it because Sylvie had the keen eye of a hawk. The second she got suspicious, she'd commence her interrogation.

Luckily for me, Sylvie's treatment wasn't finished for another ten minutes. I left a message with the receptionist in case I wouldn't be back on time and took off down the busy main street, through the gathered crowds of midday shoppers and tourists. Even though my eyes could see them, my brain continued to be occupied. Jett's statements about the club bothered me. I was ready to take his warnings seriously and investigate his claims. My thoughts circled back to Jett and the fact that the spark was still there.

What did you expect, Stewart?

I rolled my eyes at my own stupidity. The kind of attraction we shared wasn't likely to go away on its own within a few days. Deep down I had known this all along, and yet I *still* agreed to have lunch with him.

If you really wanted to move on, you could have done so with someone else—find a rebound, just like Sylvie. But you didn't. You reserved a place in your heart for Jett, and you don't want to fill it with someone else. You want him *and you need to see if you can take things slowly. You're ready to chase away the demons of your past and make room for a future with him.*

I stopped at a tiny corner café that sold gelato cones and freshly made smoothies, and bought two plastic cups of watermelon frappe before returning to the spa. Sylvie was typing furiously on her phone when I reached her and handed her a cup. Her face was glowing and she seemed relaxed. I breathed out, relieved.

"Ready?"

"Yeah. Thanks." She pointed at her watermelon frappe and took a sip as we walked out onto the street. "You were right. It was amazing. Such a shame you couldn't come."

"Yeah." I shot her a smile.

"How did it go?"

"Good. The shops kept me busy," I said. "Wanna grab lunch?"

Her entire expression changed within an instant. "I thought you were supposed to do something for the old man."

Shoot, I completely forgot about my lie.

"I didn't find what I came for," I said, grimacing. "I'll get it tomorrow. But wait until you see the shops around here. They're shop-till-you-drop-worthy."

Shit, I sounded so guilty I might as well stamp the words 'I'm hiding something' across my forehead.

"There's a pizza restaurant not far from here." Leaving the invitation open, I took a sip of my frappe and directed my vision at the next window display, pretending to admire a pair of what looked like brown riding boots with fringes. From her reflection I could tell she was still watching me with an annoyed frown. I hoped she couldn't smell fear because my hands had begun to sweat and certainly not from the heat.

"Great. I'm starving," she said.

Within five minutes, we were seated at a piazza table, sipping water as we contemplated the Italian menu.

"Are you trying to memorize your order?" Sylvie asked me.

"As a matter of fact, I am. Wanna help me?" I smiled and waved the waiter over to get our orders. He jotted it down and then I was alone with her again. My smile froze in place as my mind tried hard to come up with something to talk about, when all I wanted to do was lock myself in my room and obsess about my lunch with Jett.

Sylvie eyed me with a frown. "You're a little quiet. Is everything okay?"

"Yeah. No. I'm having this headache. Must be the heat." I wasn't lying. My head was pounding hard and I didn't know whether it was because of the sun, the tension, or a little bit of everything.

Sylvie opened her bag and fished out a small bottle of aspirin, pushing it across the table. "Take two. We can't afford you getting sick."

Literally. I had no job and no health insurance.

"Thanks." I swallowed two pills and rinsed the bitter aftertaste with a few gulps of water. While Sylvie left to use the restroom, the waiter brought our pizzas. I mouthed a heavily accented 'grazie' when the screen of my phone buzzed to life. I checked the caller. The number was private. Almost expecting Jett, I pressed the earpiece to my ear.

"Hello?"

An instant later, the line went dead. I frowned.

"Hey." Sylvie slumped into her chair and grabbed a slice of pizza. "Who was it?"

"What?"

She took a big bite and pointed at the phone.

I waved my hand. "Wrong number."

"You get phone calls abroad?"

"Apparently."

I bit into a slice of pizza and began to chew, my appetite slowly returning as Sylvie resumed her chat about her impressions of Italy and god knows what. Thankfully, she was a bit of an entertainer and never needed much input from me to lead a conversation. As I struggled to listen, my headache improved but didn't go away, and Sylvie eventually suggested we drive back to the estate.

***

The afternoon sun stood high, raising the temperature by a few more degrees. By the time we made it back it was 5 p.m. and still hot as a desert.

I lay down on my bed as Sylvie changed into her bikini, eager to deepen her tan. "Are you sure you don't want to come?" She was standing in the middle of my room, slapping half a bottle of sunscreen on her already tanned body.

I shook my head, wincing at the jolts of pain blurring my vision. "No, you go and have fun. I'll just sleep this off."

A worried frown appeared on her face. "Want me to get you anything?"

"I'm fine." I managed a fake smile and shooed her out the door.

"It must be the heat. If you need anything, just call."

"Thanks, sweetie," I whispered, leaning back against the cool satin sheets. Sylvie was right. I most certainly wasn't accustomed to the Italian weather. In the silence and the serenity of this place, my dizziness slowly cleared until I felt confident enough to stand.

I pulled the brocade curtains aside. The sun was setting in countless shades of orange and copper streaking the evening sky. From the distance, I could make out Sylvie's naked legs on an outdoor lounger facing the lake, her face obscured by a huge straw hat. Shrugging out of my skirt and into a pair of jeans, I figured I could either join her or do what I'd been waiting to do ever since Jett told me about the club. If it was the truth, there had to be some evidence somewhere.

This was my opportunity. I walked down the stairs, passed the kitchen and the living room, reached the door to the backyard, and stepped out into the fragrant evening air. My heart began to hammer against my ribcage, which was silly. The property was built on a hill, surrounded by thousands of acres of land. Even if I stumbled upon the one place mentioned in Jett's reports, it was most unlikely I'd discover what others had already found when they combed the estate in Alessandro's absence—and lost again. But the chapel, where Jett's private detective had once located Maria Lucazzone's diary, was my only lead.

Lost in my thoughts I scanned the area. According to Jett's report, Alessandro had hundreds of miles of vineyards, forests and fields, not including the beautiful backyard. Standing here on the foot of the stairs, I couldn't stop being impressed. The garden—although a little neglected—was still stunning, with tiny gravel stones building a strong contrast to the myriad of blooming flowers, and with palm and needle trees shielding the estate from prying eyes. This side of the house was surrounded by woods and mountains as far as I could see. I figured if someone wanted to hide a chapel, the tall trees would make it impossible to spy. It was the perfect place if you sought privacy.

I crossed the backyard and climbed down the steep stairs snaking toward the woods. I didn't have to look very far. Behind the huge palm trees and a dried up stone well, I could make out a gray building barely the size of a garden shed. If it wasn't for its old fashioned stone walls and a hardly noticeable cross on the roof, I would have shrugged it off as such. Maybe whoever built it meant to create a chapel that was inconspicuous. Or maybe, after Maria died, no one ever cared to get rid of the overgrown vegetation obstructing the narrow trail leading to it. Either way I didn't mind fighting my way through the bushes.

I was almost there when I heard a female voice calling out my name. My head snapped in the direction of the house.

"Brooke. Where are you? Help me."

Judging from the urgency and choice of words, it sounded like an emergency. The chapel would have to wait. Without a glance back, I dashed for the house, my brain coming up with a million bad things that might have happened.

***

"Fuck, Brooke. It hurts so much. I can't stand it." Sylvie was hysterical, shouting from the kitchen bench. As usual she was being melodramatic—and loving it. At least she wasn't crying.

"For heaven's sake. Stop being a pussy," I ordered as I focused on removing a splinter from her left foot with a pair of tweezers. "It's not like I'm sawing off your foot."

The piece of wooden splinter was so tiny I had to use a needle to push it around. We had tried softening the skin with water and soap and then with alcohol, but it was in too deep. Finally, after what felt like an eternity, I managed to grip the end of the splitter and, pushing against it with the needle, I raised it enough to pull it out with the tweezers.

"Thanks." Sylvie rubbed her sore foot, her other leg dangling from the bench. "I was walking barefoot in the grass when I stepped on a branch. Where have you been? I had to hop around the house on one foot and managed to hurt my ankle in the process."

I handed the tweezers back to her, mentally searching for an excuse. Of course I could tell Sylvie about the chapel and Jett's claims because she was my best friend, the only one I really trusted. But what was the point in scaring her based on nothing but assumptions? Besides, I wasn't ready to tell her about my lunch with Jett. Not when I didn't yet know what to do about him.

"I was thinking of going for a walk. Did you know Alessandro has his own pool? Maybe you should use it rather than the lake."

"Yeah." She tested her foot tenderly, wincing, then hobbled across the kitchen and back. "It feels so much better."

I heaved a long sigh. "That's great."

Opening the fridge, I pulled out two cans of soda and handed her one. She didn't open it.

"When are you going to see him again?" Sylvie asked.

"Who?" I blinked in confusion. Jett had been on my mind for hours, and for a moment I thought she meant *him*—until it dawned on me Sylvie had to be talking about Alessandro. "I don't know. He's really sick and every day's a struggle. Clarkson expects us to stay a week, during which I hope we'll get to talk again."

Sylvie's eyes narrowed on me. "And then what?"

Good question. "To be honest, I have no idea." I still couldn't get over the fact that this huge property would soon belong to me. The least I could do was stick around for a little bit longer, even though the initial excitement had dissipated at the outlook of living in a bizarre club's former meeting point, if not domicile.

"I do." Sylvie inched closer and squeezed my hands, her blue eyes searching mine. "Ever since we arrived here you've been on edge. You've always been a bit of a worrier, but I've never seen you so absentminded and weird." In spite of her frown, her voice became softer, soothing even. "I want you to come back with me. Let Clarkson deal with the estate, rent it out if you want, but this isn't you. It's not your kind of life. Why make yourself miserable just because you feel you owe someone something?"

I stared at her. "That's not the case at all. I'm—"

She grimaced and nodded. "You're a people pleaser, Brooke."

How could I tell her that, yes, I had accepted Alessandro's invitation because it was his wish to meet with me. But right now I was ready to stay because a mystery kept me here. I was intrigued and wanted to find out more about the estate and the people who once lived here. And if Jett was right, then I wouldn't be safe anywhere—not here, and not back home. They would come after me. The prospect felt surreal, yet scared the crap out of me.

"I'll come back with you once I'm ready," I said.

Sylvie shrugged and opened her soda can. "I need to check out my Facebook page, see how my friends are doing. I've been neglecting them."

"Sure." I wanted to point out that most of her *neglected*

friends weren't people she had ever met, but I kept my thoughts to myself.

Luckily for us, Alessandro had internet access in the library, where Sylvie could use his computer. It was an old thing that took five minutes to boot with an extremely slow connection, but Sylvie had the patience of a saint when it came to maintaining her virtual social life. Closing the door behind me, I gave her the privacy she needed and retreated to my room with Alessandro's envelope. A few minutes into flicking through family photos my phone rang, and my heart started to race as Jett's name appeared on the display.

"Found anything?" Jett said the moment I picked up.

"Well, hello to you, too." I scowled and tucked my legs beneath me on the bed, suddenly aware of how deliciously coarse the sheet felt beneath my skin. "I didn't have a chance yet. How did you know I'd be looking?"

"I know you." There was a small pause and some shuffling. In the background I could hear people talking. And then the noise was gone, as though he had left for somewhere quiet. I didn't like the idea of him frequenting a bar without me. Women would throw themselves at him and that set my skin on fire and my pulse racing. I cringed as my mood plummeted to a new low.

Boy, was I getting angry and he hadn't even done anything. "Why are you—"

He cut me off. "Any plans for tomorrow? I'll pick you

up at ten." His voice sounded so sexy, smooth like strawberries dipped in dark chocolate, and yet so rough, grating my nerve endings.

"For what?"

A part of me—probably the one covered by my panties—hoped to see him again, while the part that accommodated my brain wanted to yell at him to stop being an arrogant ass and to hang up.

"You owe me a date, Brooke."

"I'm not going on a date with you."

"Why not?"

I detected a hint of amusement in his tone and took a deep breath. "Because it's not going to happen. I need hard evidence first."

"I get it, you're angry and it's over and you have no intention of rekindling things."

Gee, he didn't get it. "I'm not angry because you withheld the truth. You did what you were supposed to do for your company." I took a sharp breath as I considered my words. "I'm angry because I don't know if I can trust you."

"Brooke, what happened is done. I'm not after the estate. I'm also not forcing you to do something you don't want to do. I'm not going to rip off your underwear and fuck you on the spot even though...I gotta admit, that's exactly what I've had in mind, numerous times ever since you walked out on me."

I choked on my breath as heat pooled between my legs and sent a delicious tingle through my sensitive clit. Instinctively, my hand wandered south, two fingers pressing against the sensitive bud to stop the growing ache. His bluntness both shocked and aroused me. Deep down I had been waiting—counting on him to do just that.

I bit my lip hard and held my breath so he wouldn't hear my labored breathing through the line.

"We still have a contract," Jett said slowly. His voice was hoarse, betraying his arousal at the thought. "You never quit on me and you know why."

"We ended it," I whispered.

"No, baby. Not in writing we didn't."

We were back to square one. Sex again, pure, good sex. I wasn't stupid enough to think I could deal with it. I wasn't making that mistake twice. Thinking of the way he touched me, the way he looked at me, I knew I couldn't handle the feelings he aroused in me.

"That's not a good idea, Jett."

Fuck, even his name sounded like sin.

"Are you alone?" His voice was sexy. It caressed my body, pushed through my pretense and touched that hidden spot that could send both pleasure and pain through me.

I nodded, even though he couldn't see me. "Yes," I whispered.

"What are you wearing?" His tone was demanding, leaving me no choice but to answer.

Oh God.

I wasn't so naïve as not to know where this was heading.

"A top and jeans." I tried to keep my tone casual.

"Take them off together with your underwear."

"Why?" My breathing came in raspy heaps. Stupid question, I know.

"Take off your clothes, Brooke," Jett ordered.

There was something about his tone that made me instantly listen to his command. Maybe it was the fact that he was not here and he was just another sexy voice on the other end of the line.

"Now," he demanded.

Cradling the phone between my shoulder and chin, I locked the door. I shrugged out of my jeans and panties, and pulled my top over my head, then unclasped my bra. The balmy air felt surprisingly cool against my feverish skin, making me all too aware of my nakedness. In the empty room, I felt exposed yet sexy. And then there was the fact that I felt horny and was up for some fun. I could hear his breathing down the line and it reminded me of all the times we had been together in bed, enjoying each other's bodies.

"Done?" Jett asked hoarsely.

"Yeah."

"Now, I want you to lay on your bed and close your

eyes. I want you to imagine that I'm there with you. Watching you." His voice was slow and deep. Leaning against he pillows, I closed my eyes and focused until I could see him before me, dressed in jeans and a snug shirt.

"I'm taking my clothes off until I'm naked," he whispered, pausing after the word naked. I pictured his body in all his glory, all hard muscles and smooth skin.

"My hands glide over your body, caressing your nipples. I can feel the softness of your skin, the weight of your breasts in my hands, and smell the fragrance of your hair."

I laughed, my nervousness getting the better of me.

"Focus, Brooke," he demanded sharply.

"Sorry."

"I want you to imagine that I'm standing naked in front of you and as I see you naked, I can tell you, baby, you're turning me on like no other. I'm hard and I'm letting you touch me."

I knew I should have stopped this, hang up—anything to keep my emotional distance. But my brain remained surprisingly pliant. His voice kept me intrigued. Everything was so surreal. He wasn't here, and yet he was—like a fragment of my imagination, willing to do what I wanted.

I cleared my throat and took a deep breath as I let his voice guide me, visualizing him and his hardness, and the way he'd touch himself. His face was a mask of want, his gaze intense with the need to please me. I pictured his eyes and their stunning green color, and his strong fingers as he moved over my breasts. I clenched my legs together to intensify the tension that was slowly building between them at the image of his majestic erection slick with want. My heart was racing in my chest, beating frantically against my ribs as I let his expert voice guide me.

"Can you see me?" Jett asked.

"Yes." Surprisingly I could.

"I'm brushing my lips across the back of your neck until you can feel my breath on your skin. I start kissing your shoulder and spine while my hands move around your waist so I can part your legs."

My skin tingled from his gruff, assertive tone.

"Your back's pressed against me, and my hand's stroking your slit. You're turning me so on, I'm bending you over until you're on all fours. I'm licking you and taste your arousal for me. Can you feel it?"

"Yes."

"Good." A raspy pause, then, "I want you to touch yourself like I'd touch you. Do it well, baby. I want you to describe the way your fingers feel inside you."

Following his command, I spread my legs and slipped my fingers between them, stroking gently, then with a little more fervor before thrusting two fingers in after he instructed me to take all the time I needed.

"Tell me what you feel, Brooke."

"I'm wet," I whispered.

"How wet?"

"Very, very…wet."

"And your fingers?"

"Two inside."

"Keep moving, Brooke." His breath came heavy, sending my fantasy into override. "You make me so hard it hurts. Keep going."

I plunged my fingers in and out of me to the picture of him in my mind and the sound of his voice caressing my senses.

"Imagine my erection between your pussy. How does that feel?"

"I like it." And I did, because my memories with him…made me wetter.

He laughed hoarsely. "I'm moving inside you slowly, imagining you wet and tight, and it feels so good for me. How does it feel for you, Brooke?"

"Good," I breathed. My thumb circled my clit, setting it on fire, my fingers between my legs, eager to follow Jett's next command.

"I'm sliding into you and as slow as I can I start to fuck you. Just inches at a time, until you begin to moan my name." He whispered so low I had a hard time focusing through the hazy curtain of sexual frustration urging me to seek fulfillment. His own arousal was apparent from his labored breathing and the picture of him touching himself shattered my last ounce of insecurity. Biting my lip hard, I rubbed my fingers through my wet folds, struggling to find my pleasure in his absence.

His voice became faint in my head as he told me how deep he plunged into me and how good it felt to be inside me. I couldn't listen anymore. I dipped my fingers in and out of me, imagining it was his body pinning me down, his erection slicing through my skin. I whimpered and pressed my temple against the cold satin pillow as my body began to shake and twist like a flame against the hard caress of my hand.

"I'm coming," I whispered a moment before the world blackened out and I lost myself in the sweet contractions of my climax.

When it was over, the phone was still pressed to my ear and the other end of the line was so quiet I wasn't sure he hadn't hung up.

"Jett?" I asked, sitting up and wrapping my sheets around my naked body. I was hesitant and suddenly ashamed. Had he heard it all? Was he shocked, maybe disgusted, by the way I had let myself get into character?

He cleared his throat but the coarseness of desire was still there, making my heart twitch in my chest.

"I'm really jealous of your fingers, baby," he whispered. I smiled. "And I think I have a problem."

"What problem?" I grinned, knowing that he was about to say one of his sexy things.

"I think I can't get enough of you," he whispered. "Do you have any idea how much I wish you were here? How much I wish I could have seen you come?"

I smiled thankful he couldn't see the blush burning my cheeks. Seriously, I could do this all night, listen to his deep voice whisper sweet nothings—or in this case naughty nothings—into my ear.

A thud echoed in the background, followed by a male voice saying something, and Jett's 'fuck you' reply.

He wasn't alone. Maybe even in a public place. The heat scorching my face intensified from both mortification and excitement.

"I'll pick you up tomorrow at twelve same place like last time." His tone was composed. Business-like. And then it dropped to a whisper. "And Brooke, I'm hurting all over for you, baby. You owe me the real deal and I'm going to take it. Running from me isn't going to help you because I've never been a quitter." The line went dead.

He had hung up on me.

Even though I had just climaxed, my body was still earning for him. I could never have imagined anything like this would turn me on—or him. It wasn't that I was uncomfortable with dirty talk. Call me cliché, but I always thought seedy phone conversations were reserved for lonely guys on a lonely night far away from the convenience of an internet connection. I shrugged back into my clothes and typed up a text message.

Don't get your hopes up. I'm never sleeping with you again.

My fingers hovered over the send button, but ended up pressing delete instead. Why warn him when I could let him simmer all night and then dash his hopes. After the stunt he just pulled on me, the jerk deserved a little pain.

9

"SO LET ME get this straight. You want to go back to Bellagio and leave me all alone here?" Sylvie asked over a hearty breakfast consisting of egg omelet and orange juice. Apart from cereals and pre-made waffles, it was the only thing Sylvie and I knew how to prepare, so naturally, we indulged in it whenever we couldn't make it to the nearest café.

Nodding, I put down my fork and pushed my empty plate aside. "I need to run some errands. You can do whatever you want. Go shopping, lounge by the pool, update your Twitter status."

"It's Facebook." She grimaced, like I was an idiot for not remembering. "I know you're supposed to do something for the old man. I thought I could come with you."

"It'll be boring." I tried to sound convincing—and failed miserably. " I'd rather you have a nice day because it's supposed to be a vacation. Go enjoy yourself. Do what you feel like doing."

"And that is?"

I shrugged. Normal people went on a sightseeing tour or lay on a sunbed, reading a book. Sylvie was a totally different species.

"Go to Milan, shopping. It's not that far. I'll be back around seven." I had no idea what Jett had in mind. My best guess was lunch, in which case we'd be done by mid-afternoon, give or take a few hours.

"You know, I might just do that," Sylvie said. "I've always wanted to visit Milan. It's the shopping capital of Italy, and I can finally get one of those Italian silk scarfs and a new *Prada* bag." Sylvie swooned and her eyes glazed over as she entered shopping heaven. I could almost see the *Prada* logo reflected in her blue eyes.

"Just do me the favor and don't go home with a guy."

"I'm not that stupid."

I sighed. "I know."

Hopefully I wasn't the one making a mistake by going out with the hottest, most persuasive guy I knew. Sleeping with Jett when he was my boss was bad enough. But going out with him as my ex-boss, who also happened to be the best lover I ever had, might be worse. It spelled instant trouble.

***

The taxi driver parked in front of the spa. I paid and got out quickly, almost tripping over my two feet as I spotted Jett leaning relaxed against his Lamborghini. Dark shades hid his eyes, making it impossible to discern whether he was absorbed in the newspaper in his hands, or watching me approach.

My heart began to thump a little harder, and my tongue flicked over my suddenly dry lips as I stared at six foot two of toned muscles. He looked so damn sexy dressed in jeans and a black shirt. His thick dark hair was shiny and unruly. I wondered whether he'd taken a shower and didn't bother to comb it before driving to pick me up. The picture of me running my hands through his hair, pulling him on top of me, made me blush so hard my skin was on fire. He was pure sin. Whoever invented the word must've done so with Jett in mind.

As if on cue, his head snapped in my direction and a devilish grin lit up his face. He folded the newspaper and tossed it through the open window into the car, then strolled toward me.

"Well, hello, I'm Jett Mayfield." He grabbed my hand in a very intimate grip. "I'm the crazy guy who called last night."

He had me at hello and crazy.

I forced a smile on my face, and prayed he'd mistake my blush for the beginning of a sunburn. Just thinking of yesterday's phone conversation with him and knowing the sound of his voice was enough to make me give in, was not only awkward—it was embarrassing and agonizingly stupid. Now was the right time for earth to swallow me up whole and make me disappear forever. Maybe I was lucky enough, and Jett had been drunk and with no recollection of my lack of refusal.

Yeah, it *was* possible. Stranger things happened.

Don't be stupid, Stewart. Just look at his grin. He knows it!

"What are you doing?" I asked, trying to sound as casual as possible.

"Establishing a clean slate." He winked and interlaced his fingers with mine as he walked me to his car. "Starting all over again. With you."

"Really?" I laughed, unable to look into his eyes. The serious undertones in his voice made me nervous.

"You look beautiful." He kissed my cheek and lingered there a bit longer than necessary. A soft tingle ran down my spine. "In Italy you don't really say I miss you. People say 'mi manchi', which means 'you are missing from me.' I feel that way, Brooke. Whenever you're not around, I feel like a part of me is missing."

A hot shudder ran through my body and every inch of me longed to touch him. That he was hot and sexy was bad enough. Did he have to be nice, too? I wanted to say something witty. But, as usual, I couldn't think straight around him.

Smiling, Jett opened the door and I entered. The smell of expensive leather hit my nostrils. It didn't surprise me in the least that people were staring at us. They probably thought we were celebrities, which couldn't be further from the truth. At least in my case.

"Where are we going?" I asked.

"It's a surprise." He started the engine and pointed at the newspaper before steering out of the parking lot. "Turn to page eight."

The newspaper was older than I thought, folded and used many times, the front page torn in several places. I flicked straight to page eight. The main headline mentioned a gallery opening. Further down was something about a charity event and pictures of high society socialites in their evening gowns, holding champagne flutes. The last paragraph mentioned various art purchases made on that evening. The date read May 8th 1991.

"It's an old newspaper." I peered at Jett, confused, as I pointed out the obvious.

"If you look closely, you'll see a younger version of Lucazzone standing next to my father. It's the only picture of the two together."

I scanned the pictures again. Although they were blurred, I recognized Alessandro. The photo must have been taken prior to his wife's death, long before his health deteriorated. My gaze shifted from Alessandro to the middle-aged man towering over him, and I recognized Jett's stubborn chin and confident smile. There was no caption—as though the two didn't need an introduction. Just a random shot at some high society party.

"Where was this?"

"New York," Jett said. "More than twenty years ago."

"That's a long time ago."

"When I was a child we came here every summer. We stayed in hotels and holiday cottages in the area, until I purchased my property on Lake Como ten years ago. All those years my father never acknowledged knowing Lucazzone. And when I asked him a couple of weeks ago, he pretended to have met him only when he decided buying the Lucazzone estate might be a good investment."

"What are you saying?"

"My father keeps pretending to have known Lucazzone for only ten years. This paper—" He pointed at the newspaper in my hand. "—shows they've known each other far longer than that. I've been asking myself why he'd lie about that."

"When did you find this?"

He sighed. "I asked a guy I know to investigate a few weeks back, right after my father told me about the club and that any exposure of it could harm the company. I wanted to find out more. Unfortunately, there wasn't much to find."

My gaze remained glued to him as I contemplated his words. Eventually I asked the one question I thought made the most sense.

"Did you confront your father about his lie?"

"No."

"Why not?"

"Because I don't know enough, okay?" Jett said. "I need to know what I'm dealing with. Who those people are. What the club's all about."

Like me, he didn't trust anyone. I bit my lip as I regarded Jett from the corner of my eye. The strong muscles of his arms were clearly displayed beneath his shirt. One hand held the steering wheel, the other rested against the window. He must've felt my gaze on him, because his attention snapped in my direction and he frowned.

"You still don't believe me, do you?" He turned back to the road, but his expression didn't soften. "Damn, Brooke. I told you I'm not the bad guy."

I chose not to answer his question because he was right. Ever since I found out he had been keeping things from me, I had a hard time trusting him. Seeing him as the bad guy was the main excuse I used to get over him. It helped me to keep my distance. Without that excuse, my brain couldn't keep my foolish heart under control.

"What do you think is going on?" I asked.

"I honestly don't know." He hesitated briefly. "My father doesn't talk. Fact is, he and Lucazzone have known each other for a long time, but he won't acknowledge it. I got him to talk about the club once, but apparently that happened a few years ago and he's out now."

"Maybe they're all hiding something," I said, matter-of-factly.

Jett nodded grimly. "That's my best bet, too. I just don't want this shit to affect you in any way."

"Yeah, see that's something I wanted to talk about." I tapped my fingers on my thigh, considering my words as my heartbeat sped up at the countless thoughts running through my mind. "You keep saying I'm in danger. But you don't have any proof."

"I do, Brooke."

Silence. I waited for him to continue. He didn't.

"What proof?"

He shook his head. "I don't want to scare you."

Oh, come on!

"Are you kidding me?" I snorted. "You do realize your whole 'I'm here to protect you' crap *is* scary, right? It's like warning me there's something or someone inside my house, but you're not telling me what it is and my imagination's left roaming free in horror movie territory."

"Okay. You know I told you about the murder victim found on the Lucazzone estate years ago?"

I nodded, thinking back to the horrendous story taking place decades ago. The victim was Alessandro's lover—or at least that's what Maria's diary supposedly said. The crime was never investigated and consequently Alessandro never prosecuted.

"Yeah, that wasn't the only weird thing happening," Jett said, "My brother and I used to watch the house when we were kids." I nodded because I remembered him telling me the story. He continued. "At times we'd see the old man leaving the house. We also noticed policemen regularly visiting the place. Laughing. Shaking hands. I have good reason to believe they were involved."

I didn't like this information. I figured in case of an emergency, I might just end up asking the wrong people for help.

I wet my dry lips and repeated the obvious because his words kept echoing inside my brain, and I needed to hear them out loud. "You think the police were involved—in the club."

"No." Jett shook his head slowly, his gaze darkening. "Thinking back, I'm pretty sure of it, considering that the murder on the estate was never investigated. With the right people covering for you, it'd be easy to kill someone and shrug it off as an accident. I think that's what really happened."

"Obviously, a man with an open throat and torso didn't kill himself."

"Exactly," Jett muttered.

As the Lamborghini sped out of the city and up the narrow country road, I realized I still had no idea where we were heading.

"Where are we going?"

His mood lightened at my sudden change in topic. "Since I'm the one taking you out on a date, I have a right to keep the destination secret until we're there."

"I don't really like surprises."

"I know, baby, but believe me this one will blow your mind."

My skin began to tingle from the sexual undertone in his voice. The temperature in the car rose a few degrees. Maybe because the early afternoon sun was shining with relentless heat. Or maybe because his right arm was so close to mine, I could almost feel his touch. Either way, I didn't like the jolts of anticipation traveling through my abdomen and gathering between my legs.

Eventually the forest cleared. From our heightened road I could see lots of sparkling water and a shore. I straightened in my seat and craned my neck to get a better glimpse. In the distance the first rows of roofs began to emerge, gathering into a messy knot of narrow properties and winding streets running between them.

"Is that the Ligurian Sea?" My brain fought to recall the tiny bits of Italian geography I had picked up on my first trip to Italy.

"No, it's still Lake Como. The sea is a two and half hour drive from here," Jett said. "It's quite nice. I'll take us some day."

Us.

My heart skipped a beat. He was making future plans— and they involved me.

He took a left turn and we came to a stop near a small port.

"Can you swim?" Jett asked as he helped me out his car and locked it behind us.

I looked up into his stunning green eyes. His impossibly long lashes shielded them from the bright light, making them appear a few shades darker than usual.

Mysterious. Dangerously hot.

"Yes. Why?" I asked, warily.

"Because we're going on a boat."

10

A BOAT WAS actually an understatement. What Jett called a boat looked more like a seventy-foot yacht with four luxury cabins consisting of an en-suite forward VIP cabin, a twin bunk cabin to port, a twin bunk cabin to starboard, and a full mid-ship master cabin with yet another bathroom—or so Jett explained. Not that I understood half the things he said, but I tried my best to keep up with his excited chatter as I let him show me around.

Upon entering the living room, the part boaters called a saloon, we walked through a spacious starboard side galley with ample space to relax, a polished mahogany dining table, and a kitchen almost twice the size of my kitchen back in New York. It had a granite countertop, fitted dishwasher, ceramic hob, refrigerator, microwave, and oven—like you'd ever need that on a boat.

It was my first time on this kind of 'boat' and walking through each of the cabins, I had a hard time not to gawk at the expensive furniture and overindulgent design focusing on shades of cream and brown. Eventually we stopped in the saloon and Jett invited me to sit down on the creamy luxury couch. Set up on the opposite wall was a huge plasma TV set and a stereo system right out of a catalog. I tried hard not to look too impressed. Truth was, Jett's boat had everything anyone could ever wish for: lots of space, privacy, and more things than the apartment I shared with Sylvie back in Brooklyn.

"Wow. You could actually live here," I said, running my fingertips over the smooth mahogany surface of a side table.

"I did about four years ago."

I felt his hand on my neck and then he pulled my hair back and his hot lips were on my skin. His butterfly kisses sent delicious jolts through me, making me shiver with both pleasure and a hint of pain that traveled somewhere south.

"I wanted to be alone with my thoughts," Jett whispered. "This was the perfect place for it. Once you're out here, far away from the oppressing boundaries of life and work, you can almost smell the freedom in the air. It's like a completely different world."

I blinked back my surprise. "The boat's yours?" I don't know why I was so surprised, when he had enough money to buy anything he wanted.

"Yeah, I bought it after finalizing my first big work project. It was much better than living in a house with my brother and father." He turned me toward him. His expression showed the same enthusiasm as before, but a shadow had descended over his mood, which made me conclude living with his family hadn't been a piece of cake.

"Why a boat?" I found myself asking, compelled by this man and the prospect of him finally opening up to me.

Jett shrugged. "Why not a boat? You wake up with the sun on your face, the air smelling of water and salt, and the wind blowing through your hair. There's no door. No bell to ring. You can just pack your bags and leave, and no one knows where you are."

He wanted to run. Like I had run many years ago. From my past. From the pain that wouldn't stop haunting me every second of the day. I wanted to ask what he was running from. Yet I didn't because I wanted him to open up to me out of need rather than obligation.

I looked up and found Jett still watching me, scrutinizing me, his dark eyes more clouded than before. He was so careful not to disclose anything about his past that he ended up showing everything in his expression. Usually, he was inscrutable. For a moment I could see he wasn't as closed a book as he always pretended to be, which was good because it showed me his arrogant and perfect façade was nothing but a disguise to protect what lay buried within his soul.

I moistened my lips and walked to the painting hanging on the wall behind him. It was just a picture of his boat with large capital letters spelling THE ROCK beneath it.

"The Rock?" I read, grimacing. "Is that your boat's name? I hope I'm not supposed to take it literally."

He laughed, gorgeous dimples forming in his cheeks. "Yeah. But don't worry. It'd take a lot to sink it. It's as solid as a rock, which is why it got its name."

I raised my eyebrows. "Aren't ships usually named after former conquests?"

"You're right." He paused and nodded, faking deep thought. "What if I told you there were no former conquests? No one who ever mattered?"

My heart slammed against the confined space of my ribcage.

Hard to believe.

And yet something in the way he regarded me—calm and serious—made me want to believe every single word.

"I might actually rename her," Jett continued. "I was thinking 'Brooke.' It has a much nicer ring to it than 'The Rock.'"

"Seriously?" I laughed nervously as I watched him move closer, stopping just a few inches away from me.

"Why would I joke about it?"

He was damn serious. I could tell from the way he stared me down with a determined glint in his eyes. My breath caught in my throat. Not because of the way he looked at me—with an intense magnetism that made me want to give him everything I had—nor because he was considering renaming his boat after me. I could barely breathe because I realized nothing had changed. He behaved as if we were still together, as if we never broke up.

As if he meant the last words he'd spoken to me the last time I saw him in New York: *I care for you enough to let you go.*

Technically, he *did* let me go —then followed me. So did he care for me? And if he did, was it a good thing? Should I welcome it, let my own feelings develop and see where that might take me?

"It might be a bit too early for renaming a boat after me," I said slowly.

He turned away, hiding his expression. For a moment, I regretted my words—until I realized I was doing the right thing. Keeping each other at arm's length. Not too involved.

"What happens when you're not here? Who takes care of 'The Rock'?" Acutely aware of the sudden tension emanating from him, I tried to steer the focus away from me.

Jett pointed at the door, ignoring my question and previous statement. "Look, can you wait here while I remove the anchor? I'll be back in a minute."

He was going to remove the anchor? Like in, sail away with me onboard?

Holy dang!

I was in big trouble.

Being alone with him on a luxury boat surrounded by sparkling blue water and no living soul in sight was the last thing I wanted, and yet I found myself smiling and saying, "Sure. Take your time."

What the heck, Stewart?

"Great," Jett said, his eyes betraying his amusement. "I'll grab us a drink on the way back."

He made it all sound so nonchalant, like he was going to get us coffee from the corner café. I knew that blasé tone of his and what it usually preceded. Don't ever trust a guy with a Southern accent, a lazy smile, and a casual stance, because he's about to sneak his way into your panties without even trying.

Pissed with myself that I didn't even think about protesting, I began to look around as I waited for him. The doors were open, and from my seat on the sofa I could peer right into the master cabin. The first thing I noticed was the king-sized bed and the small round rug on the polished oak floor. The sheets were the color of creamy chocolate, smooth and shiny like silk. The picture of me sitting down on the soft bed entered my head. I could see myself surrounded by all those pillows and imagined Jett's rough hands on my skin, his possessive tongue inside my mouth as we kissed and made love on the silk sheets, my hands tugging at his hair as he moved inside me. My stomach knotted deliciously as a pang of heat shot through me and gathered between my legs. Good thing I shaved my legs and put on my nicest lingerie.

I groaned with irritation.

Why was I even thinking of that? It wasn't like I wanted to sleep with him. That wasn't why I came here *at all*. I was so immersed in my thoughts that I didn't hear Jett coming in.

"You said you've sworn off alcohol, so I brought us iced coffee instead." He placed a long drink glass with a creamy brownish liquid and a straw in front of me as he held on to his.

I looked up, startled. My face caught fire, partly because I was ashamed of my thoughts, and partly because I *knew* he knew. It was pretty obvious from the amused glint in his eyes and the way he moistened his lips, flicking the tip of his tongue over them lazily, suggesting all sorts of naughty things. He was torturing me without so much as touching my body.

"I want to show you the lake," Jett said, "since you might want to live here when you inherit the estate." He held out his hand and I interlaced my fingers with his. His skin felt warm. Climbing up the stairs, I felt his gaze on my ass and couldn't help but sway my hips just a little bit more than usual because I wanted to have the same effect on him as he had on me.

We walked up to the deck where we lingered for a few moments, enjoying the stunning view.

"This is where I spend most of my time when I'm here," Jett said.

"It's beautiful," I whispered, realizing my words couldn't do it justice. Decorated with brown wicker outdoor furniture consisting of one love seat with creamy white cushions and a long coffee table plus a side table, it held enough space to accommodate a whole family. There were three sunbathing areas forward, aft and alongside the steering console of the cockpit.

"Let's get this baby going," Jett said. Through the glass partition, I watched him step into the cockpit and then behind the steering console. His long fingers wrapped around the helm as he expertly pushed a few buttons—and there were plenty of those. Everything looked so complicated, and yet Jett seemed as though he had done nothing else his whole life. Obviously he knew what he was doing, which relaxed me.

An instant later the boat came to life and we left the dock, slowly at first, then faster. I slumped onto a lounge chair and peered at the clear blue water around us as we moved farther from the shore and from the people walking up and down the promenade.

Being out here with the waves crashing around the boat and the wind blowing through my hair, I felt a sense of tranquility and happiness. For the first time in my life, I felt alive...and safe. As if the wind and the water could wash away the pain and the disappointments of the past ten years. As if I could leave my past behind and sail into a new future. And the fact that Jett was standing just a few feet away made the whole experience even more profound.

Boats passed as by periodically, and the shore became nothing but a narrow strip of brown in the distance. And then even that disappeared, and my mind drifted off to memories of his deep voice and sinfully sexy eyes.

***

'The Rock' slowed down—I could feel the gentle vibrations of the engine. Realizing I must have fallen asleep, I opened my eyes and squinted against the sunlight as I tried to adjust to the glaring brightness. We were far out on the lake, with no people in sight. Surrounded by mountain views, the spot looked quiet and secluded, far away from civilization. The engine whirred and then all became quiet and the boat was floating idly in the water.

Realizing it was just Jett and me now—on water,

alone—I sat up and looked at the partition. He wasn't there. A moment later, I felt his presence behind me. I turned and smiled and he rewarded me with a lazy grin.

"Had a good nap?"

"How do you know?"

He leaned forward and brushed a stray strand of hair out of my face. "Because I know what you look like when you wake up. You have a sexy, carefree look about you, like you've been to a different place."

I felt my cheeks catch fire. "Sexy, huh? I like that. I always thought I looked grumpy. Sexy definitely sounds way better."

"Even your grumpy looks are sexy." He reached out to help me up and turned me around, wrapping his arms around me so my back was pressed against his front. I snuggled against his chest and craned my neck to accommodate his exploring lips on my earlobe. My skin felt warm—hot even—and not just from the sun.

"How long have you been driving a boat?" I asked to distract myself from the sudden tension in the air.

"I took my first course six years ago, but my father taught me the basics as a child."

"That's nice," I said, leaning into him so he wouldn't stop his nibbling. "You sure know what you're doing."

"You mean the boat, or this?" His teeth grazed my skin just a little bit harder than was necessary, sending a jolt of pleasure and pain through me. His caress made it hard for me to keep my composure, so I pulled away and stepped aside to put some much-needed distance between us.

"Come on. Let's go inside." He grinned and held out his hand. I eyed it carefully, not quite trusting that he wouldn't just grab me in his arms and do whatever he had been about to do. "I won't bite—unless you want me to," Jett said.

"Why? What's inside?"

"Iced Tea? Water? You must be dehydrated." And I was. But I still didn't trust the dangerous glint in his eyes. "Besides, it's cooler inside."

"No funny business." I said.

"You know me."

Hell yeah, I did. "Which is exactly why I don't trust you when we're alone." He smiled that panty-dropping smile of his that always made me want to rip the clothes off his glorious body and wrap myself around him. Was there pride in his eyes? I groaned, irritated with myself for inflating his over-inflated ego some more. "I didn't mean it like a compliment. It's not like you're a sex god or anything."

"Why thanks, baby. I'd love to prove my worth."

Oh gosh. Why couldn't I just keep my big mouth shut?

A lazy grin lit up his face and my brain switched off for a second. Annoyed, I rolled my eyes and took off across the deck and down the stairs to the master saloon, confident that he'd follow behind.

I sat down on the couch and watched him pour us two glasses of bottled water from the fridge.

"Thanks," I said as he passed me a glass and sat down opposite from me. I took a few sips and placed the glass in front of me on the table, all too aware of his intense gaze.

Through the windows I could see the sparkling water, and the soft movement eased my tension, but not enough to make me feel less nervous around him.

"I don't know anyone who owns a boat, let alone can navigate one," I admitted. "I think it's pretty amazing. Is there anything else you've been keeping from me?"

He inclined his head. "I'm not particularly good at flying. My brother's way better than me, which annoyed my father to no end. They're both highly competitive, challenging me to beat them at whatever it was that caught their attention. But it was always the not particularly risky stuff. You know, flying, gambling, hunting, sky diving… you name it. I was more interested in other stuff."

I laughed. Was he serious? I wanted to point out that all of the things he mentioned were risky, but I decided to dive into that later. "What other stuff?" I asked instead.

He leaned so close I could see the tiny lines beneath his eyes and feel the delicious warmth of his breath. His piercing gaze met mine. "For some time I had the crazy idea to work undercover." I raised my brows in confusion and his grin widened. "You know...head hunt people. I took martial arts classes, trained in all the James Bond stuff you see on TV. I joined a gang. It was my way to handle anger." He waved his hand like it didn't matter. I almost choked on my breath.

"Wait a sec. Rewind a bit. Did you say 'gang'?"

He grimaced. "Sort of. Though not the drug dealing type you probably have in mind. Everyone said I had problems with authority, which I guess was true. I didn't listen to anyone. Not my father, not my teachers. No one."

"And by head hunting I assume you're not talking about sifting through prospective candidates to fill a job opening."

He shook his head, still grinning.

"Wow." I stared at him, open-mouthed. It was difficult to imagine Jett—the refined CEO of one of the largest and most successful real estate companies in the world—doing something dangerous, and yet I was inclined to believe him. He had struck me as the bad boy type all right when I first met him, and I was thrilled to see my people knowledge didn't suck as much as I always thought.

"It's in the past now, but I can't say I'm proud of some of the experiences I made." He ran his fingertips over my lower arm absentmindedly. His gaze was averted so I couldn't read his expression, but I didn't fail to catch the strained undertones in his voice. He was hiding something. I couldn't pinpoint what drove me to that conclusion, but I knew I was right.

"Well, we all make mistakes. It's part of humanity," I said.

The way he bit his lower lip, hesitating, I could tell he didn't want to disclose more, which was a shame because I loved hearing about his life. It made me feel connected to him. Maybe he didn't trust me enough to share everything with me. Maybe by pressing the issue, I'd be asking for too much too soon when every single women's magazine tells you to take things slowly. Obviously, I didn't want to be the pushy kind—the one who had to know -everything and ended up asking stupid questions like 'what are you thinking' or 'how do you feel about us?' I knew enough people who made that sort of mistake, and I honestly wanted to learn from their failures. He'd confide in me, eventually. Unfortunately, I had already told him one of my biggest secrets. So there was no way in hell I'd let him get away with not telling me one of his own. It was only fair he open up so we were even.

"What made you give it up?" I asked.

A few moments passed and he didn't answer. I thought he might be pissed that I took the liberty to insist on a topic he obviously wasn't comfortable talking about. And then he turned to look at me, and I flinched inwardly at the pain reflected in his expression. His eyes were deep like the ocean and filled with darkness.

I knew this was the moment he'd either share it all, or pull away from me.

"I got involved with the wrong crowd and ended up doing some very stupid things for them," Jett said. "I had to learn the hard way…it was either jail or let my father buy me out of the mess. I have changed since—" He trailed off, leaving the rest open to interpretation.

The energy he exuded made it clear something bad had happened. The image of him hiding, destroying, fighting, popped into my head and other feelings rushed through me—excitement, fear, arousal—at the knowledge he used to be someone else. Or maybe he wasn't so different now; he just hid it well. Either way, I realized my opinion of him hadn't shifted.

"I wish I could tell you more, but there's no sense in telling you something that I can't change. Something I can't explain to myself," Jett murmured. "We all have secrets. Mine may be worse than I care to admit, but I don't want you to think less of me by telling you what happened, because my past's nothing but baggage resulting from bad choices and foolish mistakes. What happened can't be undone. I'm lucky enough to be alive and that's all that counts. Maybe one day, when I'm confident that nothing can scare you off, I'll tell you more."

It hurt that he thought whatever he did would make me run for the hills, and yet I understood where he was coming from. Secrets aren't easily revealed when you have so much to lose.

"Whatever you did is in the past." My hand gripped his, giving it a light and reassuring squeeze, signalling I wasn't one to judge, just like he hadn't judged me when I disclosed my past. "It's human nature to make mistakes."

He caught my glance and something passed between us. A mutual understanding that not knowing everything was better for me. For us. For whatever there might be between us in the future.

I was okay not knowing.

"I've been there and I understand." I forced a soft smile on my lips.

"Thank you." His gaze passed through me like a current, piercing into my very core, and his thumb began to stroke my fingers. My skin tingled: strong, noticeable, but invisible. For the umpteenth time I wondered whether he could feel our connection. Two opposites drawn together like magnets. As much as I had pushed him away, hating him for the pain he caused me, I couldn't deny the fact that he was a part of me now. Wherever I went, he would be there, buried deep within my heart. Never letting him go.

"For what?" My voice was husky. "I haven't done anything."

"For trusting me." He cupped my face and forced me to meet his heated gaze. His thumb caressed my lips, his touch as soft as melted chocolate.

Kiss me.

My eyes implored him, following my heart's command.

"Sorry, I forgot my manners. Are you hungry?" Breaking our special moment, he let go of me and headed for the kitchen. My gaze followed him.

Damn him and his ability to seem so unaffected!

I cleared my voice. "Actually, I'm starving. Can I help in some way?" I walked over, unsure whether to feel happy or disappointed that we were back on easy-going, superficial terrain.

He opened a small cupboard and retrieved two plates. "I've already ordered."

"What are we having?" Standing on my toes, I craned my neck to peek over his shoulder and noticed the large silver tray on the counter. He switched off a little red button on the buffet server and removed the lid. The smell of roasted meat and vegetables hit my nostrils.

"You're not allergic to walnuts, are you? The filling might have some in it." He started to pile food on the plates, adding meat, pasta with arugula, white beans, and roasted shallots.

"Not that I know of. And even if I were, I'd take a risk just to taste a bite of this stuff. It smells delicious."

He sprinkled chopped chives on the plates and grinned. "It tastes better than it looks."

I remembered the few times he cooked for me. The food hadn't just looked good and tasted even better, it had been unforgettable. "Even better than your cooking?" I said. "Why, I'm one lucky girl."

"Wait, what was that?" He eased closer.

"What?" I took a few steps back until my back pressed against something hard.

"That look you just had." His index finger trailed down my cheek. "Was that sarcasm? Are you implying my cooking was bad?" His pretend frown barely managed to hide a lazy grin, and the glint in his eyes showed me he was joking. I sensed the direction of our conversation had changed. He was digging deeper, searching for the answer to a question only he knew; playing a game.

I bit my lip as I contemplated my options. I could pretend I didn't like it and risk hurting him, because it was most certainly not the answer he expected. Or I could play along. Hell, I was more than up for a little game.

And then what, Stewart? Open up to him so you end up hurt— all over again?

Taking a sharp breath, I met his beautiful eyes. In front of me he looked huge, dominating. But there was a fragility to him that made me realize he wasn't as intimidating as I previously thought.

"Maybe." I tilted my head, giving him full access to my exposed neck. His fingers trailed down my arms and rested on my hips. I swallowed hard and ignored the shiver his touch sent through my body. He wanted me. He wanted me bad. Right here, right now. I could see it in the way his eyes consumed me. And I wanted him, too. Badly.

Why not just give in?

Only once.

"Well, Miss Stewart, if you didn't like my last attempt at cooking, you sure as hell will have to endure my next one." His eyes turned a darker shade of green. The air charged with sexual tension, sending yet another electric jolt through my lower body.

Holy cow.

He was going for it. And my resolve was slowly waning.

Reacting on instinct, I dashed past him, heading for the deck but he was quicker. He scooped me up and carried me over his shoulder to the couch.

"Stop it." Laughing, I tried rather feebly to free myself. "Your attack is absolutely not welcome."

"Attack, huh?" He put me down on the couch, then shifted between my legs until he was lying on top of me and my hands were pinned above my head. His lips searched mine, barely touching me. Lingering. Teasing. So very close and yet too far.

"Say it." His tone came low but I registered the command in it.

"What?"

"That you like my cooking." His beautiful lips twitched with the tiniest hint of a smile.

"Uh...it's awfully—" I paused, letting him stew just a little bit longer "—good. I like it a lot."

"Say it again. I think I might have misheard." His smile was smug, his eyes shimmering with a glint of mischief.

"It's delicious. The best I've ever had." I wasn't talking just about cooking, and he knew it.

"Really? The best you've ever had?" His tongue flicked over his lips, leaving a tempting wet trail behind.

I nodded, unable to erase the stupid grin off my face.

"Then I'll let you off the hook...for now, Ms. Stewart." He shifted on top of me and tightened the grip around my wrists as his lips inched closer to mine. A moment of anticipation passed between us—a silent promise that didn't need words to convey its meaning. He regarded me with so much warmth and passion, I didn't need to delve deep into his heart to know what he was feeling.

I had never been so happy in my life, and in that instant I realized that even if I wanted to and the opportunity presented itself—I could never hurt him.

Love is when you'd rather be hurt than hurt the one you love.

Jett's lips brushed mine tenderly, making my stomach flutter as my eyes drank in the dark sea of his irises. "I hope you don't expect good manners because I'm starving," he whispered in that sexy tone of his that made it sound like he wasn't talking about the food.

Stop hearing double meanings in his words, Stewart!

"Food sounds great."

I let him help me up and sat down at the table, watching him bring our plates. He seemed slightly changed. As though a weight had been lifted off his shoulders. Tucking into my lunch, I smiled up at him. Seeing him happy made me happy, and that was all that mattered.

11

TIME PASSED TOO quickly. After our strange but intimate moment and lunch, which turned out to be nothing short of amazing, we returned to the deck and to light conversation. Jett was easy to talk to, which was one of the many things I liked about him. It was hard to believe he was only a few years older than me. The vastness of his travel experience and knowledge of the world gave a different impression.

"More iced tea?" He refilled my glass without waiting for my answer.

"Thanks." My glance traveled to the clear blue water, and the way it seemed to reflect the sunlight in a million facets.

"So you're taking it serious?" Jett asked.

"What?"

"Your alcohol celibacy."

I nodded and took a sip of my iced tea. "I do. I'm very serious about it." Maybe not forever, but right now I intended to stick with my decision. Getting drunk with Jett around was the last thing I wanted, not least because I knew I couldn't account for anything I did or said under the influence of alcohol. Besides, I needed a clear head to re-valuate our situation.

He took a sip of his own iced tea, his eyes never leaving mine. I could tell he was about to start flirting again by the way his eyes crinkled at the corners. He leaned forward, resting his elbows on the table. His leg touched mine, making me all too aware of just how close we were sitting.

"Have you considered working for me again?" His voice was playful, but there was a serious undertone to it.

"Why would you want that?" I asked surprised.

"Because I want to have you around. We make a good team."

He was right about the latter part, and having him around for most of the day was tempting. But there were so many arguments against it I had no idea where to start. For one, we were too emotionally involved to have a professional relationship. And then there was the second best argument: past experience.

"Last time didn't go so well," I remarked.

"Fair enough. But we've both learned from our

mistakes."

Did we?

"I don't have any plans at the moment. I just want to take it easy, see where things are heading." And with things I meant us. The estate. Alessandro. I needed time to make a decision with regards to my inheritance, where to live, what to do with my life.

"I have a new position coming up. It pays twice as much as you were making with me, and you would be overseeing projects as project leader, while also taking on the same duties as my personal assistant. Consider it a promotion with a pay raise. We could travel together, get to know each other. Of course, if you don't want to, I respect your decision."

"I'll think about it." I avoided his intense gaze. "But thanks for the offer." I meant every word of it.

He shrugged in that non-committal way of his that showed it affected him more than he let on. Truth was, Jett managed one of the most respected realty companies in the world, and passing on his offer would be stupid—in terms of my career. But working with him and seeing him every day would only make me fall even harder for him.

"I got you something." He walked over to the navigation area and returned with a white box then handed it to me, his hands touching mine.

"What is it?"

"Just open it."

I unwrapped the box and removed the thin paper to reveal a two-piece bikini made from tricot fabric. I scooped up the halter-top and low rise bottoms, and held them up into the light, marveling at the expensive cut and the way the material seemed to shimmer in silver facets. It was one of those luxury designer swimsuits I had always wanted but couldn't afford.

"You said white's your favorite color and I thought you might want to change into it, if it gets too hot." He ran his hand through his dark hair.

"It's—" I almost choked on my breath. "Beautiful. You shouldn't have." The only gift I had ever received from a guy was a key chain and a cup that read 'Got to be lazy.' But it wasn't the gift that took my breath away. It was the fact that in the short time we spent together in the past, he had truly listened. The color was perfect and he even got the size right. He had either searched through my underwear drawer to find out, or he had lots of experience with women's sizes. While option one seemed kind of creepy, I certainly preferred it to option two.

"Well, I hope you like it."

"I do. Thank you." I fought the urge to rise to my toes and place a soft peck on his cheek. As I arranged the top back in its box, I remembered Sylvie's warning. This was the life of the rich, who never had to worry about money. I realized that our relationship was the least of my problems. Although I was an heir to an estate, my heritage was based on a lucky coincidence while he was born into it. He had grown up rich, used to this lifestyle and to spending millions on stuff he didn't need. He could buy everything and anything he wanted. He had women throwing themselves at his feet, ready to unbutton his pants for a new dress or a pair of shoes. While I liked to think I was different, I knew he might not think that way if I accepted his gift. A man as powerful and sexy as Jett could easily replace things—and people. I didn't want to end up as one of them, because he had no respect for me.

"What's wrong?" Jett's expression reflected his concern and I realized I had been staring at the box for a little too long. "Did I buy the wrong size?"

"No, it's not that. It's just—" My voice faltered. "Why are you doing all of this, Jett?" Trying to control the shaking in my voice, I stood and walked over to the railing.

"Why am I doing what?"

I could feel him standing behind me but I didn't turn to face him.

"If you're no longer interested in the estate, why are you taking me out and do things for me?" I whispered.

"Because I like nice things and I can afford to buy them." His statement sounded more like a question and only confirmed what I already knew about him and his lifestyle.

I shook my head and laughed briefly. "So it's what you do for every woman, because you can *afford* to?"

The thought of him with others almost made me throw up in my mouth. I wasn't the self-conscious type, but I wasn't a fool not to realize that I had nothing to show off, nothing that would make his rich friends go 'wow, she's trophy wife material'—or whatever musicians, actors, and other famous people said about their girlfriends and wives. Men like Jett had women at their side that had either status or money; looks or fame. I had none of those combinations and that bothered me. I had thought his interest in me was based on his wish to obtain the estate. Now that had been clarified, what did Jett see in me that I didn't?

His hand settled on the small of my back, massaging gently as though to soothe the turmoil inside me.

"No, I don't do that for every woman. I just like you," he said. "You say things the way you see them. You're easy to talk to on an intimate level, and that's hard to find."

I turned around and he cupped my face, forcing me to look up. His eyes were as deep as the sea around us.

"You're honest and clever. You're interesting because you have something many don't have: charm, spirit, and a kind heart. And you're sexy." His lips hovered over mine, sending my insides into a raging storm of anticipation. "But what's most important to me is the fact that you're loyal. I know you wouldn't betray me."

Was I loyal? Would I never betray him? Probably yes. But were those good enough qualities to keep a man like him?

A soft breeze pushed an unruly curl into my eyes. I lifted my hand to brush it away but Jett beat me to it. His fingers sent a delicious tingle through my skin that reminded me just how much my heart was consumed by him.

It's not natural to fall, and fall so hard.

"When you reach the top the only way is down," I mumbled. "You're my peak and I don't want to plummet into the depths awaiting me when we're done."

A few seconds passed between us before he spoke.

"Maybe you think I want what others want, but that's not the case. I'm looking for things that matter. Things I can hold and treasure forever. I think you're worth holding onto, Brooke. And that's worth more in time to come than anything you think might be of importance."

My pulse quickened as his hand ran down my spine, sending an electric shiver into my abdomen.

I wanted to believe him so bad it hurt. But my parents had loved each other and yet my father still killed himself, leaving my mother behind with a hole in her heart so deep not even I, as her daughter, could ever fill.

"I told you once and I'll tell you again," Jett said softly. "I don't want someone who's perfect because I'm not perfect. I want someone who's real; someone who complements me rather than completes me."

My resolve was fading. I could feel it in the way my sappy heart began to cry with joy and the way my legs threatened to buckle beneath me, sending me straight into his open arms. Or heaven—whatever came first.

I think Jett could see it too because he pulled me closer, until I couldn't break away even if I wanted.

"For what it's worth, I still want to be with you and I know you want it, too," Jett whispered. "Just let it happen."

It was true—and for this I hated him, loved him, wanted him, and yet I wished him away. So many conflicting emotions of wants and needs. So much fear. Not because of him, but because of myself—of how deep my feelings and desires were running, and how much I would fall if I happened to lose my grip.

"What do you say?" His lips found mine, taking from them the answer he desired.

My mind was spinning, my heart was screaming, but my body knew what it wanted. It was wet and ready for him. And he knew it. I knew it. His hand moved up until he held the back of my head and our lips began to brush against each other. As he kissed me deeply, he took not only every ounce of my breath away, but also the remaining wall of my castle. For once, everything clicked into place. In his arms I felt like I was home.

12

PRESSED AGAINST ME, Jett smelled amazing—rich, and earthy, and edible, like a man should smell. His stubble rasped against my skin as he buried his face in my neck, licking and biting, teasing me. In the fog of lust descending upon my brain, I realized he was mouthwateringly sexy and I intended to taste every bit of him, whether he wanted it or not. Judging from his panting and the way his shimmering green eyes seemed to have darkened in spite of the bright rays of sun catching in them, he was very much up for it.

"Let's go inside. I want to do a lot of naughty things to you," I whispered against his mouth.

"I can't wait that long." His voice was deep and hoarse, and reflected my own desire. And oh, that accent! I had to ask him about it…as soon as we were done. If I managed to remember. Because right now I was having a hard time controlling everything, from my labored breathing to the way my heart seemed to want to storm out of my chest.

No man's scent, or voice, had ever headed straight for my panties like this. I appreciated a deep rumble just like any other woman, but Jett's baritone was heavenly. He had me panting with nothing more than a whiff and a few words. And don't even get me started on his dreamy eyes and luscious body.

I took a sharp breath and let his tongue invade my mouth with perfect precision, each lick and tug on my lips sending flames through my body as he pressed me harder into the railing and opened my legs with one motion of his knee. My nipples beaded on contact with his knowledgeable fingers and heat began to pool between my legs.

"Jett." His mouth stifled my moan. His hands continued to caress my body through my thin top and skirt. Next thing I knew my top was gone and my bra unclasped. My breasts spilled into his open palms, ready to be touched and given his undivided attention. His mouth left mine and moved south. Closing my eyes and dipping my head back, I gave in to the exquisite sensation of his rough tongue rasping the sensitive skin of my breasts. His relentless fingers began to knead my breasts while his mouth kept torturing my nipples, biting, licking, sucking—a bit of all of them at once. My head began to spin from all the different sensations flooding my body, and I groaned something that sounded vaguely like 'more.'

"I love the sexy sounds you make when you're horny, baby. Can you say it one more time?"

"More," I whispered.

I could feel the slow clenching within my lower abdomen, the heat gathering in my clit as my senses awakened to the sensual pleasure his mouth sent through my breasts. The sensations consumed me, made me want to beg him to—

Stop?

Continue?

I couldn't decide.

I moaned as Jett's mouth traveled down my belly and his tongue dipped into my navel, working his way to my inner thighs.

"Lift your leg for me," Jett said, hitching my skirt up to my waist and then my panties down to my ankles. I stepped out of them and, bending my knees, I propped my foot against the railing, my heated flesh exposed to his touch and his hungry look.

"You're so beautiful and wet." His voice came low and hoarse—filled with a desire matching mine.

And then his lips were on me, his tongue inside me, licking and thrusting through my damp folds. Slow at first, then faster, pausing only to flick his tongue over my sensitive clit, torturing me even more. A whimper escaped my lips as an electric jolt ran through my entrance and my sex clenched with need for *him*.

I gazed down at him and our eyes connected in that ancient language of sex that knows no words—just sweet all-consuming sensation. If he kept up the torture, I'd come. But I didn't want to—not yet.

"Fuck me." It wasn't a plea; it was a demand. And Jett knew it because he instantly let go of me. Grinning, he came up and captured my mouth in a heated kiss. His lips and tongue tasted of my wetness and that turned me on even more. At the periphery of my mind, I registered his hands between our bodies, removing his jeans and pulling down his shorts. My fingers moved to caress him, eager to gift him the same kind of pleasure he had gifted me, but his erection was between my legs already. Lifting me up and pressing my back into the railing, he entered me in one swift motion. A groan tore from Jett's lips as he pushed his entire length into me and began to thrust in long, hard movements. My sex began to tighten on him as he swelled marginally within me and I gasped in pleasure, the shock of how big he was almost making me come.

"More, baby?"

Jett's eyes bore into me with such intensity I felt the fragile walls of my heart crumbling at his feet. He was so beautiful, so perfect in his lust for me, I wanted to stay buried in his arms, with him inside me, forever. Our bodies united, we moved together beyond time and space, drowning in each other's desire. There was no more to the world than sensation—thrilling and demanding and aching—as our souls collided and our damp bodies met time and time again, until I knew we were about to become one.

Burying his head in the crane of my neck, I felt Jett's hot breath on my skin, whispering how beautiful I was, how much he wanted me. Against the glaring brightness of the sun, I closed my eyes and tightened on his erection. He pulsed between my legs and his breathing quickened, signalling his release was imminent.

With a last shudder, I gave myself to him as my whole being shattered around him in a million pieces. Faintly, I felt his hand on my clit as he pulsed inside me, once, twice, with my name on his lips, and his other hand buried in my hair. A hot jolt of lightning seared my clit a moment before his moisture surged through my sex. Our bodies began to melt into one another as we claimed our climaxes together as one.

Eventually, after what seemed like an eternity must have passed, he lifted me up in his arms and carried me into the bedroom. With the soft fragrance of his sheets and the heady scent of our lovemaking still clinging to our skin, I fell asleep in Jett's arms.

13

MY HEAD WAS leaning against the window of Jett's expensive car, my skin scorching with the promise of another sunburn courtesy of our lovemaking on the boat's deck. Only thirty minutes to go and I'd be back in my normal world, away from Jett's presence, and already I felt like I was missing him—even though he was sitting right beside me, steering the car through the country lanes at a leisurely speed.

The sun was setting, coloring the sky in dark shades of red, bronze, and copper. Soon the sky would darken and display the moon and the stars. It was my favorite time of the day—the few minutes between day and night, when it wasn't quite either. I was ready for my next first with Jett.

"Tired?" Jett asked, shooting me a sideway glance.

I nodded and returned his smile. "A bit. Thanks for the

date. I had a great day."

"So did I. I'd like to do it again." He winked and turned his attention back on the road.

My cheeks caught fire at his insinuation.

"The boat's amazing. No wonder you spend so much time on it." I laughed out loud, thinking how wonderful it must be to live on a boat. Be carefree. Do whatever you feel like doing.

"Once you've figured out what to do with the estate and everything's settled, we'll set sail for a week," Jett said. "Maybe even travel the world or, in this case, the world's waters."

"That sounds amazing." I leaned back in my seat and closed my eyes for a moment, savoring his presence. It felt so good to be near him, *with* him. I couldn't wait to spend more time together and get to know each other. Like *really* find out everything about him, including favorite color, hopes and wishes, the stuff of his nightmares, and what brought a smile to his perfect face. I couldn't just ask without seeming to be inquisitive fan girl material, so my best bet was to get him to talk.

"You asked me if I could swim," I began. "I can, but I wish I could dive. When I was younger I had the dream to live underwater among corals and fish, which is weird because I'm scared of drowning. I bet you can scuba dive, huh?"

His fleeting look shot to the rearview mirror and his foot stepped on the accelerator.

Not the elaborate answer, or interest, I had been hoping for. I held on to the armrest for support and thought of another angle I could go. "What are you scared of?"

"Not sure." His voice came a little brisk.

Okay.

His sudden reticence was making meaningful conversation difficult. I turned to regard him, but his focus was on the road ahead.

"Jett?" I touched his arm gently to get his attention.

He frowned but didn't turn. "Yes?"

"Are you tired? Or would you rather not talk? Because I'm fine with the latter." I tried to infuse as much nonchalance into my voice as I could muster. All guys were weird every now and then, right? If he needed a bit of space, I could give him that.

"No." He shook his head, his gaze moving to the rearview mirror again. "Sorry, baby, I'm a little distracted right now."

He was probably not interested in all my boring stuff. Of course, as a woman I tended to drone on forever, so I decided to lighten up his mood.

"There's still so much thinking to do about the estate's future, but I want you to know that I'm seriously considering your job offer." I narrowed my eyes on him.

His face was tense in concentration on the road ahead. A deep line had formed between his brows. "The pay raise sounds great and I've always wanted to be a team manager."

It was my clue to him that I wanted to work with him again. I thought the idea would please him.

No answer.

Seriously?

I frowned. That wasn't quite the response I expected. I had never seen him this quiet. Something was wrong with him.

"Do you want me to switch on the music?" I asked.

He changed gears and the car sped forward. My heart began to hammer in my chest. Even though traffic was slow, a few oncoming cars passed us by, some barely managing to stay on their side of the road.

The muscles in Jett's arms strained to hold on to the steering wheel while his eyes remained focused on the road.

"Slow down!" Maybe he was into dangerous driving but I wasn't.

"It's okay, baby," Jett said calmly.

"What? No! Slow down. What the hell's going on?"

A brief pause, then, "I don't want to scare you, but I think someone's chasing us." His words echoed in my mind.

"What do you mean? We're in a car."

"Yes, and someone's following us," Jett said slowly. I

squirmed in my seat. "No. Don't turn around."

"Okay." The tremble in my voice betrayed the sudden unease gripping my heart. My attention moved to the passenger side mirror and my heart raced in my chest, speeding faster than the car.

There was a vehicle behind us but it wasn't driving too close—not like you see in action movies. It wasn't possible that anyone was chasing us. We were in Italy, and not in a Hollywood movie.

"Are you sure it's not just heading the same way?"

"I'm ninety-nine percent sure. I've taken several turns, passed several villages, and it's still behind us." He checked the rearview mirror again. "Can you note down the license plate?"

His calm tone, which I suspected was supposed to comfort me, only managed to make me even more nervous.

I fished my phone out of my handbag and typed in the numbers and letters I could decipher from the rearview mirror, damning my phone for having small buttons that made typing with trembling fingers a nightmare.

"Should I call for help?" I asked, figuring even if I knew the emergency number, I didn't speak a word Italian.

"I've got this," Jett said. "Just get the plate."

As I made sure to save the registration number, the car behind neared us with full speed, closing in. A hundred feet, thirty, twenty, ten, three—all in a matter of seconds.

"Oh my god, Jett. Watch out!" I screamed a moment before the car bumped ours, giving us enough of a nudge to send me forward in my seat. The engine roared as our pursuers pushed to overtake us. For a second, they were almost driving next to us, the side windows so dark I couldn't see inside.

"Shit!" Jett hit the gas pedal and sped past them. My fingers buried in the armrest, I stifled a scream as the car behind us bumped us again, trying to steer us off the road.

"They're going to kill us." My breath came in labored heaps. It wasn't fear talking; it was knowledge. I just *knew* we were about to die.

"Not happening!" Jett floored the gas pedal, putting some distance between our pursuers and us.

We reached the narrow roads winding up the mountains. Jett slowed down a little as we entered the first bend.

"Go, go, go!" I screeched as the other car picked up in speed again, trying to close in on us. Any hope that we might not be a target dissipated into thin air.

"What are you going to do?" My breath came shallow.

"Are you wearing your seatbelt?" Jett's eyes narrowed on the road as we drove higher up the mountain. The car behind us didn't seem deterred by the poor road conditions, nor the steep stony wall on the driver's side and the edge followed by a plummeting abyss on my side.

"Yes." I held my breath.

"Then hold on tighter."

The road ahead seemed to narrow and merge into one lane. At our speed, the bends appeared to twist like menacing snakes. I completely forgot about those. But what worried me more was the one-way road that barely provided enough space for one car, let alone two. I grit my teeth and pressed my hand to my heart, praying no oncoming car would head our way, in which case we couldn't possibly halt on time. We'd collide, we'd crash, and we'd die.

Please dear Lord, keep us safe.

A scream formed in the back of my throat, but the sound never made its way out. Fear grabbed me, strangled me, until I could do nothing but hold on for dear life.

"Oh God, oh God," I chanted to myself as Jett maneuvered the bends, each time jerking the wheel to the max, each time sending my body through hell as we neared the edge on my side of the road. I couldn't even look behind, because each time I glanced in the mirror, all I could focus on was the abyss below. If the other car collided with ours, we'd plummet hundreds of feet into whatever was down there. Or we'd crash against the mountain cliff.

"You okay, baby?" Jett's voice was surprisingly calm in the midst of the storm. "We'll make it out of this."

How? They're still behind us, I wanted to scream, but all that came out of my throat was a whimper. Fear held me paralyzed and it was nothing like in the movies. I was sweating, the car was roaring excessively, and were those holes beneath our tires? I could feel each bump; I could feel the gravity of the car; and there was no way one could stay composed, relaxed, and cool.

The car was driving at a high speed—fast enough to send us over the edge if Jett lost control of the wheel even for a nanosecond or didn't slow down enough at the right time. Yet he maneuvered expertly through each nightmare turn. There was no way on earth somebody with normal driving skills could ever do that.

Already I could see two officers knocking on my mother's door, relaying the news that I was dead, the headline reading 'speeding couple crashing on picturesque Italian vacation' followed by the words 'tragic accident.' Poor Sylvie would blame herself. Knowing her, she'd probably blame Jett, too, thinking he tried to kill me on purpose. Life was so unfair I wanted to scream.

"Hold on," Jett said. I opened my eyes, only now noticing I must have closed them at some point. We were nearing another bend on the wicked road to hell, after which the road seemed to decline.

We had reached the top of the mountain and now we were heading back down.

This is it. My life ends here—but not before he knows my feelings.

"Jett, I need to tell you something." I tried to remain calm, which was impossible with the shaking in my voice and the freezing sensation in my limbs.

"Not now, baby." His voice oozed confidence and composure. We took the turn, after which he hit the brake—hard. My head jerked forward and a sharp pain shot through my neck.

"What are you doing?" I screamed when he unbuckled his seatbelt. The other car was out of view, but I was sure it was still behind us. Everything happened so fast, I doubted more than a few seconds passed. He placed his right arm around my seat and turned to get a better view as he went into reverse in full speed, swerving like a madman. Before I knew it, we were on a narrow byroad I didn't see before. It wasn't asphalted, and barely more than a running track with bushes scratching the sides of the car. Probably private property—but who cared?

Jett stopped the car and switched off the lights, then signaled me to stay quiet. I held my breath as I listened for any sounds. Eventually, I heard an engine and then a car passed us by, oblivious to our hiding place.

We were alive!

But it didn't feel like success.

I spun to Jett, my hands shaking so bad, I felt like crying. He leaned over and brushed my cheek, composed.

Except for the tense muscles and set jaw, there was no indicator of any sort of nervousness, as though no one had trailed us mere seconds ago. Searching for us. Trying to kill us.

"You'll be okay, baby." Jett's lips pressed against mine in a tender kiss, and then he pulled back and started the engine. "I know what I'm doing."

Before I could ask him not to drive again, to just stay hidden—because I couldn't bear another rollercoaster ride—he reversed and we returned to the main road, speeding off in the direction from which we'd come.

"We're staying at a hotel," Jett said. "Better we stay together tonight."

"Okay," I whispered, the sound barely making its way out of my throat.

I didn't argue with him. I doubted I could even if I'd wanted. My body was frozen from shock. Not even the bumpy road and Jett's speeding managed to wake me from my daze.

During the drive to the next city, my eyes remained glued to the rearview mirror, always checking, always praying no one was following us. Even when Jett parked in a hotel's guest parking lot, I couldn't stop looking behind my shoulder. Jett had to lead me, his gentle words not quite reaching my mind. Only after checking in, away from the road and the twilight chasing scene, did I realize he'd saved my life.

***

Resting on the hotel bed, it seemed to take me forever to wake up from my comatose stage, but eventually my heart and mind jolted back to life and reality. Maybe it was because of Jett's strong arms around me, soothing me, breathing his strength into me as he gently kissed my forehead. He had booked us a room for the night, and as usual, he chose to go for the most expensive option available, claiming the security was better. I wasn't convinced.

"There's nothing to worry about. It's over now. You're safe, baby," Jett whispered and pushed a glass of water into my still trembling hands, silently urging me to drink up. I forced myself to take tiny sips and swallow them down, even though my throat still felt choked.

He took the half-full glass out of my hand and placed it on the bedside table. "I need to find another parking spot for the car. Will you be okay if I leave you alone for a few minutes?"

I nodded.

"Don't leave the room and don't answer if anyone knocks. I won't be long." He stood but hesitated.

I shot him a fake reassuring smile. "Just go." Truth was,

I didn't want to be alone but Jett's car wasn't exactly standard. Our pursuers would be able to spy it from a mile away.

He left reluctantly. I leaned back against the pillows but didn't dare close my eyes. My ears strained to listen for any strange sounds. Apart from the ice vending machine in the hallway whirring once, everything remained as quiet as a tomb. After what seemed like ages, Jett returned.

"We should call the police," I said.

"No. We can't. It's too dangerous." Lying down next to me, he pushed a stray strand of hair back from my face and pulled me into his arms. Inhaling his scent, I settled against his warm body.

I remembered that he thought the police were involved in the club, consequently I agreed it might not be a good idea.

"Do you know who those people were?" I asked.

"I'll try to find out tomorrow."

He made it sound like there were many options, when the lead was pretty obvious: I inherited a property that used to be a gathering place for weirdoes. I just didn't realize *their* way to handle problems was killing the heir. Why couldn't people just get together to resolve problems through talking, preferably over coffee and cake—and not behave like war seeking apes attempting to silence us by sending us into an early grave?

I propped on one elbow and regarded Jett's beautiful face. "It's the club, isn't it?"

"Mmh." He avoided my gaze.

"I have to call Sylvie."

"Not happening." His arm wrapped around my waist, holding me in place. "In fact, switch off your phone."

"I need to warn her."

He shook his head. "People can track down a GPS. Keep it switched off."

My chin shot up defiantly. Sylvie was my best friend. I had dragged her into this mess. If something happened to her, I'd never forgive myself.

"Brooke, listen to me. They're after you and if you reach out to her, they might harm her to get to you." His tone was grave, reinforcing the warning in his words.

They.

I swallowed down the lump in my throat. Jett sat up and squatted in front of me. His hands squeezed mine and our gazes interlocked.

"I know you're scared, Brooke," he said calmly. "But you have to trust me. Sylvie will be okay. I'll text her in your name so she knows you're not coming home. And I'm sending someone over to watch the house. We stay here just this one night. Pretend nothing happened. And tomorrow I'll take care of things."

How, I wanted to ask. He didn't know who those

people were. We had no idea where to begin.

And pretend nothing happened? I snorted. Not likely. I could maybe forget the car chasing us and be grateful that we were still alive. But as sure as the sky's blue, I couldn't push the images of our various close encounters with death out of my mind, nor the endless possibilities of what could happen to us—or Sylvie.

Just because we escaped didn't mean the nightmare was over.

"Nothing happened. No one was killed." Jett's fingers began to massage the tense muscles in my shoulders. Somehow his touch calmed me a little until I felt the waves of fear slowly dissipating.

"You're safe and that's all that matters," he whispered. God, I loved that voice.

I leaned into his touch and regarded him.

"Where did you learn to drive like that?"

He blinked once, twice. "What?" Confusion crossed his features, as if he wasn't expecting my question. The reaction intrigued me.

"I don't know anybody who can drive like you. Except for my ex but he had lots of training."

"Your ex?" Jett's brows shot up. Was he jealous? Amidst the surrealism of the situation, I smiled because his sudden scowl was priceless.

Jett and jealous?

Who would've figured?

It wasn't like me to talk about previous relationships, but something told me Jett wouldn't let this one go.

"Yeah, my ex is a professional racer."

"When did you—"

"It's long over." I waved my hand. "Weeks ago."

"Weeks?" A nerve began to twitch on his forehead. He sat down on the bed, making sure not to touch me. Now he was angry.

"Jett, it's over. It wasn't even a relationship, or anything." I took his hand. "It wasn't the real deal."

It was the truth. Sean wasn't looking for commitment. Neither was I. We had an on and off relationship, a friends-with-benefits thing—more of the benefits, less of the friendship part.

"It meant nothing. I never loved him," I whispered. "He couldn't compete with you even if he wanted." His expression lit up a little bit.

"I'm the better catch, huh?"

I punched his arm playfully, my eyes willing his beautiful lips to smile. "I'm glad he and I broke up," I said.

"That's good to hear because I want you all for myself."

I wrapped my arms around Jett and buried my face against his broad chest in the hope my embrace could convey the magnitude of my feelings for him. His tension was still palpable and hundreds of unspoken questions lingered in the air. But I could also feel his unwillingness to start a senseless argument, for which I was grateful.

"Let's focus on the present." My fingers traced the contours of his chin. In spite of his stubble, his skin felt amazingly soft beneath my fingertips. He smelled so good, so manly, I could be with him, and only him, forever.

"You're right." He lay back and pulled me on top of him. I relaxed in the comfort of his arms, but my question still burned on my mind.

"So, how did you learn to drive like that, Jett?" My fingers gingerly played with the buttons of his shirt. "And don't say through driving lesson, or courses, because training alone isn't enough. What I saw is experience—and lots of it."

He heaved an exasperated sigh. Hesitating, he ran his hand through his hair, as if considering how much to tell me. "You're right. I did stuff."

Lifting up on one elbow, I tried to make sense of his cryptic statement by reading his body language, which was difficult from the way he lay on his back with his hands propped under his head, staring at the ceiling, his eyes expressionless.

"You said that before," I prompted.

"I was involved in underground car races," Jett mumbled, hesitating again.

"Okay," I prompted again.

"They're not like what you see on sports channels, Brooke. There's no one to inspect your car and change your tires. We raced for money and reputation, mostly in huge storage halls and parking buildings. Sometimes outside on quiet streets or mountain roads."

His eyes narrowed on me and a glint appeared. Sensing the magnitude of what he was about to tell me, I held my breath, not daring to move or touch him in case he changed his mind and bottled up again.

"It started after...uhm...my father threw me out when I was sixteen."

"Why did he do that?"

"Ever since my mother left, I'd been harboring a grudge against him, you know, questioning his authority and the way he used to demand respect when he had never really behaved like a father. My tendency to confront him in front of other people embarrassed him. He kept saying I was endangering his company with my behavior, so I chose to do the opposite of what he wanted. And in the end he threw me out. I stayed with my friends, many of them older than me. They kept me off the streets and taught me how to drive and how to fight, which is how things started. The fact that my life didn't mean a damn thing to me made me bold and reckless, and hell bent on winning. At some point, I was addicted to adrenaline."

"You mean fighting, like Kung Fu?"

He laughed. "Let me guess. You were just thinking of Bruce Lee?"

I smirked. "More like Jackie Chan. I used to love that guy."

"I hope not in the literal sense." His eyes bore into me. So beautiful. So deep. "It was nothing professional. No gloves, no protective headgear."

Hot, hot, hot!

Did the temperature just soar? Or was it my blood pressure sending me into the scorching desert at the images running through my mind?

"That's pretty rough," I said.

"Yeah." He nodded. "Direct body contact is rough. And you?" The sudden attempt at changing the subject didn't escape me. I wanted to hear more about his past. I wanted it so bad it hurt, and yet I knew pushing him wasn't the right way to go. Not with a man like Jett.

"Did you like sports?" he insisted.

Seriously? Did he ever look at me?

"Uhm." I laughed. "I used to swim and run, until I grew those boobs."

"So heavy lifting then, judging from your breasts…" His gaze traveled to my chest and remained there. He didn't even pretend not to be staring.

"You're such a jerk." I punched him playfully.

"Quite the contrary. It was meant as a compliment. But

just to make sure I'm not wrong, may I touch them?" He grinned that panty-dropping smile of his that always made me want to beg him to do naughty things to me. His hands cupped my breasts and his thumbs began to caress them through the thin material of my top and bra. My nipples instantly hardened, sending a jolt of pleasure through my body.

"You may not." I slapped his hands away, pretending I didn't want it, but my shallow breathing was a dead giveaway. Jett rolled on his back and pulled me on top of him. His knee pried my legs open and settled between them, rubbing gently against my sex. I suppressed a moan at the wet sensation pooling down there.

"I made sure to book a room with a whirlpool," Jett whispered. "You wanna try it?" His voice oozed sensuality and countless promises of pleasure. "We could order dinner, and then we could have desert. You get to choose. I'm game for whatever you want."

His hand trailed down my stomach and squeezed under my shirt, as his mouth began to place heated kisses on my neck.

I moaned. "No alcohol."

"You think that's the only way I can get you into bed?" His hoarse chuckle reverberated through me, making me shudder with want.

Obviously not.

"I'm in," I whispered. "Let's do this."

14

THE ROUND WHIRLPOOL was big enough to fit several people—not that the thought of others joining us appealed to me. One person was more than enough for me. I watched Jett as he slowly peeled off his clothes, with each piece revealing more of his delicious body. And then he was standing in front of me, with only his underwear to hide his impressive modesty. Towering at over six feet, his height both intimidated and fascinated me. The tattoos both attracted and aroused me. He felt my gaze on his manhood and let out a deep sexy breath, the sound vibrating through my lower abdomen. I knew what came next, and the prospect of seeing him completely naked excited me. I couldn't wait to get my hands on him.

"Let me help you," he whispered and started to undress me in slow but measured steps, his eyes never leaving mine.

Those sinful eyes that never failed to light my whole being on fire. His hands pulled my top over my head and then unzipped my skirt, taking all the time in the world when I didn't feel particularly patient.

Standing in front of him in my panties and my bra, my hands slid down his hard torso. His fingers gripped my chin and forced my face up to look at him.

"You're sexy, Brooke, but now I can't give you what you want."

"Why's that?" My voice was hoarse yet playful, pretending not to know he was talking about sex, while my hands continued to caress his naked chest. He moaned as my fingers moved further south, rubbing over the well-defined bulge beneath his shorts. "Are you giving in yet?"

"No." A soft hiss escaped his throat. "And you should stop before I change my mind."

"Maybe I don't want you to," I purred, my hand continuing to stroke his length. I almost squealed with delight as he began to grow in size before my eyes. "Maybe this is exactly what I *need*."

"No, baby." He shook his head and closed his eyes for a brief moment. His face was a mask of desire but he fought it hard, which both infuriated and delighted me because I loved a challenge. His eyes opened again and he regarded me with so much determination I knew I had to step up my game.

"So far we've focused on sex only," Jett whispered. "Today I want to give you romance because it's our first official date."

He was doing it all backwards!

My body was craving for him. I didn't mind doing him on our first official date at all. Come to think of it, we had done it already but that was just the appetizer.

"Ah, our first date." I laughed out loud. "You've given me a date I think I'll never forget for the rest of my life."

"You think or you're sure about that?" His mouth curled into a stunning smile. I wanted to run my fingers through his unruly hair and suck his lower lip into my mouth, biting and teasing so hard he'd beg for mercy.

"I was whisked away on a ship and then you saved my life." My hands moved beneath his shorts and pulled them down, revealing his splendid erection. My gaze glued to it, I licked my lips with anticipation at taking him deep into my mouth.

"Brooke, stop looking at me like that." His words carried just the right amount of a warning to make me giggle but not avert my gaze.

"What more could I want for in a date?" I said. "I think your efforts deserve a reward." My fingers wrapped around the base of his manhood and lingered there. "And I know where to start."

"Not sex. You can repay me in a different way," he

whispered.

I wanted to point out that I didn't feel like owing him anything. Truth be told, I liked the idea of pleasing him. It turned me on. It made me wet just thinking about it, picturing him at my mercy.

"How?" I ran my fingertips up and down his swollen shaft until he stopped my hand from moving, rubbing, anything that I knew would make him give in.

"You could learn scuba diving with me. Isn't that what you said you always wanted to do?"

"I thought you weren't listening," I said, surprised that he remembered my monologue in the car. "You're a really good driver. Were you even afraid when those people were after us? It didn't look like you broke a sweat."

And once again his lips curved into a wicked smile. Through my lowered lids, I couldn't see if it was because of my compliment or because he was pulling down my panties, and seeing how wet I was for him.

"No, Brooke." His electrifying green eyes brushed my breasts, and settled on the small strip of hair between my legs. Even though he wasn't touching me, I could almost feel him between my legs and the anticipation drove me crazy. "It was nothing compared to the fear I felt when you were gone. Nothing will ever top that fog of dread I fell into when I realized I might come too late...when I should've trusted you from the beginning."

My breath caught in my throat.

"You didn't know. Trust is earned, isn't it?" I said gently.

"It is." His voice was soft like the breeze. "I don't want to lose you ever again, Brooke. It was hard for me to let you go." His fingers unclasped my bra and he threw it on top of the pile of clothes to our feet. His hands moved to my breast, and the kneading and light pinching sent warm shivers through my body. His lips trailed down from my neck to my shoulders, resting there, and I could feel his breath on my skin, both his touch and words making me dizzy.

"I wanted what's best for you, what I thought would make you happy, even though it wasn't any of my business… but letting you go wasn't even the hardest part."

I held my breath and regarded him, listening hard so I wouldn't miss a word because I wanted to remember this moment forever.

"The hardest part was acknowledging I might never see you again. Realizing how much you mean to me and how much I'd miss your pretty face every morning and night. Realizing all the things I didn't do with you and might never get a chance to. But I think most of the pain came from the realization that the time we spent together was not enough for me and I couldn't force you to feel the same way."

His words were like honey. It was all so sweet, so dark,

so unexpected that it shook me to the very core. More beautiful than anything I ever dared to hope for.

"Maybe I missed you, too." I said, trying to play it cool. "It wasn't easy on my part, either." My words were already so choked, I doubted I'd be able to say much more.

Jett helped me into the whirlpool and sat down on the bottom, the hot water barely reaching his shoulders. Realizing my height wouldn't give me that advantage, I settled for the second upper step next to him, the water barely covering my breasts. The water bubbled, hiding his sculpted body, which was a shame because I couldn't stop looking at him.

As if sensing my thoughts, he turned to face me. A flicker of mischief played in his eyes and his lips trailed down from my neck to my waiting nipples. His teeth grazed the hard tip of my breast a moment before his tongue flipped over it as I buried my fingers into his hair and demanded more of his mouth's grazing and flicking. And then the sucking.

Oh God.

Either the temperature in the water just went up, or he got me boiling inside.

"I want to enjoy every minute with you," Jett said. His eyes bore into me, drinking me in, swallowing me up whole.

"As long as it lasts, huh?" I didn't remark *that* was my biggest fear—that we'd be over before we even started.

"And I hope that's a long time," Jett whispered.

In one swift motion he inched closer and lifted me up, settling me on his lap with my legs spread around him, the water engulfing my sex, prickling the soft flesh. His erection brushed my lower abdomen impatiently, demanding to be allowed entry.

"One thing's for sure, Brooke. I won't let you go easily next time. In fact there won't be a next time." His sexy whisper sent a delicious pull between my legs. His hands pulled my hips so close I could feel his large erection against the secret opening between my legs. I felt myself going wet. There was a beautiful deep ache inside me, asking to be stilled.

"You said you couldn't give me what I wanted today?" Gazing into his impossibly green eyes, I lifted my hips enough to straddle his hard shaft and, as slowly as I could, moved down, every inch sending another delightful contraction through my body. The head of his erection probed my sex, spearing my soft lips, entering me just a little but enough to send a hot wave of pleasure through me. A hard moan escaped his lips as I accommodated more of him.

"That can be negotiated." Jett's hands settled on my waist, offering the support I needed. I lowered myself onto him just a little bit more, allowing him to stretch me and fill me, until I thought I could take no more of his size—and he wasn't even half way in. I rode him, my inside clenching as the slow thrusts rubbed a tender spot. As I moaned louder, his breathing became harder. He took charge, his hand pulling my hips down until I could feel his thick, hard erection going so deep I felt like letting go. With every slide, I rocked my hips, the delicious pain radiating more pleasure, breaking more barriers. His movement reached my core, his hunger for release consuming us both and when we came, I could have sworn the burning fire merged us into one.

15

EVERYTHING WAS SO bright. The room, the colors, even my dress. I could hear myself laughing and felt Jett's arms around me as I squirmed against him, unsure whether to free myself or melt into his embrace.

"I'd do anything for you. You know that?" he whispered into my ear. "If you fell, I'd hold you. If you were afraid, I'd wrap my arms around you and take away your fears. I'd die to keep you safe, but more than anything I'd do whatever it takes to keep you by my side. For you I'd conquer anything, everything, anytime."

I smiled against his hot skin and inhaled the fresh, clean scent of his hair. So good. So soft. I felt serene, the world around us forgotten. It was just he and I, and no one else in the world.

Something soft caressed my shoulder. His lips? His hot

breath? My hands reached out to touch him—only to feel the cold, empty space next to me.

What the—

Confused, I pried my eyes open and squinted against the unnatural brightness coming from the sun spilling through the windows. My eyes slowly adjusting, I realized Jett's side of the bed was empty, the sheets crumpled in a heap.

I had been thinking he was in bed with me, only to find it had been just a dream. I grimaced, disappointed, and jumped out of bed, scanning the room for any message he might have left. Except for the jacket he had tossed over the back of a chair last night, there was no indication of him, nothing to signal last night even took place. Everything was quiet; the lights in the adjacent bathroom turned off.

Where the heck was he? Would he sneak out on me after he got what he wanted?

I grabbed his jacket. It smelled like him: manly, intoxicating. I pressed it against my bare chest and for a moment I closed my eyes to enjoy the images of us kissing—and doing other intimate stuff—flickering through my mind. Either he forgot to take his jacket, or he had left it behind on purpose, which could only mean he'd be back soon. Excitement rushed through me at the prospect of seeing him after everything that had happened between us.

The past twenty-four hours were nothing short of mind-blowing. Scary, yes, but still mind-blowing. The date, the car chase, the sex, the fact that I knew so much about him now. No idea what it all meant for us; whether we were back together. But I couldn't wait to find out. All I knew was that my fears about him were gone, replaced by a firm belief that I had been wrong about him, and he had been telling the truth back in New York. I was in danger, and he had tried to protect me from whoever had been following us.

Standing in front of the hotel mirror, I stared at my reflection and wrinkled my nose in disgust. My dark, naturally curly hair looked a tangled mess. With my makeup gone, dark circles framed my chestnut eyes and made my skin look a shade of pasty yellow. To my utter dismay, I realized I had no fresh underwear or clothes, no makeup to fake a glow, no hairbrush, not even a toothbrush. The only two things available to help me scrub up were the hotel's shampoo and soap.

At least my cheeks had a soft glow and there was a sparkle in my eyes. The signs were there: I was still in love—with Jett.

Sylvie would be so mad.

No doubt the moment we'd be back home she'd try to run an intervention, stating my fixation with him was unhealthy.

However, what she didn't know was that this love I felt for him—I didn't seek it out. I had tried to keep my emotional distance, choosing not to let Jett enter my heart. Yet this love—or whatever feeling it was that caused fluttering butterflies and a raging storm inside me—chased me, found me, and finally captured me, holding me tight amidst my fears. The more I fought it, the more it grew. The longer I hid my feelings for him, the harder I fell for him.

I knew I'd tell Jett someday, but we hadn't reached that point yet. Maybe because there was a tiny fraction inside my mind that kept warning me we might not be meant to be, and only time would tell. The best I could do with *now* was enjoy it while it lasted.

I found a trial size toothpaste and damp hotel toothbrush, which I assumed Jett used before leaving, and brushed my teeth quickly. Jumping into the shower, I let the warm water trickle down my body to soothe the ache in my muscles—courtesy of Jett's insatiable appetite for sex.

My hands were busy lathering in the shampoo when the door cracked open, making me jump.

"Brooke?" Jett asked. He popped his head through the shower curtain.

My arms lowered to cover my chest on instinct, but it was too late. Like a wildfire, a grin spread across his beautiful lips and he scanned my body up and down, lingering a bit too long on my covered breasts.

"Hi, beautiful." His voice was soft as velvet and dark as

chocolate. I'd recognize that tone blindfolded. Usually it turned me on; right now I wished I had thought of locking the door. He had seen me naked countless times but never like this: under the bright fluorescent light, with no makeup on, and no bed sheets behind which I could hide. I probably looked like shit and didn't want him to see me this way. Embarrassed, I retreated to the farthest spot in the shower and shot him a frown.

"Can you wait outside? I'll be done in a minute."

That was his clue to leave, but Jett didn't move an inch. I licked my lips nervously and kept my breasts covered while the hot water continued to trickle down my body.

"You're so hot." His tone came low. Scorching. I could say the same thing about him. "You're even more beautiful than in my dreams."

I searched his face for any signs that he was joking. His smile was gone, replaced by seriousness. His eyes were filled with passion, mirroring my lust. Slowly—as I watched him—he stripped off his clothes until he stood naked in front of me. I tried my best to avert my gaze, but couldn't. The magnetism he exuded held me tight. He was breathtakingly beautiful—a view I could look at over and over again, just like the most fascinating painting.

His chiseled chest with dark hair was on full display—all defined muscles and bronze skin. My tongue flicked over my lips as I pried my gaze away from his sculpted chest to the three rows of hard muscles on his abdomen, and finally came to rest on his erection promising to take me to pleasure heaven.

"What are you doing, Jett?"

Stupid question.

What would anyone think he was doing?

He joined me in the shower and gathered me in his arms. The water rained down on us, and for a moment I thought he'd try to get it on. I could only hope he didn't insist we do it in the shower because I didn't want to slip and break my neck.

"Can you pass me the shower gel?"

I stared at him in confusion as he just grinned at me and reached out to get the bottle, then lathered the foam into his glorious skin. I watched it run down his torso and gather in the soft hair around his manhood.

"Want me to do your back?" he asked, still grinning.

I shook my head, unsure whether he was being serious. He was behaving like we were an old couple, comfortable in each other's presence. And while I was comfortable in his presence, the entire situation had something way too intimate about it.

"Then you're ready to get out?" There was a sparkle of naughtiness in his eyes.

Struck speechless, I nodded.

Jett stepped out of the shower and wrapped a towel

around his waist, then draped one around my shoulders. I even let him pat down my wet hair, squeezing the water out of it, until soft waves and ringlets formed. He took one and wrapped it around his fingers, the light tugging sensation making my scalp tingle.

"I want you to be open for me," he whispered.

His eyes mirrored the array of emotions in his voice. For a moment I wasn't sure which direction this conversation would take—whether he wanted more or just enjoyed keeping me intrigued.

Jett's hands trailed from my breasts down my hips and then with no warning he lifted me up in one swift motion, as though I weighed nothing. My cheeks heated up at the new and intimate way he pressed me against his naked body. Gathering my arms around his neck, I let him carry me into the bedroom and lay me down on the unmade bed, our limbs entangling, mouths finding each other.

"What do you want me to do?" I asked playfully.

"I want you to be open for me," he whispered again, his eyes reflecting the desire in his voice. He pulled my towel away and removed my hands from my breasts. "I want you to be the one asking for it."

His authoritarian tone built a strong contrast to his gentle actions. His thumb was stroking my face, his wet hair was dripping on my skin, the coldness making me shiver. And yet his kiss was hot, devouring my mouth, his hand going lower to explore my breasts, my hips, my legs.

"I want you," I murmured.

"Not need me?" He raised his eyebrows, his erection pressing against my legs.

"I want you, I need you. What's the difference? I'm open to anything." I removed the towel from his hips, eager to taste him, to feel him, to have him inside me. I knew I was wet.

"You'd be surprised." He pushed me down and his hands wrapped around my wrists. Gazing into my eyes, he pushed inside me, making love to me until we were both succumbing to an orgasmic release.

***

Later I lay in his arms gathering my breath, my hands trailing up and down his sculpted torso, marveling at the smoothness of his skin and the hardness of his muscles. He was perfect.

"I hope I'm the reason behind your smile," Jett said, stroking my cheek. His statement caught me off guard. I hadn't even realized I was smiling.

"Mmh." I placed a soft kiss on his chin and regarded him lovingly.

Do people not smile after sex? Was it just hormones or something else?

Less than three days ago I had been unhappy. Actually, being unhappy was an understatement. I felt betrayed, lost, deeply hurt, and heartbroken. How strange he had been the reason why I tumbled into my second lowest point in life, and yet all it took to pull me out was for him to re-enter the picture. His words and actions had both killed my hope and rekindled it. He had destroyed and shattered my love only to conquer it again. If he hadn't persisted in trying to reach out to me, I would never have known he didn't hurt me on purpose, and we wouldn't be where we were today—in each other's arms.

"I love it when you smile," he whispered. "But I love it even more when I see your smile and know I was the one who caused it."

"Having sex three times in less than twenty four hours would make anyone happy," I replied.

"It's all thanks to you, Ms. Stewart."

"Me?" I cocked a brow. He pretty much instigated all of them. "What about you? You were the one to initiate them."

"I followed your thoughts' command. Besides, I'm just human. I can't help myself when you're around. You can't blame a man for being weak at a vixen's feet."

The way his eyes glimmered with mischief I wanted to do him again, even though my body screamed 'no more.'

"I didn't do anything," I pointed out.

"Exactly. You didn't do anything." Jett's eyes bore into me, touching my soul. "I'm not perfect. God knows I have many weaknesses, but my biggest one happens to be you, Brooke."

His words made my smile widen. He was piling on the compliments. Coming from any other man, they would've hit on nothing but a brick wall. But coming from Jett, I wanted to hear more, absorb each word, and cherish it forever. If there was one person in the world whose words were special, it was Jett.

***

Feeling a need for a bathroom break, I entangled myself from him and only noticed the tray on the table upon my return. It held two cups of coffee, two plates with croissants and another two plates of bagels with fresh cheese spread. My gaze settled on the small violet gift box almost hidden between the coffee and the plates.

"I woke up early. You were still asleep so I thought I'd get us breakfast." Walking over, Jett pointed at the tray and cleared his throat, answering the question I had been asking myself since waking. "I know last time didn't go so well but I figured why not give it another try? I hope you'll like it."

He picked up the tiny box and handed it to me.

"Thank you." My throat constricted. My legs began to

shake again, so I sat down and left my fingers trail over the gift box.

It was surprisingly heavy for its size. The shiny satin-feel paper shimmered in the sunlight spilling through the window. I untied the white ribbon, and opened the lid, then removed the black cover. Even before I saw it, I knew what it contained, but the knowledge didn't quite register in my consciousness until I saw it before my eyes. Sitting on a black velvet mount was a sleek steel watch with a silver wrist bangle and tiny gemstones that sparkled like diamonds.

"It's beautiful," I whispered.

And, judging from the feel and look, expensive.

"I thought it might be the perfect gift so you're never late again for our dates."

I grimaced at him, unsure whether to feel offended or laugh. In the end, amusement won.

"Seriously?" I glanced up, biting my lip.

"I'm just kidding. I got it a while back." He slumped down in the chair next to mine and regarded me coolly. "Call it intuition. Come on, take it out."

I gingerly removed the watch from its box, and was about to unfasten the clasp, when I noticed something was engraved on the back.

"*In the stream of life, I'll always search for you. As time goes by, you'll always be on my mind. Jett.* Did you come up with this?"

My questioning gaze searched his, begging him to tell me he had picked it up from somewhere and it didn't mean anything.

Jett nodded. "It's the way I feel."

For a few seconds, I was utterly and deeply moved, unable to say a word. My throat constricted, and my eyes swelled up with moisture. I forced myself to take slow breaths, so I wouldn't give away the storm of emotions tormenting me inside. The bathing suit was one thing—an expensive gift but nothing too personal. I could give it back, because I didn't want to feel like I had been bought. But the watch was an entirely different situation. The personal message showed me he cared about me and I couldn't be happier that we reconnected, but more than anything I was happy there was still an *us*.

I wanted him to know just how much I loved him and yet I kept silent as I kissed him in complete abandonment of my heart, my brain racing to engrave every little detail about him forever.

"Thank you. It's...I want to say beautiful but that's an understatement."

His hand touched my chin and he moved closer until we were barely an inch apart. "It's nothing, Brooke. It's just a watch. Promise me that you'll keep it."

Ever so gently he lowered his soft gorgeous lips onto mine. I breathed in his heavenly scent, savouring his proximity, the *moment.*

"I will," I whispered forcing a smile to my lips. "I will treasure it forever."

Even if things weren't meant to last, I wanted to at least remember, because in the end my memory could be the only thing left.

16

THE ROOM SMELLED of fresh butter croissants. The coffee cups were on the table, untouched, almost forgotten now. Jett's hand kept touching mine as he fidgeted with the box, waiting for me to stop gushing.

Our first night together in a hotel room.

Our first breakfast together after spending the night in a hotel room and having sex in a whirlpool.

The first gift I ever accepted from him.

I made a mental note of all of those things because, ever since meeting Jett, I had been counting all my firsts with him: the first time we used certain words and phrases, the things we did together for the first time, the first activities we planned together. My brain had become a huge scrapbook of first memories together and I couldn't wait to fill it with more.

"Let me help you." Jett took the watch from my hands and clasped it around my wrist. I held it up to admire. It was the perfect size with the right feel.

"I love it," I said again. And I did, but I also hated the feeling of not having something to give back. So I was more than eager to buy him a gift—something unique, something to remind him of this occasion, which I hoped was as special to him as it was to me.

"It suits you beautifully," Jett said, placing a soft kiss on my wrist.

"Hmm." I smiled and felt myself melting against the magic of his lips.

"I switched on your phone while you were busy in the shower." His lips trailed up my naked arm and collarbone, until he found the special spot below my chin.

"Yeah?" I moaned softly.

"Yeah."

I felt him smiling and wrapped my arms around his strong shoulders, clasping them behind the nape of his neck.

"Sylvie might have called a few times," Jett whispered.

Oh, shit!

My blood froze in my veins. How the heck could I forget her? She was probably waiting for me, worried that I wasn't back yet.

While it wasn't unusual for her to stay the night away

every now and then, it had never happened to me. Besides, we always texted our whereabouts. She'd be so mad. No, make that livid.

"I have to get home," I said.

Jett shook his head vehemently. "That's not a good idea. You're not safe. Better we try to find out who followed us first."

"But Sylvie's all alone in that house. I know her. She'll freak out if I'm not back soon."

"She's fine."

I took in his set jaw and the determined glint in his eyes. The more time I spent with Jett, the more I realized I had found my match in him when it came to demonstrating an unhealthy amount of stubbornness. Under any other circumstances I might have given in for the sake of preserving harmony, but not when it came to my best friend's safety.

"I need to see it for myself," I said.

Something flickered in his green glance. Was that annoyance? "I'd rather you stay with me at my house."

His offer sounded tempting. His house was huge, beautifully decorated, and not too far from Alessandro's estate. But—

I shook my head. "Not happening. I'm not leaving Sylvie alone in that old house. She's my best friend, Jett. If someone means me harm and I'm not there, they'll take it out on her."

"I can send someone over," Jett said.

Something told me he could continue this conversation all day.

"What do you mean?" I frowned. "A bodyguard?"

"Sort of."

I shot him an unconvinced frown. I got it. Jett had money. And lots of it. But a bodyguard—for Sylvie? How would he accomplish that without my best friend noticing? Sylvie wasn't stupid. The moment she'd find out a killer might be after us, Jett might as well hire a bodyguard for himself too, because Sylvie would end up screaming and blaming him. And when Sylvie was angry I couldn't vouch for her sanity or actions.

"Not working for me." I shook my head and finished the last drop of my coffee. "I'm sorry, Jett, but…I can't stay. You have to accept that. Now please drive me back."

"Then let me come with you."

I almost spilled my coffee. Okay, maybe I didn't spill it because it was already empty.

"Yeah, that's not possible either." I grimaced, struggling with my words. How the heck was I supposed to tell him my best friend didn't like him anymore, and I didn't want to have to face that storm?

"Why not?" Jett's eyes narrowed on me.

Oh, for crying out loud.

"Sylvie's—" I grimaced again "—out of sorts with you."
I peered up at him and almost flinched at the flicker of
anger in his expression.

"You didn't tell her about us." His eyes were
scrutinizing me.

"No, no…" I shook my head, then stopped. What was
the point in lying when he already knew it? "Yes, maybe, a
little. I didn't think it'd make a difference."

He frowned, but didn't comment. My fingers wrapped
around his hand in the hope he might feel my turmoil.

"You broke my heart, Jett, so naturally you're the bad
guy. She made me promise I'd move on from you and date
others. So—" I shrugged and laughed nervously "—she's
thinking I'm moving on."

A few moments passed during which he remained silent.
I tried my hardest to read his expression, and failed.

"Okay." Eventually, he heaved a sigh and got up,
helping me to my feet.

"You're okay with it?" I blinked back my surprise. Just
like that? During the short time I worked for him, I quickly
realized Jett never gave up. What he wanted, he got. And
what he couldn't have, he tried to get nonetheless. "No
conditions, no requests?"

"Actually, now that you're mentioning it, I'm taking you
home on three conditions."

"Of course." I regarded him, amused. Three conditions,

huh? "What are they?"

"First, you call me when you're there and have your phone switched on at all times. Second, I'll send someone over to watch over you. He'll keep to himself and you won't even notice his presence. And there's no arguing about this condition." He paused and I raised my brow, choosing not to comment because he seemed quite determined, and I just wanted to get home and check on Sylvie, no matter what. "Third, you'll have to keep your visit short. So tell Sylvie whatever story you need to tell her, but you're not staying and neither is she. Otherwise I'll have both of you picked up, and I'll use force if need be."

"That's not exactly three requests but five," I pointed out.

"It's either you do what I say, or nothing."

Talk about an inability to compromise.

"Brooke?" It wasn't a question; it was a warning, magnified by the determination in his eyes and the stubborn line on his forehead. He was back to his alpha male ways, trying to protect me, or whatever his male hormones drove him to do.

"Okay," I said, already regretting giving in so easily. "Will you drive me back?"

"Sure, baby." He winked, back in his good mood. "Just hold on tight."

I rolled my eyes at his choice of words. They seemed to

form one of his favorite phrases.

***

On the drive back home Jett kept checking the rearview mirror and the more he did, the more my nervousness increased. If it weren't for the car chase yesterday, I would've thought he suffered from paranoia. Jett drove slowly, maybe because he wasn't used to the rental car he picked up in the morning. Or maybe because he didn't want to draw any attention to us. Either way, I felt bad for his *Lamborghini.* Not that it meant anything to me, but because I knew how much he loved it.

"I'm sorry about your car," I said.

"It's not that bad. She'll be as good as new in no time." Jett winked amused and focused back on the road.

His car was a *she*?

Wow! I didn't know whether he was laughing at me, or trying to annoy me. In the end, I decided to keep my mouth shut.

Less than half an hour later, the car stopped in front of Alessandro's house. Turning to say goodbye was the difficult part. It always was. Leaving him, not knowing when I'd see him again, a part of me missing him already even though I hadn't even left the car yet.

"Thank you for the date," I said. "I'm glad I came."

He shot me his dazzling smile and ran his hand through his hair before settling on the wheel. "I'm thankful for the second chance."

"So am I."

He leaned over and our lips met in a short but heated kiss. "Remember, I want you to keep the phone switched on at all times. If you find anything suspicious—no matter how minuscule or ridiculous it might seem—call me and I'll be there."

"Got it." I nodded. My eyes remained glued to him, soaking him in. The words 'call me' triggered a memory. "Jett, did you call me two days ago, about half an hour after you dropped me off at the spa?"

His frown showed me he didn't.

I pretended not to notice. "I thought I'd ask because the number was private."

"I don't hide my number." I heard the tension in his voice, the mistrust, and the suspicion. "Did you pick up?"

"Yeah, but no one replied." I bit my lip. He studied me for a moment.

"Maybe I speed-dialed you by accident," he suggested. "Or maybe it was a friend."

"Maybe." I really wanted to believe it because it was a possibility, and yet I couldn't. In my book coincidences didn't really exist. "You're probably right and it was a friend, though with the time difference, it would've been early morning back home and I don't know anyone who'd be up at that hour."

I felt stupid for bringing this up and dragging on the conversation for longer than necessary. I grabbed my handbag from the backseat, when my eyes fell on something half covered by Jett's leather jacket and stashed in a holster. I had seen a gun before but never touched one in real life.

"Jett?" I moistened my lips, surprised at the calmness in my voice compared to the frantic beating of my heart. "What's a gun doing in your car?"

"What gun?"

I stretched to lift his jacket when his hand grabbed mine, stopping me. "Don't touch it." His eyes locked with mine.

I knew. He knew that I knew. And yet he remained silent, probably preferring I had never seen it.

"What are you doing with a gun and where did you get it?" I asked slowly, my angry gaze demanding an answer.

"Brooke, you're not safe." He shrugged and trailed off, leaving the rest open for interpretation. " I don't want anything happening to you."

Oh, sweet Lord!

"So you got a gun? Is that your answer to our problems?"

Because if it was, I had no idea how to react.

He didn't answer straight away. "Why not? If keeping you safe involves breaking a few rules, then so be it. You don't need to know more than that." He moistened his lips and turned to stare out the car window.

I regarded his profile. The thought of him having a gun didn't shock me, not after the few things he shared about his life. What outraged me was the knowledge that I *wasn't* afraid.

As long as nobody got killed and Jett didn't get into any trouble, I was fine with it.

***

I looked at the watch on my wrist. It was 1.15 p.m. In spite of a good night's sleep and a nourishing breakfast, I felt lightheaded, as though I was floating in a vacuum unable to focus on more than taking one step after another. So much had happened since I left Sylvie. The date, the proof Jett was on my side, his past, the sex, the pursuit, the discovery of his weapon, his declaration that he cared about me—which wasn't really that much of a surprise because he had said it before. But, with all the drama and emotional baggage gone, it felt different.

Real.

Yet I couldn't tell my best friend a word about it. It was time I cleared up the misunderstanding about Jett so I wouldn't have to hide my blossoming relationship from Sylvie anymore. But how was I supposed to explain everything without sounding like I had a screw loose? And—even worse—how I was I supposed to handle her reaction? Sylvie wasn't just overprotective; her vices included the inability to forgive when she felt betrayed. I had a nagging feeling that after all the bitching we did about Jett back in New York, dating him would feel like pure betrayal to her.

Taking a deep steadying breath, I unlocked the front door and entered. The house was deadly quiet, which felt strange. Unnerving. I checked the living room and kitchen, and then walked upstairs to her bedroom and knocked.

No answer.

"Sylvie?" I opened the door and peeked inside. Her clothes lay scattered all over the floor. Her handbag was on her unmade bed. I peered inside. Except for her phone and credit card, nothing seemed to be missing.

An ice-cold knot twisted inside my stomach. Sylvie never left the house without her makeup. Did something happen to her? If something happened, I'd never forgive myself.

I dashed down the stairs, and double-checked the obvious places—the living room, kitchen, veranda, and backyard. No one in sight.

"Sylvie?" I called as I descended the stony stairs leading

toward the woods. Just as I opened my mouth to try again, I spied her on the other side of the pool. She was clad in a bikini, lounging on a chair, her fingers clasped around a cocktail glass. Where the heck did she get that from?

I heaved a sigh of relief.

She looked well and safe. Heading for her, I noticed she had her eyes closed and music blaring through the earphones. I leaned over her, figuring she'd notice my presence. She didn't stir.

"Sylvie?" I squeezed her arm gently.

Her blue eyes flew open and she almost jumped in her lounger. For an instant fear crossed her face before she recognized me, and then she smiled, which was quickly replaced by a mask of anger. She was truly madly furious.

"What the fuck, Brooke! You scared the living shit out of me. Where have you been?" she shouted.

I pointed at her earphones. She removed them but her angry expression didn't change.

"Where have you been?" she repeated. "I had to call the police. I didn't know what to do."

Her eyes were wide with fear, and there were dark circles beneath them.

"Oh my God. You did what?" I sat down and wrapped my arm around her shoulders, fearing the worst—that someone threatened her and hurt her. "Are you okay? Did something happen?"

"What are you talking about? Of course I'm not okay."
Pausing, she took a deep breath and let it out slowly, as
though to calm herself. "When your best friend goes
missing in a place God-knows-where and you're expected
to communicate in a language you don't speak, obviously
you're scared out of your mind." Her finger jabbed my
chest as her eyes spewed fire at me. "You call. You act like
an adult and let your best friend know where you are. You
don't freaking *bail.*"

I had never seen her like this. Angry. Hurt. Vulnerable.

"You have a funny way of showing it," I said, pointing
at the cocktail in her hand.

"Yeah, well. Whatever shit you're going through, it's
easier when you're half drunk." She wrapped the long cord
of her headphones around her iPhone, her voice still raw
with emotion. "Music's the only thing that helps me switch
off from imagining all the things that could've happened to
you."

Drawing her close to me I hugged her, whispering, "I'm
sorry." I truly hoped she could hear the remorse in my
voice. I was horribly sorry for inflicting that much worry
upon her.

Sylvie shook her head angrily, rubbing away the
moisture in her eyes. "I thought something bad happened
to you." She sounded upset but her tone had calmed down
a little.

"I'm so sorry, Sylvie. I know I should have called but you were supposed to get a text message and—"

The hard edge in my voice made her look up.

"I got a text message which sounded nothing like you. What happened?" She eyed me up and down suspiciously. Her X-ray vision brushed over my face and crumbled clothes. "Where were you?"

The moment I had been dreading had come. Okay, where to start?

Good question, Stewart. What about the beginning?

I took a long steadying breath and let it out slowly. Her eyes fell on the watch and sure enough her jaw dropped.

"Oh my God." I could almost see her brain working. The moment she put two and two together, her frown changed into a scowl. "You went out with a guy! Please tell me I'm wrong."

She narrowed her eyes at me as she scanned my face, her jaw dropping further.

"You didn't, Brooke."

I nodded.

"You little –britch. Who is it?"

Whenever Sylvie was extremely happy or angry with me, she called me 'britch.' It all dated back to the day we were invited to her boring cousin's wedding. It was all a big traditional yawn, so Sylvie and I had the idea to ditch the party in favor of Sylvie's backstage passes to a gig—and a musician guy she had been dying to meet. Happy with my offer, but also feeling guilty to miss her cousin's party, Sylvie had combined the words 'bride' with 'bitch', calling me a 'britch.' It was a whole different story or maybe not so different now, considering I ditched her to meet Jett in secret.

"Uh." I couldn't even look into her eyes. "There's a lot I didn't tell you."

Fighting for words, I almost expected another of Sylvie's famous outbursts. What I got instead was a stare with a glint in her eyes that screamed trouble.

"Oh my God." Her voice was so low I wasn't sure I heard right. "You're dating *him* again."

"Sylvie—" I raised my hand to stop her and let me explain but she cut me off.

"The signs were there. I should have known no one changes their depressed mood out of the blue. All this time I thought you were moving on, while you were hooking up with *Jett*."

I could pretend she was wrong and buy myself time, but what was the point in lying?

"How did you figure it out?" I asked, grinning. I should have felt guilty, but I couldn't help myself. Just hearing Jett's name coming out of Sylvie's mouth and her look— her priceless scorn—made me smile.

"Come here." She wrapped her arms around me. "You

silly, silly cow! How could you think just for one minute I wouldn't notice how deeply and madly you're in love with him?"

"Is it that obvious?" I whispered.

Nodding, she laughed. "Even if I was blind, I'd still sense that stupid grin on your face every time you think no one's looking."

I laughed with her because she was right. Jett did that to me even when he wasn't around.

"Thank you," I whispered.

She shrugged, not asking what for. There were so many reasons. Like the fact that she kept proving time after time that she was the best friend in the world. We laughed until our eyes shimmered with tears—and still couldn't stop. It was almost like it used to be when were younger, and in my case, careless. All the stupid things we did and how we stuck together through every single mistake. The good, the bad, and the *outrageous*.

Just like now.

17

AFTER A QUICK shower and changing into a clean pair of jeans and a sleeveless shirt, I joined Sylvie in the backyard. We talked for an hour straight, during which I recalled the car chase in minuscule detail. Much to my surprise Sylvie came to terms with Jett being here to help me. She asked questions about Jett's reports, Alessandro's past, and even about how I felt about Jett being back in my life. She wanted to make sure I was okay, and that I was happy. When she suggested inviting Jett over for dinner, my jaw almost dropped. I'll admit her sudden enthusiasm scared me, but it was also important to me that Sylvie accepted Jett and forgave him, not least because I didn't want to hide anything from her.

We were lounging by the pool. A soft red tint covered my naked arms and shoulders while Sylvie showed a healthy golden glow that would soon turn into the most gorgeous tan, building a beautiful contrast to her blond hair and stunning blue eyes. Knowing about the estate and the car chase, she didn't seem as scared as I thought she'd be.

"I'm glad we talked," I said. "Keeping secrets from you felt terrible. I'm not good at that."

"To be honest, I already suspected something was wrong." Sylvie leaned forward and squeezed my hand gently. "I just didn't want to push you, because you were in a bad place. I reckoned you'd tell me at some point."

"Yeah." I wished I had done it much earlier.

She pushed her sunglasses back on her head, a quizzical look on her face. "Are you and Jett back together? Like, officially?"

"I don't know," I admitted, "We haven't talked about it. We're dating and he told me his feelings once, on the day I broke up with him. We might be getting serious." I shrugged as though it didn't matter. But it did. A lot. I wanted *serious*. Ever since meeting him it had become one of my favorite words.

"Might be?" She snorted. "If a guy talks feelings after you've had sex, he wants to be with you. There's no doubt about that."

"I guess," I muttered.

Something in my tone made her tilt her head. Maybe I didn't come across as enthusiastic or confident as one would expect.

"Does he know how you feel about him?" Sylvie asked.

Staring at the sparkling blue water, I shook my head.

"Why? What's the problem?"

I smiled grimly. Sylvie and I were so close and yet opposites. She knew a bit about my past and I about hers, but she denied everything she'd rather keep buried. How could I explain to her my rules about love and relationships without going into detail about what drove me to think that way? To love someone so deeply is to risk losing yourself forever. Once I admitted my feelings to him, there was no going back—no hope to ever make my heart complete without him.

"He's amazing, but—" I hesitated, my throat constricting at the thought of a future together. "I want to be with him but sometimes when I see him, I feel like I'm standing on a cliff, knowing there is no way to go but down."

I bit my lip, pondering how much I could say without giving too much away.

"Right now I'm happy with how things are. It's going great. The way I see it, Jett doesn't need to know how I feel."

Sylvie smiled and squeezed my hand. "Sweetie, love's meant to be shared. Maybe it won't last forever. But who cares? Every story has an ending. You can't stop after one chapter just because you don't know how it ends. If you love him, you should at least give it a chance. I think a life without sharing love is hell in itself. What's worse than loss?"

"Regret," I whispered, thinking back to all the times she had drilled into me just how great a bitch regret was, and why I should take risks rather than live in my safe bubble. "You're right."

"I know that. Do you?" Her brows shot up.

I did. And yet the demons inside my head kept roaring. They were the ones who kept telling me it wouldn't end well. It hadn't for my parents. Nor Jett's parents. Nor Sylvie's. Why would I encounter a different fate?

"Think about it," Sylvie said gently.

Nodding, I fought back the moisture gathering in the corners of my eyes and decided to change the topic. "Has Clarkson called?"

Sylvie shook her head and squeezed into her clothes—cropped jeans and an oversized tee that fell off her shoulder. "No, but a letter arrived this morning. I left it on the kitchen table. It's the financial reports you requested. Wanna have a look at them now?"

I wanted to ask how she knew what the letter contained, but decided against it. "Sure. I've turned into a lobster anyway."

As we returned to the house I noticed the dark clouds

gathering in the distance. The soft breeze from before turned into a strong gust blowing up the leaves, and the air carried the scent of oncoming rain. It was hard to believe that just a few hours ago the air had been so hot it had reminded me of a desert.

We entered through the backdoor and I locked it behind us. I scanned the kitchen area. It looked spotless, like Sylvie didn't use it, which was strange because she usually ordered portions that could feed a family of four—and didn't gain a pound. Maybe she had been too worried to eat. The thought ignited my guilt again.

"Did anything happen last night?" I asked. "Any strange phone calls?"

She shot me an inquisitive look. "No, it was pretty quiet here."

I had never been so happy to hear she had a quiet night in. It almost made the car chase seem surreal.

"Did you really call the police?" I asked, grinning.

"Yeah. They told me I had to wait forty-eight hours before I could fill in a missing person's report. That pissed me off big time, but other than that—" Sylvie shook her head. "Nothing happened." She blinked a few times, irritated.

I placed a sloppy kiss on her soft cheek. Ever since we moved to New York City, Sylvie and I had a code that if one of us didn't get in touch before ten a.m. the next morning, that would be a red flag that something happened. Even though she received the text and shouldn't have worried, I appreciated her concern.

"I'm so sorry. I promise I won't do that to you again," I whispered.

"You'd better not, Brooke, because you scared the crap out of me." The tremble in her voice didn't go unnoticed. "Those are the papers. Looks like there's a lot to go through." She pointed to the large yellow folder and headed for the coffee maker.

I watched her fill the filter and add water, then opened the folder and was instantly overwhelmed by the countless sheets covered with numbers and yet more numbers. Even though I knew my way around basic accounting, I had never glimpsed into the accounts of an estate as big as this one. As far as my amateur eye could see though, the numbers looked legit and the taxes paid.

"They look okay to me." I closed the folder again.

Sylvie placed a cup of hot coffee in front of me and sat down. "Can I see them?"

"Sure." Given that she had a degree in business to show off and had worked in an accounting firm until recently, I was more than happy to oblige. I handed her the folder and took a sip of my coffee, almost burning my tongue in the process.

Sylvie began flicking through the papers.

"What do you think?" I asked her, inching closer. Two minutes passed and she didn't reply. The silence was making me nervous, so I bumped her leg under the table.

"Sylvie?"

"Sorry?" She frowned but didn't look up. "Did you say something?"

"Is something wrong?"

I laughed to compensate for the worry in my voice.

"There's no debt." She looked up, her baby blue eyes searching mine.

"So that's a good thing then, right?"

Her grimace didn't quite manage to erase my unease. Maybe it was the way she clutched at the papers. Or maybe it was the way her eyes kept darting across one particular page, as though her findings rattled her. But something told me things weren't as clear as they had seemed to me.

"There's something wrong, isn't there?" I asked.

She held up a hand, her face scrunched up in concentration as she pulled three papers in front of her, discarding the rest, and started to compare them. I didn't like the look on her face. My heart began to beat fast.

I walked around the table and leaned over her shoulder, trying to see what she saw. Finally Sylvie flicked open her phone and began to punch numbers in her calculator.

"The numbers don't add up," she mumbled as her fingers pointed around the sheets to show me. "Looks like a loophole in earnings and write-offs. I'm wondering where the money's going."

Turning, she gazed up at me, her eyes reflecting my own mistrust.

"What do you mean?"

"I'm sorry, Brooke. I've no idea," she said, handing the papers back to me. "Those look like charities, but who knows. You need to talk with Jett and find someone who knows more about Italian accounting practices. One thing's for sure, the transactions were made at periodic but random intervals. The last one took place last January."

"Okay." I blinked in succession. "People donate to charities all the time."

Sylvie shook her head. "Look at all those zeroes. We're talking millions and he wrote them all off. You said Jett owns a property here, meaning he more than likely has an Italian accountant to sort out his taxes."

I knew I had reached a point where I needed help. Jett was the obvious answer.

She stopped in front of the kitchen door, her hand on the doorknob, her eyes not looking at me. "There's something else."

"What?" I cocked my head, regarding her intently. Whenever she tried to make something important sound casual, she started with the words 'also there's something else', which instantly made the alarm bells go off at the back of my mind.

"You said Alessandro didn't want you to make any alterations to the house, right?"

I nodded.

"Well, I've been wondering why there are cement bags downstairs."

"Downstairs?"

"Yes, in the basement. While waiting for you, worried sick I might add," she paused for effect, "I checked all the rooms in the house and stumbled upon the bags in the basement."

"Are you sure you saw bags of cement and not—"

"Dust? Stones?" She rolled her eyes. "I'm not stupid, Brooke."

"I never said that. It's just weird." Alessandro had been so adamant that nothing be changed about the house. I had to see it and then ask him about it. "Show me," I said to Sylvie. Not waiting for her answer, I walked past her, only stopping in the hall, so she could take the lead.

She guided me down the stairs and through a door into a narrow corridor that seemed to stretch on forever. The air smelled stale and dusty. The spare naked light bulbs above our heads cast moving shadows across the whitewashed walls. My shoes barely made any sound on the concrete floor as I hurried to keep up with Sylvie's brisk pace.

"You came down here all alone?" I asked, almost

sceptical. Who would have thought my best friend—a closet claustrophobic—would enter an underground place that resembled an oversized casket with no windows and no escape exit?

"I didn't exactly have a choice. I thought you might be trapped in the basement," Sylvie muttered. "You'd be surprised what else I'd do for you."

I smiled at the various memories of her shying away from elevators and cramped spaces, pretending she couldn't breathe.

"It wasn't easy. I thought I was going to have a heart attack."

"Look at you. You're conquering your fears. I'm so proud of you," I said, meaning every word of it. She shot me a dirty look over her shoulder and muttered something like 'just shut up.'

We reached a juncture and entered a hall with several doors. I peered into the first room. Apart from old furniture stashed in the corner, it was empty. The second and third cells looked just the same. The fourth cell was the size of a room and completely empty. Stopping in my tracks, I shuddered as unease washed over me.

"Where are the cement bags?" I asked.

"There." Sylvie pointed to my left. I turned to follow her line of vision, only then noticing the open archway hidden by darkness. We walked in and Sylvie switched on the light bulb, bathing the fifth room in artificial brightness.

The small space was stacked with racks and bottles, which led me to believe Sylvie had stumbled upon Alessandro's wine cellar. Stashed between the wall and a rack were two bags of cement, almost hidden from view, as though someone had forgotten them there.

"So what do you think?" Sylvie asked.

"I don't know." I crouched down to inspect them closer. "Maybe he needed them for renovations. It's an old building; it probably needs a lot of that."

It sounded plausible, and yet her silence suggested she didn't agree with me. I could see from the frown on her face that she didn't like my answer. And neither did I.

"When I told you I looked around, I meant *I really* snooped around and found no signs of any recent renovations. Everything looks just *old*." She made a disparaging gesture. "Why leave the bags in here with the expensive wine? Why not choose the other room where there's plenty of space? Just look at this thing." She pulled out a bottle of wine and handed it to me. I checked the stamped date before returning the bottle to the rack. The wine was over fifty years old and probably worth more than I used to make in a month in my old job.

A faint scent wafted past. I sniffed the air, focusing to catch it.

"Do you smell it?" I asked.

"What?"

"I think it's paint."

We split up, inspecting the walls, brushing our fingers over the irregular dirty white surface.

"If he had someone paint them over, whoever he hired did a really bad job," Sylvie said. "He should ask for his money back."

Sylvie was right. The paint was so irregular and rough, it looked like a child could have done a more decent job.

"The smell's strongest here." I pointed to a rack and wiped my fingertips over two bottles. "There's no dust."

"Let me see," Sylvie said. I stepped aside, only then noticing the white color staining the dark wood in places.

"I think someone painted this room, then set up the rack while the paint was still fresh. As for the rack, my best guess is it was moved from somewhere else, which would explain why there's no dust on the bottles."

We returned to the fourth room and inspected the walls. Dark traces of dust and dirt were visible where the wine racks used to stand.

"But why would Alessandro move the wine racks into a smaller room after it was painted?" Sylvie whispered behind me. "Why not just leave them here?"

Crossing my arms over my chest, I shook my head, signalling I had no idea. "I've been asking myself the same question." I paced up and down the space, my eyes focused on the wall.

"What doesn't make sense to me is why did he have just one room painted? Why not this one, too? Why not the entire basement?" I turned to look at Sylvie.

"Maybe there was no need for it. What if he had water leakage and just this one room was damp? He might have feared mold would spread through the walls," Sylvie suggested.

"The air would smell damp. Besides, you don't eradicate mold by painting it over. You can use an air dehumidifier. Worst case scenario, you rebuild all walls because fungus spreads fast," I said. "Maybe that's what he needed the cement bags for."

It was possible, and yet my words sounded unbelievable. Sylvie's doubtful look told me she thought the same. Something just didn't add up. The painted wall looked like an amateur had tried his hand at it. Why not hire a professional? Alessandro surely had enough money. And why do just this one wall?

My mind was spinning from so many questions, and each answer I came up with led to yet another question.

"You should invite *him* over, you know," Sylvie remarked as we turned to go upstairs.

No need to ask who she was talking about.

"Seriously?" I asked her. "Are you really okay with it?"

"Yeah."

We'd had this discussion before and I was eager to stand my ground. Having Jett over wasn't a good idea. First of all, both Sylvie and Jett's egos were enormous. You simply don't put two people, who each show delusions of grandeur when it comes to their meaning in life, in the same room. And then there was the fact that Jett and Alessandro weren't exactly friends.

"Ask him." Sylvie shrugged.

"You'll be good?"

"You know me." She shot me a wide smile.

"No fighting?"

She heaved an exaggerated sigh and rolled her eyes slowly. "I'd never do that."

Yeah, right!

Biting my lip, I stared at her innocent face for a few moments. I really wanted to believe her, but Sylvie could be a little too overprotective, which turned her into a dragon. But she and Jett were extremely important to me, so wasn't it about time they got to know each other? Just in case Jett and I were long-term material.

"You're right," I said. "Maybe I should ask Jett for his opinion. A male perspective's always interesting."

It was the truth. I wanted to hear his opinion because I trusted his judgment. But that wasn't the only reason I needed him around. I wanted him by my side because he was the only one who made me feel safe.

18

THE CLOCK WAS moving closer and closer to seven p.m. With every second, my heart pounded harder and faster against my chest. It had been doing that ever since my chat conversation with Jett.

Will u have dinner with us @ 7?

It had been my clue to him that Sylvie was ready to forgive him, and that I wanted to see him today. Two minutes later, his text message pinged back.

I'll bring wine.

For the past hour my stomach had been fluttering, and I was indulging in major wishful thinking. And not only because of the promise of a hot night. My phone beeped again. Expecting another message, I flicked it open. As I opened the photo attachment, I let out a spat of air, blushing.

Holy mother of pearls!

It showed a picture of me sleeping half naked on my stomach, my legs stretching out from under the covers, where my tiny nightshirt had ridden up, my hair a mess and—earth swallow me up whole—my mouth slightly open. But worst of all, the shirt I was wearing barely covered my ass. Below the picture he wrote, "Wish I could see the look on your face when you see this."

I stared at the screen in shock, my hands moving across the keyboard.

Oh God, u didn't do that.

Short silence, then my phone beeped again.

What?

The picture u just sent me!

I don't know what you're talking about?

Seriously? Now he was pretending he hadn't sent me the

picture.

I want u to delete it. I look horrendous.

A brief pause, then came his answer.

I thought the one showing your boobs was a pretty good shot, so there's no chance in hell I'm deleting it. If I want to picture myself satisfied, I just have to look at them and rewind the memories I have with you.

I looked at the picture again. It definitely didn't show my boobs. How many pictures did he take? I was about to text him again, when another text arrived.

p.s.: Can't wait to see you. I'm sick of making out with my pillow and pretending it's you.

My heart did a cartwheel. I texted him back, but no more messages arrived. Now dinner couldn't come fast enough. Sylvie noticed my frazzled state of mind but didn't comment on it. As per her instructions I showered, put on a dress of her choice, and let my hair fall onto my shoulders in cascading waves. I even let her apply my makeup, praying she wouldn't go too far. She wanted me to look amazing, and I did. Standing in front of the mirror, I regarded my mint colored, off shoulder Grecian drape dress with fine lace embroidery and hand sewn pearls around the waist. Probably designed for an evening party or gala, it hugged my figure in all the right places, and gave my slightly tanned skin a golden hue. Definitely well worth the horrendous price Sylvie probably paid for it.

"Wow. I'm so proud of you," Sylvie gushed.

"It's just the three of us having dinner. It's not like I'm graduating, or moving to Europe. But thanks for the thumbs-up."

"I know but look at you." She pointed down my body. "You're spreading your wings and learning to fly."

I turned around to inspect the dress in the mirror. "Where did you get it from? I've never seen it in your wardrobe and can't remember you packing it."

"I bought it yesterday," Sylvie said.

"So you went to Milan?" I asked.

She shook her head, touching the dress. "No, there wasn't enough time because I wanted to be back in time for you. I found this small shop in Bellagio, not far from the pizzeria we went to. Half the stuff wasn't that bad. And then I saw the dress and I had to get it. I thought it'd be a perfect fit for you." She shot me a bright smile, which made me eye her carefully. She always talked this much, but there was something in her tone that made me listen up.

"For me?"

Sylvie nodded, and her smile widened just a little bit more.

"Thank you." I hugged her tight. "But why would you get me something like this?"

"Feeling bad?" She winked.

Oh God.

Call it intuition, but I just *knew* something was fishy.

I narrowed my eyes on her. "Feeling bad for—" I was cut short by the bell. I checked my watch. It was barely six. Jett was supposed to be here at seven. I turned to Sylvie, confused. "Who's that?"

Judging from the grin on her face, something was up. "I asked Jett to be here early."

"But why?" I looked around my messy room. Clothes and shoes—mostly Sylvie's—were scattered all over the place. There was makeup, body lotion, and yet more makeup on the bed. No way would I let Jett see all the clutter.

She motioned me to follow her down the stairs to the front door. "Don't be mad, but I have a date. I figured you'd be fine without me."

"You have a what?" I almost tripped in my high heels as I tried to keep up with her.

"I've met someone."

"Who?"

She shrugged as though it wasn't important, which was

the exact opposite of what she really thought. "The guy from the bar."

No freaking way!

Why did I believe her when she claimed it was going to be just one drink? From all the people in the world, did she have to go for the local mafia?

Sylvie's hand clasped around the doorknob. Before she could open the front door, I grabbed her hand, forcing her to turn around.

"What about Jett and dinner?" My eyes spew fire, matching the angry flames blazing inside me.

"Don't worry about him. He'll take good care of you. Besides, I asked him to bring dinner, because you can't cook worth a shit. So you'll be just fine."

I rolled my eyes, ignoring her remark. I had no doubt that Jett and I would have a good time. "No, Sylvie. That's not really my concern. I don't like you going out with that guy, and you know it. What happened to 'one drink only, I'm not gonna marry him?'"

She shrugged again in that non-committal way of hers. Cringing, I clamped my mouth shut. My hopes and dreams of Jett and Sylvie spending more time together in order to get to know each other were about to run down the toilet. I wanted the ice broken between the two most important people in my life. That was never going to happen if Sylvie kept finding excuses to stay away from him. I could take care of that later. Right now my issue was her going out with a guy I didn't know.

"Sylvie, why would you go on a date with someone without telling me?"

Hypocrite alert.

Wasn't that what I had done the last few times? I began to rub my temples in the hope she wouldn't catch the guilty look on my face.

"I'm telling you now. If I can't find a decent club in the area, I need a date. Besides, I haven't had one of those in ages," she said. "I'll spill everything when I get back."

I honestly didn't want her to go and yet what could I do? I was in no position to make demands. In the end I found myself whispering, "Please be careful."

Sylvie leaned in whispering back, "When you find someone special, he's probably worth hanging on to. Don't stop trying to make it work. In fact, today's a good day to tell him how you feel about him. You take a risk, okay?"

Where the heck did the sudden Dr. Phil life coaching session come from? I stared at her, open-mouthed. Her lips touched my cheek gently and she patted my arm. That's when everything dawned on me.

There was no sense in trying to convince Sylvie to stay. I knew a lost cause when I saw one. Yes, we had been in Italy for a few days now. But as much as she wanted to fool me into thinking she was missing guys and parties, I sensed the real reason why she couldn't wait to leave me and Jett alone was to give us a chance to get back together.

"Promise me you'll text me where you are," I said.

With a sigh, Sylvie nodded and opened the door. My breath caught in my throat when I saw Jett in front of us. He was dressed in a black leather jacket, a sexy white tee, and even sexier jeans, holding a large box of what I supposed contained dinner. I grabbed it out of his hands and placed it on the side table in the foyer.

"Hey!" A smug grin lit up his face.

How could he make one word sound so deliciously sensual? For a brainless moment, I imagined kissing his butter-melting lips and wrapping my legs around his majestic body, dissolving into him, the way I did earlier today in the hotel room. Or yesterday in the Jacuzzi. Or the time before that, on the boat.

"Hi. I'm glad you could come." Sylvie stepped out to greet him, throwing her arms around him as though they were best buddies. In the silence of the evening, she whispered loud enough for me to hear. "Take good care of her. If you hurt her, I promise I'll cut off your balls and feed them to the ducks on the lake."

Jett glanced at me with an amused grin.

"You were probably drunk because I've never seen ducks swimming in that lake. But if I ever hurt her, I'll buy some for you so you can serve my balls on a silver tray. No worries, I'll keep her safe." He smiled, his gaze never leaving mine. "I'm not going to waste a second not giving her a good time."

Holy mother of double meanings!

His eyes twinkled with mischief, sending my memory retrieval system into overload.

My knees almost melted beneath me at the countless memories of us together, our limbs intertwined.

Thank God Sylvie caught none of that.

"You better take this seriously, Mayfield." She walked past him and turned around, calling over her shoulder, "Have fun, guys."

19

"SHE'S QUITE something," Jett said, as we watched Sylvie disappear around the corner.

I snorted. "Can you blame her?"

"Not really." He laughed. "Since I sensed a serious threat, I'd better start treating you well. As of now." He kissed my cheek, then picked me up in his arms and slammed the door shut with his foot, not putting me down. "Where's the kitchen?"

"That way." I pointed down the corridor and squealed as he took off, still carrying me. I could feel his hands burning my back, especially my ass, and they were beginning to roam again. I didn't mind but I wanted food first.

We reached the kitchen and Jett put me down. And then he left again and came back with the cardboard box. I peered over his shoulder as he unpacked its contents. Instead of ordered restaurant dinner, it looked as if Jett had every intention to cook for me. Again.

"Isn't it in the least weird that you're always the one who brings dinner or lunch?" I asked.

"You forgot to add breakfast." A smug smile spread across his beautiful face as he shrugged out of his leather jacket and tossed it over the back of a chair, revealing the most amazing row of pecks and biceps I had ever seen—all partly hidden under a highly annoying snug white tee. My mouth turned dry at his sight. "The way I see it there's nothing wrong with that. If I cook dinner you're happy, and I get what I want," he said, grinning.

I punched his shoulder playfully, not offended but just to use any excuse to touch him. "If I cook next time, will you do what *I* want?"

Stopping in his tracks, he cocked his head to the side as though to consider my proposal. "Maybe. That depends. Can you cook?"

I couldn't and he knew it.

"Does ordering count?"

He raised an amused eyebrow. "For all of five minutes. It certainly doesn't earn you the same privileges as a three-course meal."

"You never let me be in control."

"That's because you love me to be in control." He

inched closer and I took a few steps back until my back hit the wall.

"That's not true."

It was. I just didn't want to admit it.

His mouth came so close I could smell the faint scent of mint and that intoxicating fragrance of his that always made my knees buckle beneath me.

"Are you up for a bet, Brooke? Let's say a game of Spades? If you win, you get to do whatever you want to do to me. If I win, I can choose what I want. I have *whatever dessert* I want."

Jett stretched out his hand. I shook it with a smug smile on my face. I was the best Spades player I knew. I had never lost against anyone. The guy was in for a big kick in his ego.

"You're on," I said. "Get ready to lose, sucker."

"You think?" He propped his strong arms against the wall on both sides of my neck, caging me in. His mouth descended to trail down my neck and shoulder, his teeth removing the tiny shoulder strap.

"I like a good challenge. A test. But I don't want you to lose, baby," he whispered, his hands moving around my ass to lift me up. Wrapping my legs around his waist, I let him carry me across the kitchen and set me down on the edge of the kitchen counter. "What if I cook and you just stir?" Jett continued huskily. "You can't really do much wrong and we both get to have what we want today."

His fingers fiddled with my dress until I felt his talented hand between my legs, testing my panties and self-control.

"Sounds like someone's a big scared pussy." I moaned as his hand began to rub ever so gently, sending a first jolt of heat through my core. My legs tightened around his waist and I pulled him closer. His thighs were wedged between my legs now, his hand replaced by the bulge in his jeans. He moved in slow motion—up and down—imitating the slow rhythm of our lovemaking until the coarse material of his jeans began to chafe my clit through my panties. My head shot back and another moan escaped my lips, silently demanding more.

"I'm just concerned for you. That's all." His lips curled into a stunning smile, making me yearn to do all the unspeakable things I always wanted to do to him.

"A bet is a bet. You can't back out of it now, just because you're scared." My hands trailed down his rock hard abdomen to his jeans, ready to unzip him and give him a good ride of pleasure.

"What are you doing?" He stopped my hands, his breathing coming hard. "You haven't won yet."

I laughed. "Are you serious? Am I supposed to wait, even though you know I'll win? What happened to keeping me happy?"

"There's plenty of time for that later." He kissed me

quickly and helped me off the counter. "How was your day? What did you find out?"

And just like that our moment was gone, and Jett's expression was back to its usual casual self. The guy didn't just have an inflated ego, he had also the self control of a statue.

Damn it!

"How do you know I found out something?" I smoothed my dress, fighting the urge to smirk at him.

"From Sylvie." He moistened his lips and regarded me amused, probably inwardly laughing his head off at my disheveled state. "She said you had things to discuss with me alone and that I should bring dinner. Knowing you two, it wasn't hard to guess you must have discovered something."

He was right, as usual, but I couldn't tell him Sylvie only left us alone so I could talk to him about my feelings.

I moved past Jett to the kitchen table, doing my best not to touch him, and handed him the folder containing the financial reports.

"Clarkson dropped off the estate's financial reports. Sylvie's adamant, there's too much money coming in and going out at regular intervals."

"And you want to know what that's all about," he said matter-of-factly, making no move to open the envelope. I wondered if he had seen the reports yet. "I could show them to my accountant."

"That'd be great."

"My pleasure."

I bit my lip, unsure how to steer the conversation to the wine cellar. There was a chance I was blowing it out of proportions, and I didn't want him to think I liked melodrama.

"The basement was recently re-painted which strikes me as odd because when I met with Alessandro a few days ago, he insisted that I make no alterations to the house." Peering up, I met his questioning look. "It's probably not a big deal but I'd like you to have a look."

***

Clad in only a thin half-length dress, the air felt so cold my skin turned into goose bumps. I suppressed a shiver and wrapped my arms around myself to keep warm. I expected Jett to laugh off my implausible explanations. I even expected irritation, just not—silence. Jett remained quiet for at least ten minutes, his face an expressionless mask as he followed me down to the basement and then listened to me recalling my conversation with Sylvie. I watched him moving from one cell to the next, smoothing his hand over the walls, tapping, and moving bits and parts of the heavy rack around, absorbed in his thoughts, which he didn't seem to want to share with me just yet. In the background I thought I could hear the tapping sound of raindrops falling. The usually soothing sound made me nervous, maybe because the place gave me the creeps and my nerves were on edge. For the first time I realized I couldn't be comfortable living in this big old house all by myself.

Standing next to Jett, the seconds became minutes and I felt silly dragging him down here for no reason at all. My suspicion had been roused by nothing but my absurd need to see hidden motives where there might be none.

"Maybe we should head back upstairs. It's probably not a big deal anyway," I said. "Alessandro probably wanted to paint all the rooms, but his health deteriorated and he never got the chance."

I came to the conclusion that had to be it. The most likely reason was also the simplest one.

"Possibly," Jett replied, his voice giving away no clue with regards to what he really thought. He caught me crossing my arms over my chest and shrugged out of his jacket, then wrapped it around me.

"Put it on." His tone left no room for discussion.

"I'm not that cold, but thanks," I lied yet made no move to remove his jacket because I loved his smell. It was warm and hugged me like a cocoon. Inhaling his scent, I stared at Jett's bulging biceps as he strained to push the rest of the wine rack aside. His muscles flexed beneath the tan skin, and he let out a low groan as the rack moved an inch with a loud grating noise.

"Do you need any help?" I asked, half amused, half aroused. My tongue flicked over my lips as I watched his strong arms, his broad shoulders, and the thin layer of sweat covering his forehead. With his snug shirt and mouth-watering torso, he looked so darn sexy and enticing my body began to yearn for him.

"No. Just wait there," Jett said.

Basically, he was sending an invitation for me to stare some more.

The rack moved another inch, then a couple more. Jett's face contorted from exertion, as he pushed it to the middle of the tiny room, almost blocking the door.

"The proportions of this room aren't right," Jett said.

"Uh-huh. It's quite small." I nodded, not getting what he was talking about. It was probably a man thing. Like cars and sports. You play along, pretend you know what they're talking about, when in reality you can't stop thinking about how hot they are.

"It's an old house. They probably didn't have a good architect back then." I watched him brush his hands over his thighs to dust off his jeans and instantly wished he'd let me do it.

"That's not what I meant, Brooke," he said, turning to regard me. His eyes lingered on me a bit too long, penetrating my mind and body. I instantly felt flustered, both from the fire I saw in his eyes and the fact that I knew he sensed just how much he turned me on. "I think the room was cut in half."

"You mean there's another part somewhere?" It wasn't my brightest statement but his words made no sense.

"Listen." He knocked on the walls to his right and left. The noises sounded different—one hollow, the other muted. "It was divided. The rest is on the other side." He pointed to his right.

I stared at him in silence for a moment, and that's when it dawned on me.

"Are you sure?"

"Absolutely," Jett said.

My fingers touched the grainy surface and I knocked, listening to the hollow sound. My insides began to twist, my instincts warning me. It was as if only inches separated me from something so terrible it made me sick.

"There's only one way to find out for sure, you know?" Jett's eyes fixed on me. "We'd have to smash in the wall. We could keep the damage small, so it can be easily repaired and no one will notice."

Opening Pandora's box.

I swallowed the sudden lump in my throat.

"Alessandro's been pretty clear in his wishes," I said.

"You're the heiress. You have a right to know what's

behind that wall." Jett's voice was determined, rough, almost cold. And as usual, he had a point. "Once you inherit this estate, you automatically inherit its demons. You need to know what you're dealing with."

A shiver ran down my spine. A voice inside my head urged me to run away as fast as possible, and yet my legs didn't move. I wanted to know, and yet I didn't. I could just honor Alessandro's wish and pretend for the rest of my life that this wall didn't exist. But could I live like that? In fear. Not knowing what lay hidden beyond. Always wondering. Obsessing.

Jett inched closer and grabbed my shoulders, forcing me to meet his gaze.

"Brooke, I told you already Alessandro secrets are dangerous. I know you don't believe me, but I made a promise to protect you." His eyes were dark, glistening, demanding something from me that was difficult to give.

My heart hammered against my chest as I was torn between two options. Do it, or don't do it.

But did I really have a choice?

"Okay," I said before I could change my mind. "Let's do it."

"I'll be careful. First thing tomorrow I'll have a professional fix it and no one will know."

"Okay." I nodded, trusting him completely.

"Do you want to wait upstairs?"

"No." I shook my head. "I want to stay and help. Where do we start?"

Jett smiled. His thumb gently grazed my cheek. "Let's find a screwdriver, a hammer, anything that can puncture a wall. If we can't find any tools, we'll drive back to my house to get some."

"Can we change first? I'd rather not ruin Sylvie's dress."

"Sure." He kissed the tip of my nose and then we headed upstairs so I could slip into my old clothes. But more than that, I was eager to bide for time. If only for a few minutes, or as long as it'd take me to calm my shaking fingers and racing heart.

20

It was shortly after eight p.m. when we broke through the wall. I had changed into jeans, a long sleeved shirt and dark blue sneakers, and Jett had slipped back into his jacket. Whoever had put up the wall was in a hurry and went for drywall instead of bricks and mortar. Jett drilled a tiny hole and expanded it to several inches so he could peer inside. Although we didn't find a torch, there were enough candles in the house. We lit one and, holding it up, Jett pushed his arm through the small opening. I stayed a few steps back, not daring to look inside, painfully aware that no one would ever hide something if it wasn't terrible.

"It's okay, baby. Don't be scared," Jett whispered, his calm tone making the shivers running down my spine even worse.

Why the hell did he have to whisper? There was no one

in the house and the sound of his voice echoing from the walls was creepy, creating ice-cold knots inside my stomach.

"There's a desk," Jett said. Did I detect a hint of disappointment?

"A desk?" I asked, trying to look over his shoulder. Why would anyone build a wall to hide a desk? "Let me see."

The candle cast enough light to make out a small mahogany desk. No other furniture.

"Take down the drywall," I said. According to Jett we had no problems making a tiny opening because the wall barely measured an inch in depth. I had seen it done before on TV.

"Are you sure about that? Gypsum is easily broken and makes a huge mess."

I nodded. "Just do it. We'll worry about the mess later."

"Hold this." Jett pushed the burning candle into my hand and then kicked once right next to the small hole. And again until the wall gave in and a chunk of it crumbled to our feet in a heap of debris and dust. It wasn't large, but big enough for someone petite to squeeze through.

"Let me try," I said. Of course I didn't want to go in there alone. But I was tired, and frankly, I didn't care. I just wanted to get it over and done with. And maybe a tiny part of me was eager to impress Jett—after all he did the hard work.

"Stay here," Jett said. "You don't have to do this if

you're uncomfortable."

I hated it when people saw me as fragile. My life had never been cushioned, and I wasn't going to let his overprotectiveness change that now.

"I'm handling this on my own," I said, ready to argue if need be. Jett regarded me calmly but didn't argue. Hysteria bubbled up somewhere at the back of my throat. I swallowed hard to get rid of it and walked past him. Holding the candle up to illuminate the way, I squeezed through the opening. My heart hammered so loud I was sure Jett could hear it.

The room was dark and the air stale, swallowing up the artificial light falling in through the hole. The candle cast a faint and ghostly glow on the concrete floor, but it wasn't enough to reach the dark corners. My heart pounded harder as my mind began to conjure up images of someone hiding in the corner, ready to jump out and kill me. It wasn't just dark, it was dusty and creepy. I couldn't wait to get the hell out of here, but not before I brought to fruition what I came to do.

Jett was right. The room had been divided, though not in half. This part was almost as large as a living room. The desk was set up close to the wall. There was no chair, no other furniture.

"Brooke, do you see anything?" Jett peered inside.

"Nothing," I croaked. My mouth was so dry I cleared

my throat to get rid of the fear choking me.

The candlelight fell on a light switch on the wall to my right. I switched it on and an overhead neon light bulb flickered a few times. Bathed in glaring brightness, the room looked like any other. I breathed a sigh of relief and pressed a hand against my chest to calm my racing heart. But it was hard because the walls creeped me out. With no doors and no escape route, I felt as though I was trapped in a psychiatric ward.

"Are you okay?" Jett called. He sounded impatient and desperate to jump into the middle of the action. He was definitely not the kind to watch from a distance. Struggling, he squeezed through the hole. I motioned him to come in. He reached me in a few long strides, grinning.

"You're so stubborn," I said. "Let's hope we can get you back outside unscathed."

He rubbed his sore shoulder. "Not a good idea, I agree, but I feel useless standing around and watching you do all the work."

We inspected the desk together. It was an old thing with Chinese Chippendale style engravings and a galleried top, brass handles, and two small stationary cupboards left and right. Apart from a few ridges running across the otherwise smooth surface, the desk looked in pristine condition and was probably worth showing to an antique dealer. I ran my fingers over the horizontal panel sides and drawer linings.

"It must have been his desk," Jett said.

"And now it's left to perish away in the basement?" I asked, watching Jett test the bottom drawer. It was locked. The second one opened with a scraping sound, revealing pens, a stamp pad, and a bottle of ink. The third drawer contained loose sheets of paper. Jett laid them on the desk and began skimming through them.

"What's this?" I held up what looked like business correspondence written in Italian.

"Probably nothing important, but we'll have them translated nonetheless," Jett said. "The bottom drawer's the only one locked and I doubt we'll find the key."

He motioned for me to step back. I followed his request and almost jumped in my skin as he turned the desk upside down so he could reach underneath. It crashed against the floor with a loud thump, the noise echoing from the walls.

"Sorry." He flashed me an apologetic smile. I regarded him open-mouthed. I was never one for violence, not even against antiques.

"I hope you're not thinking about keeping it." He pointed at the desk, grinning.

"I'm not a fan of clutter," I said, watching him kick the lower drawer at its weakest spot until it broke.

I held my breath as he retrieved what looked like a black leather bound book the size of my smartphone and began to flick through the pages.

"What's in it?" I asked.

"I don't know. But Lucazzone's probably hiding it for a reason." He pushed the book inside his pocket, avoiding my gaze. But I caught the angry line between his brows. "We're done here. Let's finish up."

Finishing up was easier said than done. How was I supposed to relax with the knowledge that Alessandro had walled in his office and we had no idea why? Whatever reason he had, it didn't make sense to me. If he had a secret, why not just sell the desk, bury or burn the papers— or whatever he wanted hidden from the world. The most obvious explanation to me was that he wanted to hang on to it as evidence.

"I have to make a call," Jett said as I headed for the bathroom, ready to wash off the dirt. The warm water relaxed my sore muscles, but it didn't help to wash off the discovery of the hidden room and the scary new feelings that came with it.

As I returned to the guestroom, my body wrapped in a white bathrobe, Jett was sitting on my bed, his fingers playing with his phone.

"Any news?" I asked.

"Nobody's home. I'll have to try again tomorrow." He sounded angry. Frustrated. His gaze was still averted, avoiding me. Something was troubling him.

Ever since we returned from the basement he had been

distant. Aloof. Cutting me out from his train of thoughts.

"What's wrong?" I ran my fingers through his hair, massaging gently.

His hands moved to his pocket and he fished out the black book, then pushed it into my hands.

"I'm taking a shower." No invitation to join him. I sighed and slumped down on the bed. Maybe he was just tired and taking a shower was his way of dealing with whatever burdened him, and I accepted that.

I waited until he was gone before opening the black book to page one. There were five names. Names I didn't know. Except for one.

I stared at it, paralyzed, the name echoing inside my brain.

Robert Mayfield.

What the heck?

No wonder Jett was upset. His father had confessed to being a part of Alessandro's elite club. But maybe Jett had hoped Robert might not be *that* involved?

I stared at the names for a while, wondering why there were so few of them. I always figured a club involved more than half a dozen people.

"Jett, can I come in?" I knocked on the bathroom door and opened it without waiting for his answer, then peeked inside. He was standing in front of the mirror, wearing nothing but his jeans. His dirty t-shirt lay crumpled on the floor, as though he had kicked it into a messy heap.

"Please?" I shot him a hesitant smile, my eyes begging him to invite me in—both physically and emotionally. He turned around and opened the door wider to let me walk past. Taking a deep steadying breath, I decided to be frank about my thoughts.

"You already knew your father was involved. What difference does it make if his name is in there?"

He sighed. "You're right, I guess. I was just hoping I wouldn't find anything to back up his claims." He grimaced and ran his hand through his wet hair, hesitating at the nape of his neck. "My opinion of him has never been a good one, but I always tried my best to remain non-judgmental because he's my father."

"I know." I inched closer and placed a soft kiss on his shoulder.

"He fucked up so many times in his life, I'm not surprised about anything. I'm just—"

"Disappointed?"

Jett nodded.

"No one's perfect," I whispered, even though I knew Jett was very close to it, which was probably the result of him despising his father's ways.

"If those are the club members' names, what are the numbers on the back?" I held out the open book and pointed at the long strings of digits covering several pages.

"Could be anything. I'll try to find out tomorrow." He walked past me into the bedroom. I followed behind.

"How do you think you'll find out?"

"I have a friend who knows his way around computers."

"Do you think whoever chased us knew this book existed, and they were afraid we'd make it public?" I asked. I was grasping at straws but I couldn't help myself. "If we hand it to them, then maybe we won't have to worry about our safety and we can keep the estate." I regarded Jett intently, waiting for him to admit I had just discovered the solution to our problems.

Sort of.

"Baby, you think too much. There's no point in stipulating possible theories with absolutely nothing to back them up." His voice didn't leave much room for discussion. "I don't think your way is the way they're working. They're not as—" he smiled, struggling to find the right word "—*peaceful*."

That made sense. He used to be in a gang, so he might know a thing or two about how things worked. I figured gangs weren't really that different from elite clubs and sects. They're all made of a closed circle. No one's let in easily, and definitely not let out with a mere handshake.

As if sensing my thoughts, Jett shot me an amused look. "Let's have dinner. I don't want you to lose an inch from those stunning hips."

21

FOLLOWING JETT INTO the kitchen, I felt a hint of disappointment that he was bottling up again. I wanted to talk about our findings and possible theories, but he was more than eager to make us dinner. I leaned against the kitchen counter and watched him unpack the contents of his box, looking as hot as ever—clad in nothing but his jeans. His feet were bare and the muscles of his back seemed to flex with every move. I ignored my brain's silent invitation to run my fingertips down his spine and watch him shiver with pleasure, his beautiful tan skin turning into goose bumps under my touch.

"Wanna help me?" Jett asked. I realized the amused glint had not disappeared from his eyes.

Me and cooking?

I laughed. "Yeah, if you don't mind going to bed

hungry. You know I can't cook."

"That's why we're doing it together." He retrieved a chopping board and placed it in front of him. "We'll start off with something quick and easy. I thought we could make Spaghetti Bolognese."

Given that we were in Italy, how fitting.

I wanted to point out that no Italian recipe was 'quick and easy' to me unless it came out of the microwave oven, and judging from all the things he brought, he had every intention to start from scratch. At least he wasn't expecting we would make our own pasta. I grabbed the unopened pack of spaghetti noodles and turned it around to read the instructions.

"You watch the beef while I cut the onions. Deal?" Jett offered. He grabbed a knife from the knife rack and began to peel an onion.

"Deal."

I had always been rather slow at chopping anything, and I'd rather not have my eyes watering and my mascara running, so I placed the minced beef into a frying pan, added a few drops of oil and turned on the heat—the way I had seen it on TV. It was my first attempt at cooking something as complicated as meat. I had watched my fair share of cooking shows. They always made cooking look easy and I blamed them for my fear. But really, how hard could it be?

Half a minute later, the minced beef began to sizzle unnaturally loud and the first trickles of sweat rolled down my spine, which I could attribute to anything from my fear of cooking, the heat of the stove, or Jett's presence. From the corners of my eyes I admired his abs, so strong and well defined, and the tattoo covering his arm. I knew I had to stop staring before he noticed, but I couldn't help myself. He looked so sexy peeling tomatoes, grating carrots, and chopping up herbs; my mind kept conjuring naughty ideas of me stripping off his jeans and having sex while our dinner boiled to perfection.

Jett shot me an amused look, sending a wave of heat through my cheeks and lower abdomen. "Something smells burned."

I blinked my brain back into action.

Oh, crap!

I forgot about the meat.

"Sorry." My skin prickled from the way his eyes seemed to caress me from a distance. I flipped the meat over and breathed out, relieved. It had turned a dark brown color but it was definitely not burned.

Jett moved behind me, his hands brushing mine as he helped me stir, then added the onions. His hot breath tickled my back, making me all too aware of just how close he stood.

"Want me to remove the pan from the stove?" I asked,

unable to control the hoarse undertone of my voice.

"No, the beef's not done for another few minutes."

It looked pretty done to me.

"You never told me where you learned to cook," I said.

I felt him stiffen behind me, hesitating. "After my father kicked me out and he cut off my allowance, I took a job in a restaurant kitchen. It was either that or get involved with drugs."

"You worked in a kitchen at sixteen? Is that even allowed?"

"I looked older and lied about my age. I needed the money." He spun me around until his eyes met mine. "My family was rich, Brooke, but everything I own I earned myself through hard work and loving what I do."

"I can't get over the fact that your father threw you out. If you hadn't been the strong person you are, staying off drugs, we might not be here, having this conversation. How could you forgive him and help him after all he's done to you?"

"I'd be lying if I told you I've forgiven him." He shrugged as if it didn't matter. But it did. I could see it in the hurt in his eyes and the hard lines around his mouth. "I hated him for a long time, but he's still my father, Brooke. If it wasn't for the shitty stuff he did to me, I wouldn't be who I am now. The trials of our lives make us strong, determined to succeed, to be different, both in body and spirit."

He took the spoon from my hand and stirred one more time, then added the peeled tomatoes, chopped carrots, and grated cheese to the mix.

The air was charged with tension. I could feel his struggle to remain calm in the midst of the hurricane raging inside, and I asked myself how much stronger that hurricane must have been when he was younger. A part of me wondered how many people knew the story of his life and upbringing—his true side, not the one he showed to his prospective business partners and the journalists writing about him in their stories.

He was beginning to trust me. Another first. Another step that proved to me he was serious about us. Affection's easy to gain, but trust is hard to get and yet so easy to crush and lose.

Jett took a deep breath, his eyes turning cold again. "You can forget what people said and did, but you never forget how they made you feel. You can forgive the people who hurt you, but you will remember what they taught you." His gaze searched mine, waiting for warmth and understanding, which I was more than eager to give him.

"He's not a bad man, Brooke. He was a strict father, and he threw me out because he believed in discipline, whereas my mother—she only thought of herself when she left us. She didn't stay in contact. She loved her drugs more than us, which was so much worse than anything my father ever did. At least he *cared* enough to stay. He helped me out of the hole I dug for myself. I can forgive him because he did what he had to do, but I'll never forget how he made me feel."

His eyes glazed over, his mind recalling memories I couldn't reach. I brushed his back gently and his attention returned to me. "Can I forgive my father for seeking the perversions of whatever Alessandro's club occasioned? Possibly. Will I forget the kind of man Robert is? Probably not."

He added the pasta to the boiling water, avoiding my gaze, but I caught the glint of anger shimmering in his eyes nonetheless. It wasn't aimed at me; it was at his family—the people who should've loved him unconditionally, yet betrayed him when he needed them the most. In that instant I understood why he thought his father deserved a chance. Robert had been there for him once, or at least more than Jett's mother, so Jett felt a sense of obligation toward the old man.

I imagined myself having Robert Mayfield as my father. Stern, hard, unrelenting, maybe even merciless. Having someone like him in my family, having to accept him just because he was my father, the only parent I had after the other one left. It wasn't a beautiful picture.

As if sensing the dark direction of my thoughts Jett

smiled at me weakly, and the warmth in his eyes returned, enveloping me like a safe bubble.

"I'd do anything to avoid being like them," he said softly.

I kissed the palm of his hand, wishing I could make him forget, or at least ease the burden of memories weighing down his soul. Returning his smile, I let my fingers glide up and down his sculpted arms. I wanted to help him forget, if only for a few minutes, and the only way I knew how to do that was to give him my passion. Looking up at him, I trailed my hand from his nipple to his abdomen. The top button of his jeans was undone and I could make out the happy trail of dark hair that always enticed me.

"Are you horny?" His piercing eyes turned a darker shade of green. I could see his instant desire in the way his jeans tightened around his groin and the way he watched me.

"A bit." I bit my lip. "And you?

"I'm always horny when you're around." He laughed, his voice hoarse and erotic, filled with a silent invitation. "You're sexy. You set everything on fire, and you know I can't keep my hands off you when you're looking at me like *this*."

He tugged at the belt of my bathrobe, opening it slowly. My blood rushed harder and my breath came faster. Towering over me, he looked at me with his sexy bedroom eyes, the kind of eyes that said everything along the lines: *I want you. I need you. And if you don't give me what I crave, I'll take it. And you'll like it. You'll love it. You'll want more.*

And I did. I wanted him. I wanted him so badly that I buried my hands in his hair, and I pressed my body against him, my desire burning through me like hot lava, burning my mind, burning through every barrier that held me back. His fingers caught hold of my hips, pulling me against him, and his mouth descended upon mine so hard, heat pooled between my legs.

"I fucking want you. I want you so hard." His fingers trailed down my thighs and then up again, his scorching touch sending my pulse into a frenzy. "I want you so much, I don't want you to be with anyone but me."

His hot lips moved to the corner of my mouth while his thumb stroked my cheek, the other hand caressing the sensitive spot between my legs. A soft moan escaped my mouth as he started to kiss my shoulders. His teeth grazed my skin. I imagined them on my nipples and on the inside of my thighs.

An unpleasant smell reached my nostrils.

"It's burning."

Our dinner was burning. Pushing Jett away, I reached out to remove the pan from the stove but he beat me to it.

"That's not the only thing burning here." His sexy smile made me melt like chocolate under his double meaning forbidden promise. "It's crazy how much you turn me on."

He switched off the stove, his fingers moving so fast I couldn't follow. One second I watched him brush aside the clutter covering the oversized kitchen counter, and the next second both of his hands cupped my ass and lifted me onto the counter. My bathrobe barely covered my naked body as he started to kiss my shoulders and my nipples, the bulge in his slacks rubbing hard and deliciously against my entrance.

"Jett," I whispered. "Is it really a good idea to do it here?"

"What's wrong with it? We've never done it in the kitchen. It's only a matter of time, so we might as well do it right here, right now."

"Good point."

How could I argue with that?

The tip of his tongue moistened his lower lip, leaving a glistering trail of moisture behind. My fingers clawed at his back, pulling him against me. His thumb started to rub my clitoris until I felt my juices slowly gathering between my legs, and then ever so slowly, he dipped his finger inside me, the rotating motion making me moan.

"You're turning me on," I whispered against his shoulder.

His finger moved faster, matching the pace of his thumb, as he thrust it in and out. I raised my hips and wrapped my thighs around his waist. My stomach quivered.

My whole body trembled for him as his thumb continued to stimulate my clit.

"I want you inside me."

"Not yet," Jett whispered. "You're so wet. Do you hear that?" He laughed quietly into my neck as he slid a second finger into me. My sex clenched around him, welcoming him with a squishing hum. "That's the sound of love, baby. That's how I know I turn you on."

Holy mother of pearls!

Did he have to be so blunt? My cheeks caught fire. I opened my mouth to protest, but he shut me up with a hot rich kiss, his talented fingers continuing to do their magic tricks, bringing me closer to the edge.

Holy cow.

This guy was good. Really good.

Higher and higher waves of arousal washed over me, and my head began to spin in the vortex only Jett could create. I didn't mind the vulnerability—lying naked on the kitchen counter. I didn't mind that the kitchen had two large windows and anyone could see me in the heights of lust. Hell, I didn't even mind Jett watching me circling my hips shamelessly against his talented hand. What I minded was not having him inside me when my orgasm was near. From the even thrusts of his fingers, I knew his little torture would get me there quickly.

As if sensing my thoughts, Jett's fingers pulled out of

me. "Are you ready for a deeper plunge?" His voice dripped with insinuation, as his thumb continued to circle around my clit.

I felt the prod of his erection against my sensitive entry and ran my hands down his chest, exploring the hardness of his muscles beneath my fingers. He kissed me as he spread my legs wider, his tongue tangling with mine, sucking it, nibbling my lips, while the length of his erection rubbed against my entry, spreading the moisture of our arousal.

"You have me, but are you mine?" Jett whispered, his deep voice sending another delicious pull through the depths of my sex. Did he have to talk when I was balancing on the edge of insanity, waiting for him to give me the final push? I was wet and in need of release; if he wouldn't give it, then I'd go for it and take it.

"I'm yours, Jett." I moistened my lips, the lust savaging my body, throbbing so hard I was ready to *demand* his rawness fill the emptiness inside me. I lifted my legs higher, my hips silently pleading with his hard shaft to enter me.

"I'll take you at your word."

His large erection slid deep into my wet sex, filling me, taking every inch I had to offer. I quivered with delight at the way his shaft felt inside me—moving, thrusting—slow but immensely deep. His groans became louder and faster as I matched his movements. With every pound my nerve endings caught fire anew, until my sheath contracted around him, sucking him deeper into me, creating a feeling of closeness and intimacy as he impaled and stretched me. Lost in him, I let go of everything but the sensation of him slamming into me.

Jett dipped his tongue into my mouth, mirroring the fast movements of his hips, his hard flesh plunging deep inside me. He told me how tight I was, how beautiful I was in my need for him, and how he felt my orgasm building as I arched my back to welcome his thrusts.

"Brooke," he moaned my name, a moment before my vision blurred and I bucked against him. Waves of pleasure rocked my body. A moment later thick hot moisture exploded inside me and he climaxed against my damp body, consumed by the pleasure my body had given him. And I drowned in the sea of release, the air heavy with our scent mixed the smell of herbs.

**

We were still panting when Jett buttoned up his jeans and helped me off the counter. I wrapped my bathrobe against my shivering body and tied my wet hair at the nape of my neck.

"Are you okay?" Jett placed a soft kiss on my forehead.

I nodded, figuring I didn't need a mirror to know that my cheeks were red and I was smiling, matching the grin on his face. I had never made love in a kitchen, so another first for us.

We cleaned up the mess and erased any proof of our intimate session in silence, enjoying each other's presence without the need to talk. By the time we were done it was a little after ten. Jett followed my glance to my watch and wrapped his arms around me whispering, "Tired?"

"Very."

"It's been a hard day. Do you care for a pre-midnight snack?" His eyes twinkled with mischief and for a moment I wasn't sure whether he was talking about food or sex—until he drained the pasta in a sieve.

"I'm starving," I said, ready to take whichever of the two options he offered. "You finish dinner while I get changed."

"Don't take too long, woman."

I giggled and moved past him. Upstairs, I slipped into a clean pair of jeans and a long-sleeved shirt. I was halfway through the foyer when I noticed Jett standing near the window, in the darkness of the living room.

"You scared me." I laughed uneasily.

"Shhh." He pressed a finger against his mouth and motioned me to step closer. I tiptoed to him, wondering what the heck was going on.

"What's wrong?" I whispered because his paranoia was contagious. He pulled the curtain aside so I could look. It took my eyes several seconds to adjust to the darkness and my brain another few seconds to process what I was seeing. A man was standing near the house, his features blurred in the moonlight so I couldn't make out his face.

"Stay here and be quiet," Jett whispered.

"Are you crazy? I'm not staying behind," I whispered. He shushed me by placing a finger on my lips, motioning me to stay. I watched him sneak to the door his hand wrapped around a gun. It had to be the same one I had seen in the car. He must have hid it in his jacket or in the grocery box. My hands covered my mouth to stifle a scream.

Oh God!

He was going to shoot and someone would get hurt.

My heart hammered so hard all I could hear was my blood rushing through my veins. And then my mind began to spin with possibilities. What if the other guy carried a gun too and he shot Jett? What if Jett killed him and we'd end up in even bigger trouble? What if there were more people outside waiting for Jett to walk blindly into a trap?

I wasn't going to let my guy die. He had to stay inside— with me— and keep that door closed so that nobody could enter and we could call for help.

"Jett, no." I whispered after him, shaking my head, signalling to stay. But he ignored me. Before I could move an inch, he was outside. Paralyzed by fear, I pulled the curtain aside. The intruder was gone and Jett disappeared out of my vision.

I wasn't going to stay and wait for disaster to strike. Before I could change my mind I dashed out the door as quietly as I could, aware that my breathing sounded like I had a saxophone inside my chest.

The night was pitch black. The moon hid behind thick clouds but the air was surprisingly balmy. Apart from the chirping of crickets, I could hear no sounds. I moved past the white balustrades and down the stone stairs, gravel crunching beneath my feet as I took a left turn toward where I *thought* I had seen Jett disappear through the window. My eyes were slowly adjusting to the darkness— good enough to show me the way, but too weak not to mistake tree shadows and branches for people. Still, my courage was stronger than my fear. It was true. Love gave me courage.

I walked around the house, almost reaching the front porch when Jett and another guy appeared in my line of vision.

"Drop your weapon before I shoot you." Jett's voice was cold, unrelenting. A voice that would not hesitate to hurt someone, a voice I had never heard before. A voice so damn sexy I would've smiled with pride at the fact that he was my man—if I wasn't so scared. A twig snapped under my feet. Jett turned his head sharply and in the darkness his gaze fell on me. I could almost see the angry lines around his mouth.

"What the fuck? Go back inside, Brooke."

Holy cow, he was hot when he was angry. His tone kept me transfixed to the spot, unable to follow his command.

"What did I tell you, Brooke? Get back inside," Jett hissed.

My feet felt like they were glued to the spot.

"Turn around," Jett ordered the man.

"Jett?" Holding up his hands, the guy spun around. The first two things I noticed about him were his black leather jacket draped around his arm and the tattoos on his naked biceps.

It was the same guy from the bar—the one Sylvie couldn't keep her hands off.

I blinked several times as I tried to match the man standing in front of Jett to the memory inside my head. Strong jaw. Pierced eyebrow. Sturdy build. And he was tall; almost as tall as Jett. Yeah, it was definitely the same person, and he still looked like a drug dealer.

"He must have followed us from the club," I said. "Should I call the police?"

"That's your girl?" the guy said. I couldn't help but notice the amusement in his tone. "I'm glad you found her, man."

"Kenny." Jett slapped his shoulder. "I was about to shoot you. Yeah, that's her."

"You know him?" I inched closer. Jett wrapped his arms around me and pulled me close, grinning.

"This is Kenny. We go way back," Jett said.

He stepped closer to me and extended his hand. "I'm Kenny. Jett's friend."

"Nice to meet you." I shook his hand, my heart still pounding because, in all honesty, I couldn't shake off the feeling he *was* involved in some shady business.

Your girl.

My mind circled around Kenny's words. Was that how Jett had titled me around his friends?

"What are you doing here?" Jett said, oblivious to the sudden burst of affection invading my heart. "Now it makes sense why I couldn't reach you."

"Went on a date." Kenny grinned.

I blinked because the answer was so obvious and yet I had to ask. "A date? With whom?"

"A blond girl—Sylvie," Kenny said.

Sylvie went on a date with *him* and didn't tell me? "Where is she?" I asked.

"She told me she couldn't use the front door because someone was home, so I walked her around the house. I had no clue you guys were in there. I thought she was living with her parents." Kenny seemed like a nice guy. Friendly. Good manners. Definitely not how I pictured him at all. And he was Jett's friend. I found myself warming up to him.

"Do you want to come in?" I asked. "We were about to eat but there's enough food and drink for everyone."

Jett raised his brow. I shrugged and smiled at Kenny in the hope he'd accept my invitation because I wanted to get to know Jett's friends. I wanted to know everything about him.

"Thanks," Kenny said.

We switched on the lights in the hall and were halfway to the kitchen when I spied Sylvie through the open living room door. At the sight of Kenny, she smiled and opened her mouth to explain. I cut her off.

"Yeah, I know. He told us already. Turns out he and Jett are friends."

"How long have you been involved?" Jett asked.

Sylvie's jaw dropped. "What the fuck is wrong with you? Do I look like I'm crazy and participating in a sect?"

"It's a club," I said. "And I think Jett was asking about Kenny and you."

Jett turned his head back to me, mild annoyance shimmering in his eyes. "I told you not to tell anybody."

"She didn't," Sylvie said. "I'm just psychic."

I laughed at her sarcasm. My laughter died in my throat at Jett's glare. "We've been best friends forever. She'd never betray my trust."

Sylvie's chin shot up and her eyes sparkled with pride.

"That's true. I'm the most trustworthy person in the world. Your secret's safe with me—even safer than with the CIA, and I've heard they keep secrets pretty well."

"Right," Jett muttered.

We were in the kitchen when Kenny said to Jett, "You pulled a fucking gun on me. Were you trying to impress her, man?"

"No need to. Did that already." Jett grinned and winked at me.

Earth, swallow me up whole!

"Sorry, I didn't want to interrupt you guys," Sylvie whispered.

"You didn't."

I forced a smile to my face and prayed she would mistake my blush for the beginning of sunburn. If she had entered the house a few minutes earlier she would have caught us in the middle of an intimate sex act.

"We were busy cooking. Right, Brooke?" Jett said. "I was teaching her how to prepare meat."

Kenny let out a low chuckle.

"Aw, that's nice," Sylvie said, oblivious to the shame burning inside me at Jett's double meaning, and the way his hand rested possessively on my ass like it belonged there.

22

I WOKE UP to the chirping of birds. The sun was shining, bathing the bedroom in a golden glow. Jett's side of the bed was empty but he had left a note on the nightstand.

I'll be back around 4. Stay in and keep your phone switched on! And thanks for dessert. It was THE best. Jett x.

Dessert. In that instant my mind transported me back in time to our love making, and I felt my cheeks heating up from the memory of him kissing me so deeply I forgot the world around me. I couldn't wait for more of that.

After a quick shower I put on clean clothes and then checked in on Sylvie. She was asleep, her long legs tangled in the sheet.

I sat down on the bed not so gingerly and pulled the sheet aside the way she always did when she woke me up.

"Hey," I said. "Wake up, sleeping beauty."

Groaning, she squinted and pulled the sheet out of my hand and over her head.

"Give me five minutes? I'm so tired."

"Sure. I'll be in the kitchen." I tickled her feet and she screamed, pulling away.

"Go away, Brooke."

Laughing, I left because Sylvie had a short temper, and it was only a matter of time before she threw a pillow at me.

I opened the back door to let in fresh air and brewed a pot of coffee. Sitting outside on the porch overlooking the woods, I sighed with pleasure as my mind began to rewind last night's firsts: first sex in the kitchen, first time meeting a friend of Jett's, our first dinner with friends. I almost squealed with delight at the realization that our relationship was developing beyond the bedroom. But what made my heart melt, and not because of the warm morning sun, was the fact that Jett had introduced me as 'his girl.' That was the most important milestone to date.

Half an hour later, just as I was about to get my second coffee fix for the day, Sylvie made her grand entrance, her usually perfect hair a big tousled mess.

"What?" She glared at my suppressed smile.

"Looks like you had a roll in the hay with Kenny."

"Rolling's not the only thing we did." She pointed to an empty wine bottle on the kitchen counter. "We helped ourselves from your future wine cellar and drank the whole thing in the pool."

My brows shot up. "At four a.m.?"

"I'm an early bird." She sat down at the kitchen table and hugged her naked knees to her chest. I pushed my mug of coffee into her hands.

"Sounds like you had fun," I said.

"We did, right before your guy demanded that Kenny accompany him to god knows where, and I went to bed." She took a big gulp out of my coffee and sighed with pleasure. "So what do you think of him?"

"Who? Kenny?"

She nodded.

Hesitating, I considered my words. She had never asked me about my opinion before. The sudden interest unnerved me, not least because I didn't know Kenny and had no idea what Sylvie wanted to hear. Jett had introduced Kenny as a computer expert and one of his oldest friends from 'earlier days,' so I could only guess they went through a lot together. Jett had turned his life around. Maybe Kenny did the same. At this point, I didn't want to come across as judgmental or overly enthusiastic, but I didn't want to see Sylvie hurt either.

"He's hot." I met her eager gaze and realized she was

hanging on my every word. Damn. "I think that even though he looks like a bad boy, it doesn't necessarily mean he'd ever let you down."

"Really?" Her blue eyes sparkled with delight, as though I had just confirmed her own thoughts.

I nodded and decided to change the subject. "Do you know where the guys are?"

"They didn't say." She tied her long blond hair at the nape of her neck and took another sip of coffee.

"It was a long night for you, huh?" I laughed at her expression as she lifted a hand to high-five me. Her eyes were a rich shade of baby blue—the kind of eyes that fooled you into thinking she was innocent, when in reality all she wanted was to have fun.

"Want more coffee?" I asked.

"I'd rather have breakfast. I'm starving."

I opened a cupboard and retrieved a box of cereal when my cellphone rang. I checked the caller ID, remembering Jett's instructions not to respond to any calls—not even from Alessandro's lawyer.

"It's Clarkson!" I said to Sylvie. We watched the phone ring a few times and then it stopped and a text appeared announcing that I had a voice message. I pressed the phone to my ear and listened.

"Good morning, Brooke. It's Ken Clarkson. I hope I'm not intruding. I'm sorry to inform you that Mr. Lucazzone suffered from a stroke last night. He's in a coma and the doctors cannot confirm that he'll make it. As your attorney, I will keep you up to date. Thank you, and if there is anything you need, please let me know."

His voice was polite but straightforward, almost unaffected. It was hard to believe that he was relaying bad news.

"What did he want?" Sylvie filled two bowls with cereal, poured milk on top, and then placed one in front of me. I watched the cocoa rings dye the milk a chocolaty hue.

"Alessandro had a stroke and the doctors don't know whether he'll ever wake up."

"I'm sorry, Brooke." She wrapped her arms around me and held me tight.

I took a deep breath, forcing my mind to stay rational. I wasn't attached to Alessandro, but I couldn't shake off the sadness at hearing he might not make it. Even though we weren't related by blood, he was a family member after all. Until we had concrete proof of his actions and intentions, I didn't want to see him as a bad person.

"I hope he'll be okay," I said.

We ate in silence and cleaned our bowls when Sylvie said, "I feel sick," and bolted out the door. I followed her into the bathroom and gathered her long hair at the nape of her neck as she emptied the contents of her stomach in the toilet.

"Are you okay?" I asked, stroking her back. She nodded. Frowning, I helped her up and re-arranged her clothes.

"I'm fine," she said weakly.

"Maybe the wine was too old." I had never seen her sick before and it was the most plausible explanation. Either that, or the hot weather and lack of sleep were catching up with her.

She held her hands under the cold-water faucet and then moistened her face. "Actually this was the third time. I was sick the last two days."

I passed her a towel. "Why didn't you tell me before? You need to see a doctor."

"I don't think I need to." She met my gaze. "My period's eight days late."

"You think you're—" I couldn't even finish *that* word.

"Yeah, I think I'm pregnant." She sat down on the cold bathroom tiles and pressed her back against the wall, her face buried in her palms. A pregnancy was one of her worst nightmares. The few times we talked about marriage and children, she had been adamant she never wanted any of those, which is why she always insisted on protection.

I squatted down in front of her, and grabbed her hands. "Are you sure?"

"No. Obviously, I'm not."

"Let's get a pregnancy test."

"What, now?"

"Yeah, now." I pulled her to her feet and squeezed my arm around her waist in case her nausea returned. Even though Jett instructed me to stay in, my best friend's peace of mind was a priority. "We get the test. No shopping. No other delays. And no telling Jett we were gone."

She smiled. "Sure."

***

On the way to Bellagio I held Sylvie's hands to comfort her.

"As long as we haven't seen the test results, there's no need to worry," I whispered. "It could be stomach flu or food poisoning."

"My period's always on time," she whispered back, ignoring my plausible explanations.

"Aren't you on the birth control pill?" I asked. We both were. She nodded. "Then you're okay. Trust me." I could only hope I wasn't overly positive, but the chance of a pregnancy was so minimal, I didn't see the sense in reinforcing her worries. "You cannot possibly fall pregnant within a few hours."

She looked up. "Actually, this isn't the first time Kenny and I did it."

"When?"

"Uhm…" She buried her face in her hands again, hiding

from me.

"Sylvie?"

"I'm sorry, Brooke. It was the day when you went on a date with Jett."

Was that the time he showed me his boat? "The day you said you went to Bellagio instead of Milan?"

She nodded.

"You didn't." I gasped. "You lied to me!"

"So did you!"

I couldn't deny that.

"Geez, Sylvie. You could have been abducted." My head was spinning from all the horrendous things that could've happened to her.

"I'm sorry. I didn't want to tell you because I thought you were hurting, and I wanted the focus to be on you. It just didn't seem fair that I had found someone I liked while your heart was broken."

"It's okay." I squeezed her hand reassuringly. "You said you were sick several times in the last three days. Technically, Kenny couldn't be the father."

"Who then?" She peered at me, confused—and then realization dawned on her. "Shit. I hope I'm not knocked up by that asshole."

With asshole, she was referring to her ex, a married man who first tricked her into believing he was single, and then that he wanted a relationship with her. Just like Jett, Ryan happened to be her boss, with the only difference that he fired Sylvie when his wife found out about the affair.

"Let's just hope it's food poisoning," I whispered.

23

TRAVELING TO BELLAGIO to get a home pregnancy test was a bad idea. Not only did Sylvie end up buying three, she also managed to convince me she needed a whole lot of other stuff. As soon as we reached the main street she dragged me from shop to shop, and she ended up with a new pair of shoes, a light summer dress, and a bottle of après sun lotion for me—which I'm pretty sure I didn't really need...that much. On the bright side, she didn't dawdle trying on clothes because she looked amazing in anything she wore. Miraculously, the whole shopping spree took her only half an hour.

It was shortly after noon when the taxi driver stopped in front of the house. I was about to unlock the front door when my cellphone rang again. I fished it out of my handbag and checked the caller ID. It was Jett.

"Where are you?" he barked. My heart skipped a beat.

"Stop worrying. I'm fine," I said. It was the truth. We were still living and breathing. Basically, nobody got hurt so he didn't need to know my little secret.

He let out a long breath. "Good. We're on our way back and should be there in twenty minutes."

He hung up and I relayed the message to Sylvie.

"We need to hurry," she said.

I followed her to the bathroom and sat down on the floor, realizing she was going to use the pregnancy test.

"I can't read the instructions. They're in Italian. But we should be fine anyway. You see this stuff on TV all the time." She tore one of the foils to remove the test stick and held it up to me. "What do I do now? Stick it into a glass of urine or what?"

How would I know?

It wasn't like I had ever needed one of those.

"I think you need to turn the test stick so that the purple side of the handle is facing you. And then you hold the other side into your stream of urine."

"Okay. Turn around."

I tried not to listen to the gushing sound. Barely a minute later, she tapped my shoulder. "You can turn around now."

"Finished already?" I sat up and regarded the stick in her hand.

"Yeah. What's next?"

"I don't know. I'd say put the cap back on and then put it on the table."

"For how long?"

"A few minutes, I guess." I thought back to all the TV advertisements I had ever seen and not paid attention to when I should have. The knowledge would have come in handy.

Sylvie turned on the water faucet and washed her hands. I stroked her back. "You'll be okay. Even if you're pregnant, it's not the end of the world."

"I know," she whispered, staring at herself in the mirror. "But I'm not ready to be a mom. I don't want to be a single mother raising a kid."

We stood in silence as the seconds ticked by.

"I can't look. Can you look for me?" Sylvie said eventually.

"Sure." I lifted the pregnancy test and held it up to examine the pink colored band in the small window.

Sylvie peered over my shoulders. "Am I pregnant?"

"I don't know. I think two bands stand for a positive result, so I'd say no."

She let out a whoop of joy, her smile dying on her lips almost instantly. "What do you mean 'I think?'"

I shrugged. "It's not like I'm an expert or anything."

"Why can't they just mark it P for positive and a smiley

for *not pregnant?*"

I laughed at her attempt at infusing humor. "You should give it another go in case you didn't hold it under the stream long enough."

"Oh right. I thought dipping it in there was enough." She smirked and grabbed another test. I turned away to give her privacy.

"Hey, Brooke. On the off chance I'm not reading this right, can you try the third one? Comparing my result with yours would make me feel better. I don't want to think I'm not pregnant and then find out I am when it's too late."

"Sure. Just give me a minute." I took the stick from Sylvie's outstretched hand and waited until she walked out of the bathroom, leaving the door ajar. Using a pregnancy test when I wasn't pregnant was definitely strange, but I had done stranger things to help Sylvie out.

A minute later I was done and called Sylvie back in. She held out her hand. I handed the pregnancy test to her and she placed it on the marble counter.

"With your result we can't be wrong," she said.

"Yeah." I sat down on the edge of the bathtub and tapped my fingers against my thigh, waiting.

"Brooke," Sylvie whispered. Sensing the sudden tension in her voice, I turned and followed her line of vision, my heart slumping in my chest. "Didn't you say two bands means pregnant? Yours is showing two."

I snatched the test from her hand and stared at it, my mind unable to comprehend the meaning of it all. There were two lines, which had to be a mistake.

"Oh shit." Sylvie laughed. "*You* are pregnant."

"I can't be." My voice failed me as I tried to make sense of the situation. "Did you switch the sticks? If you did, it's not funny."

"It's not a prank. I'd never do that." Which was true. She didn't like jokes, or playing games.

I frowned. "Honestly, it must be a mistake. I'm on the pill. My period is due any minute. Maybe I got it all wrong and one band means pregnancy and two means nothing. It could be an Italian thing or the brand differs from those advertised back home."

I felt myself panicking but couldn't stop it.

Take a deep breath, Stewart.

"You're kidding, right?" Sylvie said. "The instructions are in Italian, but in the end all pregnancy tests are the same and they work the same way."

Oh God!

Denial is bliss.

I shook my head. "No, you're the one feeling sick and I'm okay. Besides, my period—" I broke off, unable to process the shock. My period was never really on time. It changed like the weather. So that argument wasn't valid.

"It can't be, Sylvie," I murmured. "I never forget to take

the pill. Every single day, at the same time. It must be false positive."

"Nothing's a hundred percent safe, and particularly not if you're sick or there's something wrong with your hormones." She squeezed my arm gently. "Like you said, it's not the end of the world."

"I only tried to be supportive when I said that." I thought back to my first trip to Bellagio. Jett and I were staying at his house. During one dinner, I got intoxicated and sick. It wasn't my proudest moment, which is why I must have repressed it and never told Sylvie about it. Maybe the few glasses of wine messed with my hormones.

"It's a false positive," I whispered. "It has to be because we've only been dating for a few weeks, and it doesn't happen that fast."

Sylvie threw the pregnancy tests in the garbage bin and grabbed my arm, forcing me to follow her to the library.

"What are you doing?" I asked as she sat down in front of the computer.

"Googling pregnancy tests."

"The guys will be back any minute."

"Let's hope this old thing's fast." She heaved a long sigh as we waited for the computer to boot. It whirred idly, like it had all the time in the world. Waiting wasn't good. It made me anxious. I could feel dark clouds descending upon my head.

"That's it," Sylvie said, turning on the browser and navigating to a search engine. Her longer fingers moved over the keyboard effortlessly and then, with one click, I had my answer.

Two bands…positive.

"You're pregnant. Congratulations!" Sylvie said, grinning. "It's not me; it's you."

I glared at her, ignoring the sudden urge to pour a glass of water over her head. I felt so faint my legs threatened to buckle beneath me.

"Brooke? Oh, shit," Sylvie said. "Come on. Sit down. Don't be upset. You know I didn't mean it like that."

"Impossible. The test— " Sitting in her chair, I took a deep breath and let it out slowly. "—is wrong. I don't feel pregnant." Lying to myself gave me a false sense of relief, so I kept going because it was easier than facing the truth.

"We'll repeat the test, maybe even go to the doctor's to check your blood results."

Which meant waiting at least a day or as long as it'd take to get an appointment. I couldn't wait. Sylvie grabbed me in a tight hug and I rested my head against her chest, letting her stroke my hair, her soothing voice barely reaching me. "Don't worry, Brooke, it'll be okay." She kept repeating those stupid words I said. "It's not the end of the world."

It is the end of the world. Definitely.

"No." I shook my head. "I'm doomed."

I wanted to be a mom one day; just not at this point. The thought of telling Jett filled me with dread. A pregnancy so early, when we barely knew each other, could ruin my relationship. He'd run, like most men do. He'd run as fast as he could, and that would hurt me more than anything in the world. I didn't want to lose him because of a mistake. A stupid mistake occurring under the influence of alcohol.

"You'll have to tell him," Sylvie said, deleting the browser history and switching off the computer. "It might seem scary now. But once you do, you'll find out whether it was just a fling or more. And if he breaks up, which I hope he won't, then you can either let it define you or strengthen you. And there's always *that* option," she whispered. "You can get rid of it and he'll never know."

I thought about it for all of three seconds. "That's not me."

She smiled and brushed my hair off my face. "I know and I would never encourage you to do that. It would destroy you, haunt you for the rest of your life, and that's a lot worse than the pain you'd feel if he let you down."

24

IN THE SILENCE of the house we heard the car pull up outside and the doors slam shut. Figuring I was too shaken to face Jett, I hid inside the bathroom. Through the walls I still could hear them downstairs, chatting and laughing. I pressed my feverish forehead against the cool wall tiles when a knock on my bathroom door made me flinch.

"Brooke?" It was Jett. The strained undertones in his voice betrayed his worry. "Sylvie said you're in here."

"Wait." Jumping to my feet, I straightened my clothes and stepped out of the bathroom, closing the door behind me. I curled my lips into a smile, praying it looked genuine enough to fool him. My pulse leaped as he lifted me up in his arms, and my stomach began to flutter at the way his lips brushed against mine, exploring my mouth as though we hadn't seen each other in weeks.

"Are you okay?" he said after putting me back down.

"Just a headache. That's all." It wasn't even a lie. Ever

since discovering my possible pregnancy, I felt physically sick and my head was a throbbing pulp.

"Where were you?" I tried to keep my tone casual in my attempt to steer the conversation to him.

"We had the license plate checked. It was a waste of time. It's not registered and thus fake." He smirked and grabbed my hand. His fingers interlaced with mine. On any other occasion, his touch would have pleased me, but today it only managed to make me feel even worse.

"I'm sorry."

"Don't be, baby. Kenny's hacking into Lucazzone's computer today. I'm confident if there's something, Kenny will unearth it."

He walked downstairs to join Kenny and Sylvie. I felt Sylvie scrutinizing me, watching my every move. I grimaced at her in the hope she'd get the hint to act normally. The last thing I needed was being examined like a bizarre specimen at the local zoo. Jett wasn't stupid. He'd catch that something was wrong in a heartbeat.

"Did you tell her about the computer?" Kenny asked. At Jett's nod Kenny turned to me. "Are you okay with it? The hard drive will be destroyed beyond repair and you'll have to throw it away."

Sylvie shot me a sideway glance. I could smell her fear in the air and gave her a noncommittal shrug. She had deleted the browser history so we had nothing to worry about.

"Sure, Kenny. Do whatever you need to do. It's not like I intend to keep it."

"Good." He snatched his rucksack and headed out, calling over his shoulder, "Because it can go two ways: Either we get into his computer, retrieve the information, and destroy the disk in the process. Or we find nothing, but the hard drive's done. Either way, what we do will leave a trail behind. A pro will be able to tell and there's no going back."

I swallowed hard. If Alessandro decided to check, he'd find out that his guests had been snooping around the place. Did I really want that?

"Brooke." Jett nodded at me encouragingly. "We talked about this in the basement, remember? You have a right to know."

"I know. I just—" I exhaled a slow breath. I could always tell Alessandro the computer broke down and I bought him a new one. "Okay."

Kenny laid out all the tools, then started to disassemble the computer, explaining each step.

"If the hard drive was erased, a pro might take weeks, maybe even months to retrieve the data. If you use a good data destruction software, no one will ever recover anything."

"We don't have weeks or months," Jett said.

Kenny shrugged. "I'm just saying, man. The fact that you used the internet means the hard drive's not destroyed, so he probably performed a wipe-out. What was the guy's name again?"

"Lucazzone," I said. "So how long do you think *you'll* take?"

"That depends. Maybe an hour."

Kenny continued his chatter as he removed the hard drive and pushed it into what looked like a black box, which he called an enclosure, and connected it to his computer. It all looked so complicated and, judging from Sylvie's expression, boring. All I could see was a black screen—until he opened a program and the data transfer began.

"The software's doing its own rewriting during the data retrieval process. We're burning the entire information as an ISO image on this disk to make sure we have a backup," Kenny said, popping a mini CD-ROM into his computer.

I could see Sylvie was bored out of her mind from the way she suppressed a yawn, which made me laugh. She suffered from a short attention span, and in particular when a conversation involved sports, computers, or anything with no relation to fashion, men, or parties.

"So boring," Sylvie mouthed. "Come on."

I shook my head.

She grimaced and turned to Jett, gesturing at me. "Do you mind if I borrow her?"

"You have thirty minutes, then I want her back," Jett said.

Sylvie pulled me into the kitchen and closed the door behind us.

"You okay?" she whispered.

I hated when people asked that question. The desired answer is yes, even when you don't feel like it.

"Don't ask," I said.

"I just want to make sure you're okay."

"I'm fine." I groaned inwardly at her skeptical expression. "Please, Sylvie, I don't want to think about anything anymore. *Please*?"

"Sure." Pouting, she sat down and regarded me. I grabbed the opportunity to change the subject.

"Remember when I told you a private investigator found a diary in the chapel?" I waited until she nodded before I continued. "I've always wanted to locate it."

Her eyes narrowed conspiratorially. "Do you want to—" She trailed off, leaving the rest unsaid.

I looked out the window at the lush green scenery and the dense woods stretching as far as I could see. "It's stopped raining. I say we go check out the chapel."

"Is it far?"

"No. Come on. I'll show you."

Our flip-flops sank into the damp earth, and the grass and fallen twigs scratched our feet as we made our way down the staircase and through the bushes.

"It's nice," Sylvie remarked as we finally reached the chapel. I walked around the tiny building and tried to peer through the small window. The glass was too dirty to make out much, but the wild rosebushes near the door told me at some point someone must have cared enough to plant them.

Sylvie pushed the rosebushes aside and moved past them, barely paying attention to their fragile beauty and the way they seemed to huddle together to protect themselves from nature's unpredictable forces.

We split up as we circled the chapel and finally found what we were looking for: a small door with a tiny but intricate cross engraved into the wood. I tried the door and to my surprise it wasn't locked.

"I'm going in," I said. Sylvie stared at me with an expression that screamed sheer dread. As if the thought unnerved her, she took a step back.

"No way. I'm not going in there. Sorry, you're on your own."

"It's in the middle of the day. What do you think could possibly happen to you?" Her face made me smile. "Okay, stay here."

I pried the heavy door open and stepped into the semi dark room. It was bigger than it looked from outside—

maybe the size of a bathroom—and accommodated two benches set up in front of an altar. The walls were covered in religious paintings. At the front of the altar was the sculpture of a sitting angel, his eyes cast on the concrete floor, appearing to be in deep thought, his face a mask of melancholy. I wondered whether Maria had felt that way during her marriage. I didn't know a lot about the woman, but I had a strong feeling the chapel hadn't been just a place of worship; it had also doubled as a refuge.

Kneeling, I made a cross sign and sat down on a bench, my gaze scanning the dirty window—the only source of light. Branches scratched against the glass and the unnerving sound carried over like a silent warning. In that instant I felt something in the air—a shiver of sadness. This place was filled with hopelessness, just like the woman who had come here to seek spiritual comfort. Maybe something terrible happened and she was ashamed of Alessandro's actions, and this was the only place of peace she could find.

"Found anything?" Sylvie called, jerking me out of my thoughts. I turned to see her standing in the doorway with her arms crossed over her chest and a frown darkening her features.

"Not yet," I said.

"Hurry up. This place gives me the creeps."

Jett's report specifically mentioned the diary had been buried, but the floor and walls were made of stone. I commenced my investigation by searching under the benches and altar for any hiding place large enough to fit a book or a diary, then brushed my hands over the stonewalls to make sure I wasn't missing a loose stone. I checked the religious paintings twice before I returned to Sylvie, convinced whoever removed the diary never put it back in its hiding place.

"If you wanted to hide something personal, where would you put it?" I asked.

Sylvie shrugged. "I'd do what normal people do and get a safe."

I laughed. "That's not exactly hiding. Anyone could force you into giving away the lock combination."

"I guess." She paused. "You could always bury a hole in the ground."

"That's a good one." I scanned the yard and the overgrown thicket. Maria could have buried her diary anywhere on the estate, including under the rosebushes leading from the chapel to the backyard and around the house.

"What exactly are you looking for?" Sylvie asked. "I mean, even if we find the original hiding spot, the diary isn't there."

"You're right." I bent down and ran my hand through the damp earth, letting it crumble between my fingers. Jett told me the PI took the diary and then one day it was lost.

How could I explain to Sylvie that I was trying to find out what kind of life my great aunt had once led?

"I was hoping I might find something—anything that would help me visualize her life." I smiled, realizing just how ridiculous I sounded. Human life's so much more complex than a few diary entries. Even if the diary was still buried here somewhere and I found it, I couldn't possibly read her emotions and the kind of person she was from a few words strung together. Judging from Sylvie's skeptical look, she thought the same.

A strong wind rustled the leaves and raindrops began to drizzle down.

"Let's get back inside. I'm cold." Sylvie said. "We'll dig up the whole place another day."

I was about to follow her, when a movement in my peripheral vision caught my attention. I scanned the woods. All I could see were trees, their wide crowns casting ominous shadows, and yet I couldn't shake off the overwhelming feeling of being watched.

"Brooke?" Sylvie called. "Are you coming?"

"I thought I saw something." I turned away from the woods reluctantly.

"Of course. If I inherited an estate with an eerie chapel, I'd think it's haunted, too."

She was laughing at me. I slapped the back of her head gently. "That's not what I meant. It looked like a tall figure dressed in black."

"Now you're creeping me out. Can we please go inside?" Sylvie whispered.

"It was probably nothing anyway." I tried to infuse as much confidence into my voice as I could gather, but my glance trailed back to the trees. "I'm a little paranoid." My words didn't sound particularly convincing.

"I would be too if someone tried to kill me," Sylvie said, yanking at my arm. "Nothing against you, Stewart, but I feel safer around the guys."

We barely reached the house when the rain turned into a torrential downpour. Sylvie locked the backdoor behind us and I switched on the lights. She brewed us our obligatory afternoon coffee while I stood in front of the large bay window, staring at the puddles of rain and my reflection, unable to shake off the feeling of being watched.

***

We decided to drink our coffee with the guys in the library. The moment we entered, Jett's arms moved around my waist and stayed there, his chin resting against my head. I could feel his heart beating in unison with mine as his body heat warmed my skin.

"Why are you wet?" he whispered.

"We visited the chapel."

He looked at me but didn't break our embrace. "How is it?"

"It's beautiful." I paused to consider my words and found that none could do it justice. "You should check it out one day. See for yourself."

"Did you find anything yet?" Sylvie asked, her hands resting on Kenny's shoulders, her eyes fixed on the computer. My eyes moved from her to Kenny's arms and for the first time I noticed one of his tattoos looked like Jett's.

"We're getting there," Jett said, his lips descending to nuzzle my neck.

I tried to twist my way out of his arms. He didn't let go. "What have you found so far?"

"We haven't checked everything but—" Jett held up the disk and smiled triumphantly "—the entire hard drive is on *this* disk."

There was something in his tone that made me look up. "What's on it?"

"It's going to take days to go through everything but we found a file containing a spreadsheet with numbers. I've written a couple of them down," Kenny said, pointing to the indecipherable handwriting on a sheet of paper.

"What do you need the numbers for?" Sylvie picked up

the paper and walked over to me so we could look together.

"The first three digits of each and every number match the corresponding line in the black book," Jett replied. I met his glance and something passed between us. "They're all here. Look them up."

I counted the rows. There were thirty-six in total—the exact same total of numbers. The first row on the paper started with the same three digits like the one in the black book.

"Okay," I said. "The corresponding lines start out the same, but after three digits the code seems to change?"

Jett nodded.

"What do you think they are?" I asked.

"If you count the number of digits, I'd go for sort codes, bank accounts, or passwords," Kenny said. "And since Jett has financial relations here, I suggest we drive to his bank and make a discreet enquiry."

"I could give my advisor a call and ask to see him today," Jett said.

"And if that doesn't work out, I'll hack into the bank's system," Kenny said.

"Nothing new there." Jett grinned at me, revealing his gorgeous dimples. "Kenny's the best money can hire. No wonder he's so popular."

A professional hacker? Holy cow.

I had assumed that was just a joke. I bit my lip to hide my shocked expression.

"That's so hot," Sylvie mouthed to me.

Of course she was into bad guys. And if they could do something as illegal as hacking into a bank's database, they immediately attained 'keeper' status for sure.

25

WE ARRIVED IN Bellagio in Jett's replacement car. Jett drove, Kenny sat in the passenger seat, while Sylvie and I huddled together in the backseat. My head was throbbing so hard, I felt slightly nauseous. Maybe it was the prospect of being pregnant, or maybe my nausea was the result of being pregnant. Either way, I was scared out of my mind.

I rested my head against the cold glass window and closed my eyes, the sound of the rain splashing down on the asphalt relaxing me. All I could think of was how my life had changed into a mess. Just when I thought it couldn't get more complicated, life twirled up another whirlwind of chaos, pushing me into unknown territory.

There's nothing more frightening than not knowing what the future will bring. A baby was one of the biggest challenges I could think of. I had no job, no money, and knew nothing about raising kids.

"We need to get some aspirin from the drug store," Sylvie said to no one in particular.

You have enough aspirin to last you for a year, I wanted to say when I noticed her conspiratorial smile and consequent wink. She wanted to get rid of the guys, of course.

"There's a large one on the main street. We could pop in quickly," Jett said, making it clear he wasn't going to let us out of his sight. His worried gaze brushed over me in the rearview mirror, and I shot him a weak smile.

A few minutes later the car came to a halt in front of the drug store. This was our chance to get out before he found a parking spot.

"You stay here. We'll be back in a minute," I said, opening the car door before Jett could argue.

"Be quick," he called after us.

The rain was falling so heavily, we dashed for the store, eager to take refuge. Through the glass windows I could see Jett and Kenny's eyes following our every move. Figuring we had no time to waste, we headed straight for the counter.

"We need more pregnancy tests," Sylvie said to the same lady, who'd served us on our first visit. "One from each brand you have in stock."

The woman nodded and smiled at me, probably sensing my turmoil.

"Oh, and a pack of aspirin," Sylvie added, nodding toward the window.

"Why do you need so many?" I whispered, pointing to the tests.

She shrugged. "What if they're faulty? We want to be sure either way."

We paid quickly, hid the pregnancy tests inside Sylvie's huge designer bag, and walked out holding the plastic bag containing the aspirin.

"Thanks," I whispered to her before we reached the car. I really appreciated her support.

"You know I'm always here for you, no matter what."

With a questioning glance aimed at me, Jett started the engine and joined the main traffic, heading for the bank.

"Where's the paper?" he asked as soon as he had parked the car. Kenny handed it to him and Jett folded it in half.

"Okay, this is what we do next," Jett said. "You stay here with the girls while I meet with my bank advisor and pretend I have to transfer money to two accounts. Don't come after me and don't leave the car."

"Got it," Kenny said. And then Jett was gone.

***

The silence in the car felt awkward. Sylvie played with her hair, Kenny stared out the windows, and I was busy fidgeting with the hem of my shirt. I used the moment to get a good look at Kenny, not least because he seemed to genuinely care about Sylvie and I sort of wanted her to date one of Jett's friends.

From up close, I couldn't deny Kenny was attractive. His strong features and cropped dark hair gave him a somewhat rough and manly edge—quite the opposite of Sylvie, who looked as sweet as a pie. If someone could see past the tattoos that covered half of his neck, his left arm, and his whole shoulder and back—or so I was told—he might just scrub up well enough to meet Sylvie's rich parents. I smiled at the prospect, until I realized he lacked two important features: money and success. Sylvie never talked much about her parents, but it was enough to know they valued social status higher than personality.

"The spreadsheet's the only thing you found so far?" Sylvie asked Kenny.

"No." He threw us a fleeting look over his shoulder. "I've discovered a whole lot of other stuff, but it's all irrelevant."

Focus on I.

He had not yet shared his findings with Jett. I swallowed hard.

As if on cue, Kenny's eyes rested on me. His expression was impassive, but his eyes twinkled. I couldn't help but feel slightly alarmed. Did he know? Could he somehow have tapped into our search engine history and stumbled upon the word 'pregnancy?'

"What stuff?" I narrowed my gaze and a silent warning passed between us.

"Favorite bookmarks like certain sports pages, Facebook pages and Wikipedia. Cookies people always fail to delete… that sort of thing." He didn't smile, but his dark blue eyes twinkled again. "Like I said, all irrelevant."

My heart banged hard against my ribs.

He knew.

I could see it in his eyes. Hear it in his words.

"I guess *he* wasn't careful enough," I suggested, meaning I hadn't been careful enough to erase any traces and because I was the soon-to-be owner, Kenny probably thought the info material on pregnancies concerned me.

"I'm good at this stuff. I pick things up. It's like they just fall into my lap." Kenny leaned back in his chair and put his iPod speakers on, the sound of hard rock making me even more nervous.

Damn it, Stewart.

Of course deleting the browser history wasn't good enough when it came to hiding something from a professional hacker. Sylvie and I forgot to clear the cookies, and that's probably one of the first things someone like Kenny would check before trying to recover previous versions of the hard drive. I was ready to bet my pay check he could probably retrieve any sort of information, including the time one used the internet long after I reset the browser.

"What is he talking about?" Sylvie whispered.

I shrugged and shook my head.

After what felt like half an hour, Jett finally left the bank. My stomach fluttered as I watched him cross the street. Tall. Mesmerizing. Dark hair and perfect bone structure. A body to die for. It made me almost anxious to know he was with me.

He opened the car door and slumped into the driver's seat. From the way he threw the bag to Kenny before slamming the door shut, I could tell he was angry.

"Anything?" Kenny asked, switching off the music.

"Nothing." Jett started the engine and steered the car out of the parking lot, his face emotionless. He was pissed off big time though, which was obvious from his driving— faster than usual.

"What did—" Sylvie began. I elbowed her gently and shook my head, my glare uttering a silent warning.

Jett's hands tightened on the steering wheel until the white of his knuckles showed through his skin, but he remained quiet. Knowing Jett, letting him calm first was the only way anyone would get him to talk. He'd start the conversation when he was ready.

Half-way back to the estate I noticed his muscles

relaxing a little.

"I checked the first two numbers, and then I tried three more," Jett finally said, breaking the silence. "They're not bank accounts. The file we found is a dead end."

"Maybe they're passcodes," Kenny suggested.

"Passcodes to what?" Jett's frown line deepened.

Unaffected by Jett's frostiness, Kenny leaned back into his seat and shrugged as Sylvie and I kept swapping curious glances.

"Maybe someone deliberately created confusion, so you wouldn't find out the answer," Kenny said. "The right combination could be linking the first three digits of the first half of the list with the last three digits of the second half. It's just a suggestion. I doubt anyone would make this easy on you."

"Or they could be different kind of accounts. Not necessarily bank accounts," I chimed in.

"I can't go back without raising suspicion," Jett muttered. "Either you find out more, or you hack into wherever you think is necessary to give me something I can work with."

"That was exactly my plan, bro." Kenny opened a foil wrapper and shoved a piece of chewing gum into his mouth, before tossing the whole pack to me and Sylvie, leaving a piece near the gearshift for Jett.

26

BY THE TIME we reached the estate Jett's bad mood had lifted. We had walked up the stairs when Jett pushed me behind his back and motioned Kenny to be quiet. I scanned the area anxiously and my gaze fell on the front door. It stood ajar, just a few inches, but strangely enough, my first thought was that I might have forgotten to lock it when we left.

In spite of my heartbeat spiking, my mind remained surprisingly calm. Maybe because the rain had stopped and the sun was shining, clearing the dark clouds and making it seem surreal that someone could have broken into the house in the middle of the day.

Pulling out his gun, Jett instructed me to hide with Sylvie behind the bushes on the other side of the house, and stay there no matter what. And then he and Kenny were gone.

"Come on," I whispered to Sylvie, dragging her to the nearby bushes. We fought our way through the dense undergrowth, careful not to scratch our arms and legs. Reaching the backyard, we stooped down and I wrapped my arm around Sylvie. Our gazes remained glued to the closed balcony door and the house beyond while I listened for any sounds.

I began to count the seconds inside my head when a gunshot echoed to my right, then another, and a startled yelp escaped my lips. My heart stopped dead in my chest and I found myself leaping up and running across the open terrain around the house and through the front door—my legs shaking bad, my lips trembling with Jett's name on them, my mind unaware of the fact that if anyone decided to shoot I was an easy target.

"Jett," I shouted, running straight into his arms, happy to find him safe. The foyer was as silent as a tomb and Jett was alone—the realization sent a jolt of ice through my veins. "Where's Kenny?"

"He took off after the guy."

"Are you hurt?" I brushed my fingers over Jett's arms and chest, checking for any wounds.

"No, but listen. I need you to stay inside, hidden. Okay?" He kissed me absentmindedly and turned to leave. I gripped his upper arm, a rather feeble attempt at stopping him. "Please, don't go. I don't want you to get hurt."

"I'm not getting hurt, baby," he whispered.

"What's going on?" Sylvie asked, her face a ghastly shade of white.

"Kenny's following the intruder," I said.

Her hands moved up to her chest. I wrapped my arms around her and pulled her aside. "He'll be okay."

For the first time I noticed the place was ransacked. Almost every drawer had been opened and the contents scattered onto the floor.

"Maybe we should lock ourselves up in the kitchen," I whispered to Sylvie, figuring that was the only place with an escape exit through the backdoor and plenty of weapons in case we needed to defend ourselves.

We waited in the kitchen in silence until we heard footsteps departing. Ever so gently, I locked the kitchen door behind us, grabbed a big butcher-like knife from the knife rack, and motioned Sylvie to hide behind the kitchen cupboards. Forcing myself to breathe quietly, I listened for any sounds.

***

"Brooke?" Jett's voice called from the hall. The strained undertones betrayed his worry.

"We're in here," Sylvie shouted.

My hand still clasped around the knife, I unlocked the door and opened it. Jett and Kenny were standing in the hall, their faces hard, betraying nothing. Sylvie jumped into Kenny's arms. I was tempted to do the same with Jett, but refrained from it.

"Are you guys okay?" she asked, clinging to Kenny for dear life. "We've been worried sick about you. Thank God no one's dead."

"We're okay," Jett said. "We couldn't get them though."

Them?

I raised my eyebrows and hid my hands behind my back so he wouldn't see the knife, or my shaking fingers. "How many are we talking about?"

"Two. One broke in; the other one waited in the car. They sped off."

"Was it the same car that chased us?" I asked.

"I don't think so," Jett said. "They wore ski masks and the car had no license plate, but I'm pretty sure it wasn't the same car."

"They spoke English. Right, bro?" Kenny said to Jett. "I heard the first one yelling something. You almost hit him."

"You *shot* him?" I asked Jett, horrified.

What did you expect, Stewart?

Of course I knew violence was to be expected in such a situation, but the knowledge didn't make it any easier to accept.

"I didn't hit him," Jett mumbled. "Unfortunately. Let's check what they took." I stared at Jett open-mouthed. There was something in his look—just a tiny flicker, but enough to show me he was hiding something and was trying hard to divert my attention from it.

"Jett, what's wrong?" I scanned his body to make sure he hadn't been shot. "Are you hurt?" My hands brushed his arms. That's when I noticed the tiny blood splatters on his shirt.

"It's just a scratch," Jett said. "Don't worry about it. I've seen worse."

My throat tightened at his words. Who would say something like that?

"How did it happen?" I pulled at his arm to force him to sit down. He flinched but didn't move.

"Knife. I didn't seem him and he surprised me."

"Let me see." Ignoring Jett's protest, I pulled his shirt up and gasped at the two-inch wound on his torso. It was no longer bleeding and it didn't look deep, but he'd need at least proper sanitizing, if not stitches. I didn't want his beautiful skin blemished, nor did I want him to endure any sort of pain.

"We're going to the hospital."

"It's just a scratch, baby," Jett said, pulling the shirt back down.

"We need to treat that." I glared at him, annoyed by the determined look in his eyes.

"I said not now." He pushed my hand away and started off down the hall toward the library.

Damn his stubbornness and unwillingness to give in.

I hurried after him and stopped in the doorway, ready to argue some more when Kenny let out a string of expletives.

"What's wrong?" Jett asked.

Kenny pointed to Alessandro's computer. It was still there. "Everything that's important is gone."

"What do you mean by everything?" I asked slowly.

"The financial reports, Lucazzone's papers, the book, and the disk."

I stared at Jett open-mouthed. My vision blurred and my head felt so light, I thought I might faint on the spot. "Everything?" I whispered.

Kenny nodded.

"Fuck." It was the second time I heard Jett swear.

***

We tidied up the place so Alessandro's household staff wouldn't notice the break-in. As far as I could tell, except for the evidence nothing else was stolen, nothing was broken. We worked hard to make the place look like it had before. Even though every piece of evidence was gone, Jett insisted we leave. We didn't go to bed that night. After cleaning up, he gave Sylvie and me just half an hour to pack our belongings, which turned into two hours because Sylvie had acquired too many things during her brief shopping sprees and couldn't fit them in her suitcases.

"Do you think they'll come back?" I asked Jett when we were alone in my guestroom, sitting on the bed, my suitcase zipped up at our feet. Jett's arms wrapped around my waist and he pressed me against him.

"I'm not sure," he whispered. "They have the book and they have the hard disk. They have everything they wanted. There's nothing to come back for."

He was avoiding my question, so I turned around and peered up at him.

"But it's not over, is it?" I asked him. I could see it in his eyes, in the way he bit his lower lip, in the way he struggled to control the angry line between his brows.

"They have no reason to." He averted his gaze, still not giving me a straight answer. "But it's not safe for you to stay here. I know it's your house. I mean it'll be your house some day, but staying here's not a good idea." He took my hand and pressed his lips against the back of it. "Come back home, baby. They might have what they wanted, but I'll feel better if you're with me."

"What about Alessandro? The lawyer called to say he's in a coma."

"We'll figure things out. Okay? Just trust me. We'll come back, if need be. There's no point in you staying, not when you don't know how long it'll take until he wakes up."

And not when we don't know who we're dealing with. I was sure Jett skipped that part.

"Okay." I let out a sigh. "I'm coming home."

"Great. I'll get the company jet ready." His frown lifted a little and his hands cupped my face. His lips were so close

I could feel his warm breath on my skin. "And Brooke? You are expected to start your position as the new team manager with immediate effect."

"I'm hired?" I smiled at the way his lips grazed mine, teasing me. A sense of anticipation washed over me at the thought of spending more time with him. "I can't wait."

"Well, in your case, I wouldn't be too excited. I've heard your new boss can be demanding." He put on his stern face. "In fact, he likes to spend his time with his favorite female employee, having sex in the office when no one notices—not that he gives a damn about that."

I laughed at his audacity. "I can deal with demanding."

"And he can be annoying when he wants something. Are you sure you have what it takes?" He trailed his fingers from my ankle to my knees and then the inside of my thighs. My breath hitched.

"I have a splendid reference from my last boss," I said, grinning.

"Indeed?" He rode his fingers just a little bit higher. "Are you talking about the stingy SOB who hired you on the spot without so much as a job interview?"

I nodded. "Yep. I had to quit."

"Well, we want to avoid you having that kind of boss in the future. You're not easily fooled, Ms. Stewart. And you're very good at what you do. I can certainly use someone like you on our team. Congratulations. You have the job." He held out his hand then pulled it back again.

"What?" I asked warily.

"I forgot to mention something." He waved his hand as if it wasn't really that important. "I was told by very reliable sources—" I grinned at him because I knew he was talking about me "—that I'm insatiable and I can't help it. It's the effect you have on me and you're the cure. Is that going to be a problem?"

"You're welcome to ask for it *anytime*."

"Anytime. Now that sounds tempting." His fingers gathered beneath my panties, sending shivers of pleasure all over my skin. "I'll take you at your word, Ms. Stewart. You might want to think twice before scaling this particular deal with me."

"Anytime." Shushing him, I pressed my fingers against his mouth and raised my lips to meet his heated kiss.

27

One Week later in New York City

WE WERE LYING on the soft rug in the living room of Jett's amazing apartment. My head rested on his chest, his arms wrapped around me, the warmth from the fireplace engulfing us like a cocoon, taking us to a place where love could light up the sky and nothing was broken. Jett's fingers caressed my back as I listened to his strong heartbeat. In the midst of the stillness, his breathing returned to normal. I moved closer to him and my hands trailed down the almost faded scars on his body, telling so many stories I didn't know. Stories that reminded him of the many dark places he had seen and the many dark things he had done—just like the scars in my heart that reminded me how risky it was to love.

"Having you around me all day long is tempting," Jett whispered.

I laughed and shook my head in confusion. "Why? What

would you do?"

"For starters, I would chain you to my bed and do all the things I've always wanted to do. I'd kiss you in every kind of way I know and in all the possible places I could find. And I wouldn't let you go because you belong here, with me."

"You're crazy." I lifted my head to look at him and ran my fingertips over the tiny stubble covering his chin. Since returning from Italy we had been so wrapped up in our world, enjoying every second we had together, that we barely managed to leave the house. That he wanted more delighted me. "I wouldn't want you to tie me to your bed because you don't play fair. I'd rather *you* be at *my* mercy."

"You'd have to learn to cook because I couldn't possibly live off cereal and takeout," he pointed out. "And you'd have to stop smiling like this because it gets me every single time, and I can't stop lusting after you. Every time you smile, I want more."

The flames leapt at the logs hungrily, casting a golden glow on our naked bodies. In the soft light his green eyes were so deep I could drown in them.

My smile widened. His gaze lingered on me, as if he could see something I couldn't. What did he see in my smile that other people didn't?

"I enjoy taking care of you because, honestly, I kind of like the idea of you needing me," he whispered. "I'm my true self when I'm with you. I feel like I don't have to hide."

"Why's that?" Sensing the serious direction the conversation was taking, I propped up on my elbow so I could regard him. His fingers intertwined with mine and he lifted our hands, watching the slow dance of the flames's shadows on our skin.

"I don't know." He shrugged. "It's not just that I'm attracted to you on a physical and mental level, it's also the fact that I love being *with* you, around you, inside you. Everything you do makes me want to kiss you like there's no tomorrow."

His lips sealed mine and desire swept through me, making me high, so high, reminding me how far I could fall, and he still didn't know I was pregnant. The first pregnancy test had been positive, and the next, and the one after that. There was no denying, no matter how many times I tried. I had postponed telling him for a week. It had been one poor excuse after another.

"Jett?" I broke off contact with his lips, my voice shaky. The sudden silence hung heavy in the air.

"Mmh?"

A few seconds ticked by. His beautiful green eyes were probing, waiting. I felt like I was trapped in his spell—unable to escape. I swallowed hard as I considered my words. I wanted to be what he wanted because I knew I was what he needed. But sometimes what we need isn't what we want.

Sylvie was right. I needed to know if what we had was the real deal and whether we had a future together. I had to know if I was wasting my time. I was ready to get hurt—if that was the only way to find out. There was a chance it wouldn't work out because love means falling and overcoming the fear of height. And God knows, I couldn't even climb up a rope without feeling scared, without feeling tiny and helpless when looking down. My love for him made me feel that way: vulnerable, powerless, afraid of what the future might have in store for us.

Jett's eyes narrowed on me as though he could sense my

struggle to gather my courage.

"We have to talk," I began.

His worry lines deepened. "You're not going to quit on us again, are you?"

"No, that's not it." I moistened my lips.

"That's great to hear because I think we have a good thing going." He seemed relieved. Of course he couldn't possibly imagine the magnitude of the situation, which made what I had to say all the more difficult.

"Are you happy?" I asked, unable to hide the tremble in my voice. "What if things were more complicated than this?"

"Why are you asking?" He looked at me, listening. "Did anything happen?"

Biding for time, I stood and put on his shirt, then walked across the room to the couch. I could feel his gaze on my back, his confusion palpable in the air. I retrieved the white box I had hidden inside my bag and walked back to him, then sat back down on the rug, facing him. In spite of the warm temperature, I was trembling from the icy fear gripping my heart.

"What's this?" Jett asked, staring at the box in my hands. I pushed it toward him. In the soft light, the white wrapping paper shimmered in a million facets and built a beautiful contrast to the blue ribbon tied around it.

"A gift." My throat constricted. "Open it."

The bubble holding my emotions in check was beginning to burst. As much as I tried, I couldn't stop the first tear trickling down my cheek. I wiped it away with the back of my hand and watched him open the box.

"You don't have to keep it," I whispered, just in case he felt obliged to.

Jett inhaled a sharp breath and his eyes widened. And then, ever so slowly, he pulled out the two tiny pink baby socks and held them up, his eyes searching mine. I could see the emotions on his usually unreadable face. Surprise. Shock. Disbelief. Then surprise again. His eyes moistened, which in turn forced more tears to roll down my face.

"Are you sure?" His voice sounded choked.

"I found out when Sylvie thought she was pregnant and she wanted me to do a test so we could compare the results. It's a long story." I stopped, realizing I was jabbering. "I know it's way too early in our relationship."

He started to smile—and this time it was a different kind of smile. It conveyed excitement, and there was a spark in his eyes that I hadn't seen before. The air was heavy with promise. My hands were shaking but so were his as he wrapped his arms around me, hugging me tight.

He breathed out, forcing me to look up at him. "It's perfect. That's the best surprise I've ever had."

A sense of relief washed over me. "Really?"

"I can't believe it. We need to celebrate." He picked me up and swirled me around, then put me down, his excitement surprising me. "I'm happy. I'm shocked. But in a good way." He brushed a stray strand of hair out of my face, still smiling, and there was so much warmth in there I knew he wasn't lying.

"I would do anything for you," he whispered. The serious undertones in his voice gave me chills.

"Strange that you should say something like that. I had a dream about it." I thought back to the morning after the car chase, when I woke up alone in the hotel room.

"A dream?" His twitching lips betrayed amusement. "I hope it was a hot one."

I slapped his arm playfully. Most of my dreams nowadays were hot—and involved him. But he didn't need to know that. "The only thing I remember is you saying you'd do anything for me." I waved my hand, embarrassed that I had brought it up. Lately, I seemed to have a hard time keeping my big mouth shut and not making an idiot of myself. "It was just a dream."

"It wasn't a dream." Jett trailed the back of his fingers down my cheek. "I thought you were asleep."

My eyes searched his as my foolish heart began to turn all sappy on me.

"And the part where you said—" I started. My pulse thumped like a drum in my ears.

"All true," Jett whispered, brushing his lips against mine. "I'm in love with you."

My whole being trembled—I could feel the tremors inside me, in my veins, in the beating of my heart.

"I'm sorry I pushed you away." I broke off, unable to meet his impossibly green gaze. "But I was never in love until I met you."

"Brooke." He grasped my chin and forced me to look at him. His eyes reflected the glowing fire, the golden flickers inviting my wish to melt with him. "You say it as though that's a bad thing. You know I love you. What's wrong with you loving me back?"

"I'm afraid that we're not going to last," I whispered, "and I'd rather we take things slowly in the off chance things don't work out."

"That's the most stupid thing I've heard. We're going to last, Brooke, and do you know why?" His eyes bore into me, forcing me to listen and comprehend every word. "Because you and I—we fit together. What we have is real."

"And if we fight and you grow bored with me?" That had been my fear ever since I felt myself falling for him.

"Then you'll have to remind me of the many things that made me fall in love with you in the first place. Like your smile, your laugh, your voice, actually everything about you." His fingers traced the contours of my lips as his voice lowered to that sexy whisper I adored. "I can't promise we'll never have problems, because that would be a lie. People fight, love, argue, talk, forget…that's the way life works. Things can get broken, but whatever happens I won't love you less."

"Are you sure?"

He placed a hand on his heart. "I can feel it. I want you to be with me. I want this—our baby. I want you. Nothing in this world can change how I feel about you."

His eyes were glistening and there was so much warmth in them, I knew I was seeing the truth. That's when the tears began to pour down my face. *Really* flow. I wiped my cheeks with the sleeve of his expensive shirt, soaking it.

"Don't tell me I've just said something wrong," Jett said, pulling me into his arms.

I shook my head and laughed between the tiny sobs forming at the back of my throat. "They're—"

Happy tears.

I forced air into my lungs. "If you mean one tenth of what you just said, I'm the happiest person in the world," I whispered, my voice threating to break off again.

"You're everything to me," he whispered in my ear. "You are my love, Brooke. Losing you once was hard. I don't think I could possibly survive it a second time."

"You had me at 'everything.'" One look at him and he had me. Jett owned my heart, my body, my soul.

Inhaling his intoxicating scent, I buried myself in his waiting arms and closed my eyes against the cascade of butterfly kisses descending upon my face, forgetting the world around us.

His green eyes, his whole being, and the things he did for me to keep me safe had taken me by storm, captured my heart, and etched a love inside my soul that could never be erased. And there I had been thinking I'd lost him; that the secrets he had kept from me destroyed everything we had—only to find they only brought us closer together.

Yes, love happens in the blink of an eye. It can change a person. I know because it changed me. It changed him. It helped us ascend to a more meaningful existence. And what's more to the story: I gave him my heart, and Jett didn't crush it.

He made me his.

I knew he wouldn't let me fall. Even in my darkest and gloomiest of times, he wouldn't let me drown.

The End

Jett and Brooke's story continues in the powerfully sensual last instalment of the Surrender Your Love trilogy

Treasure

your

LOVE

COMING SOON!

Once you have found love, treasure it.

Experience how their past is challenging their future, and dark secrets can shatter love.

A THANK YOU LETTER

There are so many things I want to say at the end of a book. The story of Brooke and Jett teaches that love can be found in the most unusual places and it's not always obvious at first. If there's just one thing I learned from writing CONQUER YOUR LOVE it that no matter who you love, don't give up. Fight for it. Conquer it, because in the end, love is worth the effort.

Of course this story is fictional and there's no resemblance to the living or dead, but between you and me, many people inspired it:

My grandparents, who raised me as my parents.

My best friend, who is in so many ways just like Sylvie. I adore her quirks and the ability to see the bright side in everything she does. She's funny and sarcastic, and everything you could ever wish for in a friend.

My two children and, of course, the experience of love.

I'm immensely grateful to those who've spread the word on Facebook, on Twitter, and on their blogs, and who have supported me by telling their friends and family.

I want to thank all bloggers for their support. My journey as a writer started with you and I thank God every day for meeting amazing people like you.

And because reviews are hard to come by for indie authors, I want to thank those who have taken the time to leave a review, no matter how short.

My gratitude also goes out to my kick ass editors, Janet Michelson and Shannon Wolfman. You've done a tremendous job. You guys absolutely rock.

Most important, my immense gratitude goes to you, my readers, for reading and giving this story a chance. Without you, this book would not have been written.

THANK YOU from the bottom of my heart.

Jessica C. Reed

Connect with me online:

http://www.jcreedauthor.blogspot.com
http://www.facebook.com/pages/JC-Reed/295864860535849
http://www.twitter.com/jcreedauthor

Made in the USA
Lexington, KY
03 July 2013